"But I'm their mother!"

Judge Winslow banged his gavel. There was only one solution. "Grantham Hale and Phoebe Rutherford," he intoned, "I hereby sentence you to be parents together!"

Grantham gasped. "But these are my kids, my family!" These kids were his whole world! He watched in horror as Phoebe Rutherford rose to her feet, her clingy black dress calling attention to her curves. Her white-blond curls were so much like those belonging to his quadruplets that Grantham's chest squeezed tight. Angrily, she whirled around to face Grantham. And pure emotion surged through him.

It was *her*. His earth angel, his savior. The stranger who, one long-ago night, had soothed him and helped heal his aching soul. Grantham had never even learned her name. And yet, with her, he'd spent a night he could never forget....

Dear Reader,

I'm so excited to bring you *Verdict: Parenthood*, the second book in my BIG APPLE BABIES miniseries!

These love stories are set around "Big Apple Babies," an adoption agency that is backed by anonymous matchmaking millionaires, one of whom is unmasked in every book! While each story stands alone, much-loved characters always pop up their heads, so we can see their lives progressing. Of course, BIG APPLE BABIES is about far more than just babies. So be prepared to meet some sexy Manhattan men with lots of attitude and heart....

This month, meet wealthy widower, Grantham Hale, a man who becomes an overnight daddy—to quadruplets *and* twins. Grantham's one hundred percent male. But is he man enough to handle *six* Big Apple Babies—without a wife?

Turn the page and find out. And experience Manhattan's special magic, which can be felt everywhere—from the swanky Upper East Side, where this story is set, to brightly lit Broadway and the old-world charm of downtown's Little Italy.

Please share all the magic with me as BIG APPLE BABIES' characters take on lives of their own, and we discover how—no matter where they are—people who were meant to be always magically find each other and fall in love.

Look for all the upcoming BIG APPLE BABIES books!

All my best,

Jule McBride

Jule McBride

VERDICT: PARENTHOOD

Harlequin Books

TORONTO • NEW YORK • LONDON
AMSTERDAM • PARIS • SYDNEY • HAMBURG
STOCKHOLM • ATHENS • TOKYO • MILAN
MADRID • WARSAW • BUDAPEST • AUCKLAND

For Malle Vallik, writer and editor—
for your many encouraging words, invisible feathers in
my own dual caps that helped me take flight. May your
own quills always have sharp points.

ISBN 0-373-16699-0

VERDICT: PARENTHOOD

ABOUT THE AUTHOR

When native West Virginian Jule McBride was little, she kept her books inside her grandmother Helen's carved oak cabinet, to which only Jule had a key. Only later did she realize that the characters she loved weren't real and that someone called a "writer" conjured them. That's when she knew one day she'd be a writer. In 1993, that dream came true with the publication of Jule's debut novel. It received the *Romantic Times* Reviewer's Choice Award for "best first series romance," and ever since, the author has continued to pen heartwarming love stories that have met with strong reviews and made repeated appearances on romance bestseller lists.

Books by Jule McBride

HARLEQUIN AMERICAN ROMANCE
500—WILD CARD WEDDING
519—BABY TRAP
546—THE WRONG WIFE?
562—THE BABY & THE BODYGUARD
577—BRIDE OF THE BADLANDS
599—THE BABY MAKER
617—THE BOUNTY HUNTER'S BABY
636—BABY ROMEO: P.I.
658—COLE IN MY STOCKING
693—MISSION: MOTHERHOOD

HARLEQUIN INTRIGUE
418—WED TO A STRANGER?

HARLEQUIN LOVE & LAUGHTER
23—WHO'S BEEN SLEEPING IN MY BED?

BIG APPLE BABIES

on the Upper East Side

Strawberry Field   The Great Lawn

Rink   Lake   The Reservoir

59th

Zoo   Pond   Museum   Central Park   Fifth Ave.

Plaza Hotel

Madison   97th Street

Park Ave.

60th   Lexington   70th   80th   86th   90th

Chapter One

High time you did me a decent turn, ladies.

From a painting at the front of the crowded courtroom, the three Fates smiled placidly at Grantham Hale. Angelic women with dewy rose-milk cheeks, they were draped in ethereal white dresses. One spun the threads of fate, the second gathered, the third clipped. And Grantham grinned. Somehow, in a crazy twist of overnight fate, he'd become the proud adoptive papa of twins *and* quadruplets. Ah, anything was possible, he thought on a sigh. A man's dreams really could come true.

Ignoring the camera flashes and curious questions from the media, Grantham glanced to the three double strollers surrounding him. His quadruplets—Lyssa and Kirby, Langdon and Nicolas—shook their downy white-blond ringlets, while his sandy-haired, golden-eyed twin boys, Stanley and Devin, gazed up adoringly, gurgling. Shaking rattles and offering pacifiers, Grantham wished he was already home on Park Avenue getting his life back to normal. Or as close to normal as it could get with six one-year-olds riding tandem. Doubts suddenly niggled at him. How *was* he going to manage all six babies without his wife?

Or at least a nanny.

Grantham's trusted personal assistant, Caroline Dapinsky, would only go so far. At helping care for six babies, she would definitely draw the line. With a start, Grantham realized the Fates were still gazing at him from on high, as if to say they'd think of something.

Well, you'd better think fast, sweet ladies.

And maybe they did.

Because Grantham heard a sudden commotion and glanced toward the courtroom's gated area. Behind one legal table was James Sanger, a balding, burly attorney from Big Apple Babies adoption agency, who'd been instrumental in helping Grantham get the babies. Behind another was Suzanne Billings, a citizens' action lawyer who'd called today's hearing. She and a woman who was wearing a black dress and scarf both scooted over, making room for three new arrivals, all of whom Grantham recognized as high-profile defense attorneys. What were all these F. Lee Bailey types doing here?

The honorable Judge T. Winslow seemed to be wondering the same thing. Corpulent, red-faced and fully robed, the cantankerous eighty-five-year-old judge glared from his elevated bench, looking like Wrath incarnate, his piercing blue eyes glacially cold, his thick eyebrows drawn sagely together, his expression thunderous.

"Need I remind you people that this is *my* court," he growled. "*Family* court. And no attorneys, no matter how well-known, may simply waltz in and make themselves at home. I've decided that today's case is closed!"

As the judge angrily slammed down his gavel to

make his point, the six babies chortled and Grantham bit back a smile. Instinctively, the babies guessed what Grantham knew for a fact—that the old man's bark was far louder than his bite. Grantham glanced at the newly arrived lawyers. He couldn't recall the names of the two men, just the woman's. Joyce Moon.

The thirty-something woman rose, making her straight dark hair sway against the back of her plaid gray-and-white blazer. "But, Judge Winslow, you *must* hear this! Suzanne Billings and our client asked us to come today because you've got a real problem—"

"*I* haven't a problem in the world, Ms. Moon," Judge Winslow intoned dryly. "But *you* are about to be fined for contempt!"

Joyce Moon stood her ground. "Judge, Grantham Hale can't be awarded custody of those quadruplets!"

What? I already have custody! Grantham's heart stilled, and something inside him shattered. Wouldn't he ever learn? Hadn't his wife's abrupt, horrible death taught him that something bad was bound to happen when things were too good? He took quick hawklike inventory of his six babies, sure that each—quadruplets *and* twins—would be snatched away before he could even take them home. Oblivious of the fact that a lawyer was tampering with their precious little lives, Lyssa tossed her head and Kirby giggled. Grantham's wide-eyed sons, all four of them, seemed spellbound by Judge Winslow.

The man did look thoroughly intimidating. "Ms. Moon, need I remind you that Big Apple Babies adoption agency was on trial here today. Not Mr. Hale. Last night, I personally awarded Mr. Hale full legal custody of the quadruplets in question. Case closed."

"But, Your Honor," Joyce Moon continued in a rush. "Please listen! The mother of the quadruplets is your very own great-granddaughter, which is why you were named guardian and next of kin when—"

Judge Winslow's color was deepening by the minute. "I am well aware the quadruplets are my great-great grandchildren, Ms. Moon. Just as I am acquainted with the fact of my great-granddaughter's—" the judge paused long enough to shudder "—indecent behavior and untimely end. However—"

"But she isn't dead, as presumed!"

An eternity seemed to pass in the silence that followed. Grantham realized he'd been holding his breath and slowly exhaled. Everything seemed so quiet. *What do you mean, not dead?*

Judge Winslow looked shocked. "Excuse me?"

Grantham watched in horror as the woman next to Joyce Moon floated to her feet, her black, curve-hugging, calf-length knit dress calling attention to the delicate arc of her spine. A dark scarf was draped over her head as if she was either in mourning or fancied herself to be Greta Garbo, and as she rose, it slipped from her head to her shoulders, exposing a mass of long white-blond curls that were so much like those belonging to the quadruplets Grantham's chest squeezed tight.

Judge Winslow leaned forward, narrowing his eyes and peering hard at the woman as if noticing her for the first time. Suddenly, he began to choke. "My pills!" he gasped, rummaging in the folds of his black robe, his cheeks turning purple as plums. "My pills! Where are my heart pills?"

His hands shaking uncontrollably, Judge Winslow quickly rested a pill bottle on his massive scarred desk, fumbled with the child-proof cap, then hurriedly pressed two tablets between his trembling lips. As he gulped some water, court security officers began rushing to his aid, but the judge sent them such a withering stare over the rim of the water glass that they all stopped in their tracks. "I do have problems with my heart," he thundered. "But at least you now know I *have* a heart, however contrary to public belief. May we please proceed?"

Seeing that the judge was fine, Grantham's grip tightened possessively on Langdon and Nicolas's stroller, and he glared at the blonde's slender back. Was she really Phoebe Rutherford, the mother of the quadruplets? And could she claim his children? Telling himself he didn't care what she looked like, that he merely wanted to see what he was up against, Grantham willed her to turn around.

Instead, she said in hurt voice, "Didn't you even recognize me, Granddaddy?"

"I beg your pardon?" Judge Winslow glared from the bench, looking positively appalled. "Need I remind you that at my advanced age, I've outlived two wives. I have five siblings—two living, three dead. Six sons and daughters, three by each wife. Fifteen grandchildren at last count, which means twenty or so great-grandchildren—of which you, Phoebe Rutherford Adair, are only one. There are even more great-greats." Judge Winslow leaned forward. "Do you honestly expect me to remember every fruit—or was that nut—on my family tree?" His voice lowered, becoming barely audible. "Especially if that *nut* happens to hang from a Rutherford branch?"

Her voice was contrite. "Well, I'm sorry I made you choke, Granddaddy. Are you all right?"

"No, I am most certainly *not* all right!" Judge Winslow exploded. "You can't be Phoebe! Not Phoebe Rutherford Adair! We had every reason to believe you were..."

Dead.

The woman tossed her head indignantly, making the soft curls dance. When her voice turned haughty, Grantham guessed taking a high tone ran in the Winslow-Rutherford genes. Not that he wasn't on equal footing. The New York Hales could be arrogant beyond compare.

"Don't say you're happy to see me!" Phoebe exclaimed.

"I am not entirely sure I am," the judge shot back.

"Well, then, excuse me for living!"

"I shall *try*, Mrs. Adair," Judge Winslow intoned dryly.

"Rutherford," Joyce Moon quickly interjected, gripping her client's arm, as if to ward off a family squabble. "Phoebe took back her maiden name immediately following her divorce."

Grantham's eyes settled on the Fates again, and this time, he cursed them soundly. Days ago, the elderly judge had been named next of kin to the quadruplets who were now in Grantham's care, and it had been recently established that their mother, Phoebe Rutherford, a woman who'd lived an undeniably decadent life, was presumed dead.

But apparently she was alive, well and right here in the courtroom. How could things have gone so wrong? Grantham's eyes darted to James Sanger. The lawyer from Big Apple Babies stared back grimly. Unfortunately, Jake Lucas, the agency executive, had temporarily left the courtroom with his son, Tyler, and girlfriend, Dani Newland. Grantham sure wished the three were still here, offering their support.

Judge Winslow sighed heavily. "Ms. Moon, do you or do you not intend to explain Ms. Rutherford's disruption of my courtroom?"

"It should be obvious, Your Honor! Your great-granddaughter is legally contesting Mr. Hale's adoption of her children."

Emotional control was a Hale legacy, but this situation was so intolerable that Grantham rose to his feet. "She can't contest! I've fought too long and hard to get these kids!" His fierce amber gaze settled on the judge. In spite of the judge's legendary willfulness and reputation for being unconventional, Grantham did hold him in the highest regard. He and Tilford Winslow had met socially, had business dealings, and now the elderly man was the great-great-grandpa to four of Grantham's six children. Because of that, Grantham restrained his temper. "Please, Tilford—I mean, Judge Winslow—we know Phoebe Rutherford was declared to be an unfit mother before she died—"

"I didn't die!"

Grantham ignored the dissenting voice. "Besides, Judge Winslow, she's related to you. So you can't sit on the bench for this. We have to adjourn. We have to find an impartial judge. We—"

"Young man."

Grantham gripped the stroller tighter, steeling his insides, bracing himself for whatever was to come, his eyes turning watchful. "What?"

"I'll have no grandstanding," Judge Winslow huffed. "All I allow in my courtroom is commonsense law! This is *family* court, which means we're here simply to explore matters of the heart and of the truth. Now, are you quite through?''

Grantham met the judge's piercing gaze dead on. "No, I am *not*. This *is* a matter of the heart. *My* heart. I..." How could he explain that losing these kids would make his damn heart break? "I just want to say that...that these kids are my whole world. Each one is a dream come true. They're everything I've worked for since my wife passed on. They're..." His hand swept over the strollers. "The family Celia and I planned to have together. My wife was right around the corner from Big Apple Babies, just minutes away from signing the adoption papers that would give us custody of the twins, when..."

Because he still hated talking about Celia's death, Grantham's voice trailed off. "I...had to start the whole adoption process all over again."

Judge Winslow's expression was grave. "Mr. Hale, I'm well aware of what you've been through. We all appreciate your extreme courage and perseverance. But—"

"No buts!" Grantham exploded. Wincing at the sudden loss of his usual self-control, he strove for a more neutral tone. "After ten months of undergoing media scrutiny, of having caseworkers all but live with me, I was finally awarded custody of two boys last week—two boys I had every reason to *believe* were the twins Celia and I were supposed to adopt.

"Then it turned out I'd received two look-alike brothers—" Grantham glanced at Langdon and Nicolas "—who, along with their sisters, Lyssa and Kirby, form a set of quadruplets. I know Big Apple Babies has now been cleared of any negligence in the mixup, but I..." He paused, suddenly feeling raw, exposed and vaguely uncomfortable because of it. "But I—I've already bonded with those two boys. And they can't be separated from their sisters. And, as of a week ago, the twins were legally mine."

Judge Winslow cleared his throat loudly. "Your point?"

"My point is that all six babies are *legally* mine now—and you can't take them away! So far, only Langdon and Nicolas have been living with me, but today they're *all* coming home!"

Damn. He'd just lost his temper again. Grantham blinked against the sudden white flares of the camera flashes that punctuated the end of his explosive, heart-felt speech. For better or worse, he knew his story was sensational. While much power came from being his father's sole heir, Grantham had remained a slave to the memory of his beautiful society wife. Valiantly, a month after Celia's tragic death, he'd gone forward, determined to adopt the babies they'd planned to raise together. And the media, by reporting on his fidelity and devotion to Celia's memory, had helped him get his kids. The love story had brought New York City to its knees.

"Please," Grantham implored, his voice low. "This is my family."

The judge raised a bushy eyebrow. "Are you quite through now, Mr. Hale?"

Not by a long shot. I'll fight for these kids. Grantham held back another rush of uncharacteristic anger—at Judge Winslow. At the Fates. Maybe even at God. Feeling venomous, Grantham seated himself. "Yes, sir."

Judge Winslow nodded curtly, then pursed his lips and turned to Phoebe Rutherford. "Ah, yes." He sighed loftily. "I should have known the Rutherford fish would rear its ugly head in the Winslow gene pool again. So, Ms. Rutherford, could you so kindly explain your sudden, disturbing return to the land of the living? And, pray tell, why do you think you deserve to be within a thousand yards—no, let us make that *miles*—of those babies?"

It was Joyce Moon who answered. "Judge, we know Phoebe's on record as having some difficulties—"

"Difficulties?" Judge Winslow gasped. "Oh, please do not spare my tender ears. In fifty-odd years on this family court bench, I do assure you, I've heard it all. This Rutherford relative of mine has long been engaged in scandalous behavior—"

Joyce Moon's index finger shot into the air. "'Scandalous' might be a bit harsh—"

"Harsh?" Judge Winslow roared. "She's been charged with public intoxication, indecent exposure, check fraud and extramarital affairs! I dare say, life with her must have *felt* like eternity. Perhaps her dearly departed ex-husband passed on last week of a most unfortunate heart attack simply to avoid her! In her checkered past, my great-granddaughter has never once shown any signs of remorse or reform or—"

"But she has, sir! She—"

"How dare you interrupt me!" Judge Winslow was on such a roll now that he could have been preaching a fire-and-brimstone sermon instead of presiding over a Manhattan courtroom. "In spite of the hard proof," he continued, "my great-granddaughter has continued to maintain that her husband fabricated evidence against her in order to destroy her reputation and gain custody of her children. Not even a restraining order could keep her away from her now-deceased husband's property in Bel Air.''

"She entered the home to see her own babies!" Joyce Moon protested.

"Exactly!" Judge Winslow thundered. "And in doing so, she broke the law. Then she vanished without a trace. Given her decadent life-style, she was quite naturally presumed dead." Pain crossed the judge's features, and he shook his head. "And here she is again. Haunting us like a ghost."

"Talk about grandstanding," Grantham couldn't help but comment under his breath.

The judge's voice was ice cold. "I heard that, Mr. Hale."

"Please, Your Honor," Joyce Moon interjected smoothly, "I assure you, your great-granddaughter is now completely rehabilitated. She was presumed dead, but she was really away, seeking counseling. Now, if I may..." The attorney swiftly circled the table, approaching Judge Winslow with a thick file. "I submit to you all the documents proving her misbehavior, of which you've so kindly already informed the court. It's all here—all the information collected by her husband's PI prior to his filing for divorce. You'll see she was denied appeal four times last year when she tried to get visiting rights to her children..."

Anger had left Grantham. Now he could listen in morbid fascination. He almost felt sorry for Phoebe Rutherford. She might be alive, but she'd definitely dug her own grave. Surely, with her track record, they'd never let her anywhere near the kids.

Judge Winslow scrutinized the evidence of Phoebe Rutherford's wrongdoings, his nose inching ever closer to the file. "Oh, I should have remembered you were educated at Berkeley!'' he suddenly exclaimed, spewing the word Berkeley as if it was the vilest curse. Shaking his head and addressing no one in particular, he continued, ''That's where her hippie parents went.''

''But Phoebe's not a hippie, sir!'' Joyce Moon crooned helpfully. ''And she *did* drop out of Berkeley.''

Judge Winslow's exaggerated groan vibrated in the silent courtroom. ''My, my. And a dropout, too! Now, why isn't *that* a surprise?''

Joyce Moon didn't back down. ''She spent months in A New Leaf rehabilitation center, sir. The receipts are all there in the file.''

''Thank you, Ms. Moon. I assure you, I can read.'' Heaving a great sigh, Judge Winslow finally closed the file as if to say he *had* read—and quite enough, thank you very much.

''We know Phoebe Rutherford has led a life of sin,'' Joyce Moon declared, her voice rising passionately. ''And yet we also know she's a changed woman. Reformed, penitent and willing to make restitution. No matter how she behaved in her past, she's first and foremost a mother, and she loves her little babies....''

Grantham winced at the heartfelt plea. For a second, it affected him. Until he glanced over Phoebe Rutherford's dream team. Lawyers of this caliber were bound to make an impact. Grantham rose to his feet again. ''This woman can't simply charge into a courtroom with the best legal defense in the country and be heard this way,'' he said coolly. ''And, Judge Winslow, you *cannot* make a legal decision involving your own relative.''

Looking indignant, the elderly judge raised an eyebrow in Grantham's direction. ''How many times do

I need to say it? This is *my* courtroom. And in it, I will not be dictated to, not by you or anyone. Is that clear, Mr. Hale?'' Without allowing a response, the judge turned to Joyce Moon.

"Judge," she said quickly. "We have grave doubts about Grantham Hale being an appropriate guardian for these babies."

Grantham's lips parted in unspoken protest. Were these lawyers really going to start making insinuations about *his* character? He felt as if he'd been punched.

For the first time, James Sanger, the attorney for Big Apple Babies, spoke up. "I'd like to remind everyone that these proceedings are highly irregular," he said, his voice tight. "Not only does Mr. Hale already *have* custody of the children, but his impeccable résumé is a matter of public record.

"At thirty-two, he's on the board of directors of two international companies and at the helm of his own advertising agency where he only promotes products he believes in, such as natural foods. A tireless voice of civic boosterism, he also advertises city projects free of charge, such as the recycling effort and the winter coat drive for the homeless. For ten months, Mr. Hale has endured constant scrutiny. By the press. By Big Apple Babies adoption agency. And now my client would like to be left alone with his family!"

My client. The words echoed in Grantham's mind. It was as if he was on trial.

Joyce Moon had the decency to murmur, "Well, it's true we have no *hard* evidence against Mr. Hale."

Judge Winslow was clearly losing his patience. "Your tone implies there are other kinds of evidence, Ms. Moon. So, what exactly do you have on Mr. Hale?"

Grantham's veins suddenly rushed with ice—and his hand rose to his heart. Beneath his button-down shirt, under his silk Hermes tie, was a cross on a gold chain. And hanging next to the cross was a diamond-studded wedding band—one that didn't belong to Grantham's wife.

Just touching the ring made Grantham's mind race—to another time, another place. To a sumptuous hotel in Los Angeles, and to the red-haired stranger he'd met the month after Celia died. Anger flared inside him. He didn't know what he'd do if these lawyers had dug up information on...her.

He didn't even know her name. But he'd spent the most significant night of his life with her. Even now, the emotions slammed forcefully into him, stealing his breath. Because when nothing in the world could reach him, when he'd lost his desire to live without Celia, that one woman, a stranger, had broken through to him and helped heal his soul.

She hadn't left behind a glass slipper, of course—only the diamond-studded ring that Grantham wore next to his heart. Inside, in tiny script, was the message, "Love isn't love until you give it away." Grantham had lived by those words ever since. The woman and the words were what had inspired him to try to get single-parent custody of the twins.

He'd hired a PI, hoping to find her, but without her name, he knew he never would. The press, of course, had never known of the affair. Would his one indiscretion somehow cause him to lose his babies now?

"Judge Winslow," Joyce Moon was saying persuasively, "you've seen evidence of Mr. Hale's explosive temper today, right here in this courtroom. And a substantial trust fund exists for those babies, not to mention an account for use in their upbringing."

Judge Winslow sighed. "Are you implying that Mr. Hale was motivated to adopt because he would gain access to money?"

"That's preposterous," James Sanger protested indignantly. "He's the heir to the Hale estate. Besides which, he's made his own fortune through diligent, honest hard work."

"Then why," Joyce Moon shot back, "would he withdraw one million dollars from the quadruplets' account this very morning, mere hours after they came into his custody?"

Grantham heard curious gasps. Then the whisper of graphite pencils on tiny notebooks as reporters scribbled. Cameras started to flash. And James Sanger shot Grantham a quick, questioning glance.

Judge Winslow prodded, "Mr. Hale?"

Grantham thought of his wife, who had always said he was as steady as a rock. He kept his voice even. "I'm not here to defend myself. Legally, it was absolutely within my rights to use that money." He had good reasons for doing so—even if he was sworn to secrecy about what he had done. Under threat of death, he would refuse to answer these questions. His jaw set. Phoebe Rutherford's legal dream team was of the sort that could catch a saint with his pants down.

Joyce Moon turned to him. "Surely you can tell us how you dispensed the money."

"I can't," Grantham said simply.

Joyce Moon let the comment hang in the air for a long moment. "Well, legal or not—" everything in her tone suggested Grantham's actions were not "—the quadruplets' mother finds it deeply disturbing that Mr. Hale has already withdrawn money from an account set aside for the upbringing of her babies.''

Grantham's tone was chilling. "*Her* babies?"

Joyce Moon ignored him. "Besides which, the wealthy never overlook new ways to generate income. And between the trust and usable account, the amount of money Mr. Hale has received tops the two-million-dollar mark." Ms. Rutherford's ex-husband was nearly as wealthy as Mr. Hale!

James Sanger's voice was tight. "We've established that Mr. Hale was *already* a millionaire."

A few times over. Not that it was giving Grantham any comfort at the moment.

"He's not after the babies' money," James Sanger repeated.

"Then why did he take it?" Joyce Moon demanded.

Grantham had no choice but to remain silent. Even if it came down to losing these babies, he had vowed not to speak.

"Mr. Hale?" the judge prompted.

Grantham allowed himself a sigh of frustration. The newspapers were going to crucify him. "Judge Winslow," he said, "there are countless reasons you should take my side in this, not the least of which is that my use of that money was legal and doesn't need to be justified."

Judge Winslow cleared his throat. "Quite right."

When nothing else was forthcoming, Joyce Moon chided, "Well, let's just forget about that missing million dollars. I still want to know why this man would want six babies. He's thirty-two, single, rich. And he is quite handsome." She shot Grantham an appreciative once-over that, in other circumstances, might have made him smile, but that now made his blood boil.

"Last year, the *New York Post* voted him the sexiest man in Manhattan. So isn't it a bit odd that he'd want to shut himself off from the world—and so soon after the tragic loss of his wife—with six babies?"

James Sanger said, "I'm sure Mr. Hale feels lonely after his loss, but—"

What Mr. Hale was starting to feel was murderous.

Judge Winslow looked angry. "I have heard enough!" He raised a liver-spotted hand, and the room fell dead silent. Slowly, the judge turned and glowered at Phoebe Rutherford, then he turned and glared at Grantham. And then, still holding up his hand for silence, he sagely bowed his bald head as if in prayer and intoned, "Please. I need a moment's respite in which to think."

Grantham shook his head. What was there to think about? These kids were his. He placed his palm over his heart again, feeling the ring beneath his shirt. After losing Celia, he was so sure he'd never want to marry—or love—again. Only the amazing encounter with the stranger had helped heal him.

Even now, he could barely believe that woman had been real. She was a more like a savior-angel, a godsend, a heaven-sent gift. After their one night together, he'd realized that love really wasn't love until it was given away. And he had so much love left to share with these kids. That was why, after that night in the hotel in Los Angeles, he'd devoted himself to getting the twins, his and Celia's family. And now they—and the quadruplets—were his.

Yes, Grantham had been touched by two heavenly women in his life—Celia and the red-haired angel. Only to be thwarted by Phoebe Rutherford, a devilish woman clad in black with wild blond curls and an arm-long list of sordid transgressions. Staring at her back, Grantham tried not to notice the sinfully shapely curves, the delicate spine. He tried to tell himself that his male reaction was to be expected. After all, he'd gotten an enticing earful about all the female naughtiness of which the woman was capable. Any widower in his right mind—or body—would react. Now, if she'd just turn around…

Slowly, Judge Winslow raised his ponderous head. "I'm afraid I see only one solution."

Grantham glanced protectively over his babies. Why did he feel as if his life and the lives of his children were about to be broken apart and shaken up like pieces to a jigsaw puzzle? "These proceedings are out of order," he protested.

Judge Winslow ignored him. "Phoebe Rutherford and Grantham Hale," he intoned. "Please rise."

Grantham allowed himself a long-suffering sigh. "We *are* risen."

Judge Winslow raised his gavel. "Phoebe Rutherford and Grantham Hale," he continued, swinging the gavel downward, "I hereby sentence you to be parents together!"

"What!" Grantham exploded. "No way is that—that *tramp* getting near my kids!"

Phoebe Rutherford whirled righteously. Just as quickly, she gasped, clutched her heart and staggered into Joyce Moon, who caught her as she fell.

Grantham could only stare.

Because it was *her*. His earth angel, his savior. The woman he'd met in the hotel in Los Angeles. The woman he'd hired a PI to find. The woman with whom, on the lowest night of his life, he'd shared himself completely—mind and heart, body and soul.

The woman whose diamond-studded ring he'd been wearing for ten months, pressed against his heart.

But she'd been a redhead, Grantham thought in shock.

Then his eyes leaped to the three Fates again. Draped in their ethereal white dresses, they spun, gathered and clipped the threads of his fate.

And this time, Grantham could swear they were laughing.

Chapter Two

She'd just lost everything, including her babies, so the very last thing Phoebe Rutherford Adair should have noticed was a man. But then, as her mother always said, Phoebe was the queen of putting on a brave face. And right now Phoebe was desperate for any distraction that might dam yet another flood of tears. Yep, her eyes were already red and itchy, and the next tidal wave was pressing hard against her eyelids, making them ache.

Besides which, he was some man.

Perched on a bar stool in one of the swankiest hotel bars in L.A., he was tall and broad-shouldered, dressed in nice jeans, a pressed white shirt and a tan corduroy sport coat. His boot heels were hooked over a floor-level brass rail that ran the full length of the bar, and while the rail was otherwise populated by a trim line of fancy high heels and alligator loafers, this guy somehow made his cowboy boots look right at home. Obviously, they'd seen more polished brass rails and plush carpeting than cow pastures.

Not that he was from L.A. In fact, everything about him seemed to say he was from somewhere else and just passing through. Phoebe fantasized that maybe he was even from another time, since he had such a proud warrior's face, bronzed by the sun, and sun-kissed golden hair that waved against his coat collar like a Raphael angel's.

Slicked straight back from his high forehead and shoved behind his ears, the hairstyle—if it could be called a style—accentuated the sculpted, striking face, the bronzed skin over high cheekbones, hollow cheeks and cleft chin. His eyes were wide-set, a deep, golden amber that never wavered in the bar mirror, and he had perfect, straight white teeth. And while an unusual bow-shaped mouth lent him raw, undeniable sensuality, a slight bump in the bridge of his nose gave him a certain haughty arrogance that was turning the head of every female who happened by.

Including Phoebe.

Yep. His face held proud integrity, but his eyes hinted at kindness and self-control, as if he'd managed to harness at least most of his darker passions. All his parts combined—the looks, the austerity and the aura of old money and power—made for a truly heady mix.

Phoebe still wanted to cry.

So she kept thinking about him. She imagined most women would steer clear. Wise ones, anyway. Because he looked as if he might demand too much of a mate—the very best of everything within her. Just one glance, and any self-respecting woman had to wonder if she could ever live up to his expectations.

Phoebe had to wonder.

But, of course, this was all projection. The fact was she couldn't meet anybody's expectations, the mere

thought of which made tears threaten all over again.
What had she done that was so wrong? she wondered.
What had made her husband hate her so much? Well,
whatever it was, she'd failed—that was a legal, un-
contestable fact, as of today. When she thought of her
babies, pain twisted inside her, and she forced down
another punishing sip of her martini, hoping that
would somehow help.

It didn't.

Not even the stranger's magical eyes could soothe
and distract. Still, each and every time Phoebe's eyes
strayed to his and those gorgeous amber eyes meshed
with her blue ones, she seemed to absorb the shock of
the man somewhere deep inside herself. Fighting the
sudden urge to tame the disheveled mass of her shoul-
der-length red hair, she tried to look away.

But it was too late. He'd caught her staring again.
He was getting up, coming over and, as if he meant
to visit awhile, he was bringing his drink. It was
straight whiskey, by the looks of it. Phoebe couldn't
even see any ice cubes.

As he got closer, she swallowed hard. Moments ago,
she'd fled from a courtroom, her heart completely
shattered. When, through the plate-glass window of
the bar at the Wilshire Arms, she'd seen this overstuffed blue love seat half-hidden by potted palms,
she'd plunged through a brass-trimmed revolving
door, made a beeline for the love seat and collapsed
thankfully onto the cushions. Swiping at her cheeks
and trying to sound confident in spite of her trembling
voice, she'd said to a waiter, "I guess I could use a
good stiff drink."

The waiter had smiled sympathetically, then politely

raised an eyebrow and inquired, "Can you think of any particular *kind* of drink, miss?"

Phoebe couldn't. She never drank, so she'd wound up ordering what Nico always did—a very dry martini with an olive.

It was awful.

It burned her nose and made her eyes water. As she watched the stranger approach, she was sure she'd start crying, maybe because of nothing more than the punishing taste of the martini. But really, she wanted to cry because she'd just been declared unfit to care for her four beautiful, precious babies.

Just don't think about them right now, Phoebe.

She wasn't the type to cry over spilled milk. Martinis, either. Nope, tomorrow she'd get right to work on the legal appeals that would get her babies back. Meantime, she had to stay strong. She had to think positive. She needed distractions.

At least that's what she'd been telling herself—until all six or so feet of pure, muscle-bound, living, breathing male distraction stopped right in front of her. He silently waited, standing so close she could smell his faint cologne and feel his heat and the raw power of his body.

Staring, suddenly aware of the pulse ticking in her throat, Phoebe tried to muster an apologetic smile. She felt somehow compelled to put her best foot forward. Something—pity, maybe—stirred in the depths of his liquid amber gaze.

His voice was heartbreakingly gentle. "You really don't have to try to smile for me, angel."

Only now, when it didn't disappoint her, did Phoebe realize she'd already been imagining that voice. It wasn't gravelly, but deep and resonant, as rich as his clothes and clear as a bell. But the words cut her to the quick.

"Sorry," the man murmured, clearly wondering what he'd said wrong.

"My husband—ex-husband—used to always tell me to smile for him," Phoebe explained in an angry rush, feeling it necessary to account for the tears springing to her eyes. "It was always when—" She paused, fighting the urge to cry. "When we were going out, to his client's parties...." And in her hurt tone, she realized, it was all there for this complete stranger to hear—how Nico had treated her like a prop, and how she'd always clung to him in public, flashing brilliant smiles as if they had the perfect marriage.

The stranger gently said, "I said you *don't* have to smile."

"I know. And I do appreciate that."

Oh, Phoebe really did. More than this man could ever know. But she suddenly wished he wasn't watching her quite so carefully, and that she wasn't so strangely aware of his good looks and energy and heat. Even his slightest movements seemed to draw her eye—the tightening of his fingers on the glass, how he shifted his weight. She decided her heightened perceptions were due to the fact that she was wound so tight after what had happened with Nico in the courtroom.

You really don't have to try to smile for me, angel. In spite of the words, Phoebe sent the man another fleeting curve of her lips. "Sorry about all the smiling," she explained. "My mother always said Queen of the Brave Face was my secret Indian name."

The guy's luscious bow-shaped mouth quirked. "Native American," he corrected decidedly.

"Touché," she returned. "And I think that's French."

He raised an eyebrow. "French."

She could swear he was staring at her mouth and thinking about French kisses. But, of course, he didn't kiss her. Instead, he lifted his hand, palm out.

"How, Queen of the Brave Face," he said. "I guess that's Indian for hello."

It was such a silly thing for such a good-looking, thoroughly masculine, whiskey-drinking guy to do that, all at once and completely unexpectedly, a genuine fledgling smile broke through Phoebe's false one. "Uh, *how* to you, too," she managed to say. "What? Is this practice in case you ever meet my mother?"

He chuckled softly. "Maybe."

Bravely sipping her martini, trying to keep her feelings at bay, she continued, "Look, sorry to have an outburst on you like that. I guess it's just my personality. I...get carried away. And I've been known to have a sassy, tart tongue."

His thick golden eyebrows knitted above his noble-looking nose, then his lips twitched. "Yeah, you look like a real tough cookie."

She didn't. She'd been crying her eyes out, and she probably looked a mess. He looked so unlike Nico. So fierce and protective. Like a good listener. Not that Phoebe was about to bare her soul to a stranger. Nope, she wasn't the type to dump her problems. Lightly tossing her red hair, she gave a soft, embarrassed laugh and said, "Well, maybe not. But I usually have a better sense of humor."

He shrugged. "So do I."

"Look, I know our eyes met in the mirror...."

"Met?" His lips curved into another wry, thoroughly sexy smile. "I got the distinct impression our eyes already met, shook hands, shot the breeze and then headed somewhere else. Angel, pardon me for saying so, but you were staring."

A warm flush rose to her cheeks, this time feeling oddly bothersome, carrying a twinge of something she barely dared to recognize as her sensual response to him. "Well, you stared back," she countered.

And he still was. He hadn't moved one of his countless muscles. He stood there—towering over her, staring, clutching his drink. She started to tell him to sit, then thought better of it.

He said, "You know, maybe you're right."

Phoebe squinted. "About what?"

"About your having a tart tongue."

"Look," she ventured, "I…I know I was staring at you. And it would be a complete lie if—"

"If?"

She blushed. "If I didn't admit it's because you're kind of—oh, okay, *really*—striking-looking, but…"

When she didn't finish, he merely knocked back a swallow of his drink, then surveyed her, the color of his eyes deepening when he squinted. Finally, he said, "But what?"

"But—" She glanced around the fancy hotel, at all the polished glass and brass, at the many crystal vases of fresh fragrant, long-stemmed flowers in the lobby. In the bar, finger bowls of floating white blossoms graced the tables, and musicians were setting up to play later in the evening. Phoebe's breath suddenly caught. Everything was so lovely, hinting of luxurious upstairs rooms resplendent with everything needed for dizzying, gratifying romance of a sort she'd only dreamed about. She thought of her babies again, and felt tears threaten. "Uh, there's no easy way to say this."

He raised his golden eyebrows. "Then just say it."

"I'm very definitely not here, uh, looking for a pickup."

"Oh, good." He shrugged. "I wasn't really trying to pick you up."

"Oh." Feeling flustered, Phoebe felt color stain her cheeks. She wasn't proud of it, but she almost wished he'd shown some interest, if for no other reason than her own husband never had. Her eyes dipped from his granite-chiseled face down the long length of his powerful body. She wasn't sure, but guessed he was a businessman. He looked like the suit and tie type. The jeans and sport coat were probably about as casual as he ever got. When, at eye level, she noticed his hand-tooled leather belt and how his jeans molded over his slender hips and muscular thighs, her mouth turned cottony.

Don't cry, she thought, trying to tell herself it was a darn good thing this guy wasn't interested. Hadn't Nico told her, time and time again, that she hadn't known what to do with a man even though she'd had one? She tried to mask her feelings, keeping her brave face intact. "Well," she said, "if you're not trying to pick me up, then what *are* you trying to do?"

The man suddenly laughed, a deep resonant laugh, then he said, "You know, angel, I honestly don't have a clue."

Almost against her will, Phoebe laughed, too. "Heaven knows," she returned. "I really don't think I do, either."

Then something warm and sweet and human passed between them. Their laughter tempered to a shared smile, and Phoebe stared deeply into his eyes. The irises were like tiger's eye stones in a streambed, liquid amber tinged with flinty black. All at once, her chest squeezed tight because she noticed his eyes held pain that was every bit as deep and heart-rending as her own. What had happened to him?

She cleared her throat. "Well, I...I guess if you're not really trying to pick me up," she said softly, nodding toward the sofa next to her, "you can go ahead and sit down. But I can't promise I'll be much for conversation." In fact, she was probably mere seconds from bawling her eyes out again.

When he sat, he left a very safe distance between them, then he rested his large, bronzed hands on his well-muscled thighs. Barely perceptibly, one of those sexy hands tightened on the whiskey glass. After a long moment, he said, "Guess you don't drink much."

She colored. "Never. What gave me away?"

His mouth quirked, then that warm, slow chuckle teased her ears. "The way you wince every time you take a sip. That was the big hint."

"And the little hint?"

"The way you shudder."

She mustered a smile, eyeing his drink. "Looks like you're an old pro."

His eyes stirred, black and gold like his whiskey, all warm color swirling together with a hint of lights deep inside, of emotions that ran deep. "At some things, anyway." His eyes strayed to his glass, and he amended, "Not really... I take it you're not celebrating."

"Nope." She took another sip of the martini, this time almost choking. Frowning into the glass, she said, "I swear, this drink smells exactly like the astringent

I use on my face. Do you think it's the same stuff, just with a different label?''

His smile broadened, not that it met his eyes. ''You like cranberry juice?''

She nodded. ''Definitely more than skewered olives in facial astringent.''

He shot her a wry half smile and signaled a waiter. ''Let's try a Cape Codder, please.''

The next thing Phoebe knew, she was holding a drink that turned out to contain cranberry juice and vodka. ''Yep,'' she pronounced after a first, tiny sip. ''Definitely more user-friendly.''

His sympathetic wink made the corners of his eyes crinkle. ''Martinis probably aren't the best drink for beginners.''

She sighed, suddenly wanting to talk about what had happened to her today, then not wanting to burden him with her problems. She shot him another quick, brave little smile. ''I...guess I should be celebrating,'' she ventured. ''My divorce was just final.''

''Ah, the gay divorcee.''

Hardly. Her attempted smile suddenly faltered. Darn Nico. Self-consciously, Phoebe shoved her hand deep into the blazer pocket of her powder blue suit—only to find her wedding ring. She'd been in court, facing Nico, when she realized she was still foolishly wearing it. Twisting it off, she'd let it fall into her pocket, determined not to let her ex-husband see her wearing it. Now she thought of the words so carefully inscribed in the band. *Love isn't love until you give it away.*

Oh, Nico had given it away, all right. To every blonde, brunette and red-head who came within a half-mile radius. He'd seemed particularly prone—and prone was definitely the word—to redheads, which was why Phoebe had dyed her hair. Toward the end, she'd been willing to try anything.

The man scooted a tad closer. "You okay, angel?"

Phoebe nodded. "Yep."

But she wasn't. She could still hear the finality in the sound of the judge's gavel coming down. As if she was someone else, she could see herself running from the courtroom weeping, staggering down the sidewalk and winding up here.

"Sure you don't want to talk about it?" he said softly.

Gazing into those kind, luscious amber eyes, she suddenly said, "I...I just lost everything. The house, money, my car." Those were the easy things to talk about. "Not that I ever cared about those things. But...but—"

But the children. Oh, Nico had taken everything, all right. Her pride, her dignity, her self-respect. But the babies? Nope, she definitely couldn't talk about them. What she was feeling was far, far too painful to verbalize.

She couldn't even *think* about them. Or about how, a month ago, Nico had locked her out, even though the babies were only a month old and really needed her. She'd been staying in a small, furnished room— at least until today, when the landlady evicted her. No doubt, Nico had somehow gotten to her. For months, he'd been using his money, influence and expertise as a high-power image consultant to do exactly what he did best—destroy Phoebe's reputation and take away the babies.

He'd manufactured countless horrible trumped-up charges against her—public intoxication, indecent exposure, check fraud, affairs. *Affairs,* she thought. What a joke. She couldn't even please Nico, much less anybody else. She'd never even met Sven Nordstrom, the man with whom she was supposed to have had such a big hot romance. In fact, she'd never even slept with a man other than Nico, and she was one of the few women she knew who'd been a virgin on her wedding night. Maybe if she'd been more experienced with men, she'd have known how to be woman enough to please and hold on to her straying husband. Then she'd still be at home with her babies. Panic welled inside her. Right now, all she had to her name were the clothes in the carryon she'd left in a bus station locker this morning and the few dollars in her wallet.

"You sure you're okay?"

The stranger's clear, gentle voice drew her from her reverie. "I—I loved him," Phoebe found herself saying, her voice stunned. "At least I *thought* I did. But he...he just destroyed me in court."

"Destroyed you?"

She nodded. He'd made her look so criminally incompetent that she'd been declared unfit to be a mother. But she was such a good mother. Hysteria bubbled inside her. What was going to happen to her four kids? Who was taking care of them? Nico didn't even pay attention to them. But their nanny, Selena, did. At least that was a relief.

"I...just wish I'd never gotten married," she managed to say. "My parents divorced years ago. And my mother travels a lot. She's an archeologist. So, wanting stability, I guess I just got carried away and rushed headlong into it. I was so young, just twenty-three..."

"And now you're so old?"

She shot the stranger another fleeting smile—and

for a moment thought she'd drown in his gaze. "Twenty-six."

"Ancient."

She decided he looked a couple years older, maybe thirty. She smiled again, then glanced away, thinking of how desperately hard she'd tried during the first two years of her marriage. She'd been so sure a baby would help, and although fertility therapy was necessary, she'd put all her willful enthusiasm to the task and gotten pregnant. She'd been so excited about the quadruplets. But her relationship with Nico had only gotten worse. He criticized her. He cut her down. Then he quit coming home.

And, like a fool, Phoebe had kept smiling through it all. She'd tried harder and harder, until she was sure she couldn't try anymore. And then she'd get up, dust off her knees and try all over again. Her cheeks warmed, and she felt another blush rising. Almost forgetting the stranger next to her, she whispered, "Why couldn't I ever do anything right?"

And how am I going to get my babies back? Tonight, she should probably take a bus to her mother's in Cat's Canyon, and then try to find a legal-aid attorney. Trouble was, she'd been trying—and failing—to reach her mother for a month. That meant she might have left town for one of her digs. And heaven only knew how long she'd be gone.

"Angel," the man said simply.

Turning toward him but keeping her gaze lowered, she forced another smile. He reached, and with a feather-light brush of his thumb, grazed her lip as if a touch alone could finally make her stop smiling—or make that smile genuine again.

His voice was tender. "Don't you ever stop being so brave?"

"'Fraid not." Phoebe raised her gaze slowly, until she was staring into those amber eyes, her own wide and questioning. Her lips parted, and out of habit, she tried to broaden her smile one more time. But a sudden dry sob escaped her lips.

The man drew in a sharp breath, as if her hurt was his own.

"What did I do that was so wrong?" she whispered.

Swiftly, the sexy stranger set aside his drink. His strong arm circled her back, and one of his huge, warm hands squeezed her shoulder. "Nothing," he said emphatically. "Absolutely nothing."

"But I must have!"

He didn't contradict her, just rubbed her back, the touch gentle. Heat streamed into her cheeks. "I...I couldn't please him." Her intonation left no doubt as to her meaning. Sexually, she hadn't been enough of a woman. It was so horrible, Phoebe couldn't believe she'd finally confessed it to anyone, much less to a complete stranger. But then, she didn't even know this man's name. She'd never see him again.

"It wasn't your fault," he soothed.

If only Phoebe could believe that. But Nico had come to hate her. He'd fought dirty, blackening her name, making people testify against her in court. As Nico built the case against her to take away the kids, all their mutual friends turned on her. Even her great-grandfather, Judge Tilford Winslow, whom she rarely saw but dearly loved. When she'd called him in New York for help, he'd looked into the case, then said she looked guilty. He said the law would have to decide. And today it had. She'd lost her four babies.

Even now, Phoebe could smell their soft skin and feel the downy fuzz of their hair teasing her cheeks when she held them close. For a whole month, while she'd been staying in the furnished room, she'd missed the sweet ache in her arms from lifting them, the strong grasp of tiny fingers squeezing around hers and the loud, life-affirming squalls of their lungs.

Hysteria bubbled in Phoebe's throat. What good was the law if it wrongfully separated a mother and her babies? Not that she thought for one minute she wouldn't get them back from Nico—she would. She'd have to start those appeals bright and early tomorrow.

"I don't have anywhere to go," she whispered, still hoping against hope that her mother hadn't left town. "Nowhere to turn..."

The man's voice was low, beckoning her. "Turn to me," he whispered.

His arm tightened around her back, drawing Phoebe so close that if she allowed herself to relax, her cheek would be pressed against that solid, masculine chest. Her nose might smell beyond the scents of his cologne and his clean white shirt, to what was purely man. Her ears might hear his heartbeat.

His breath stirred against her cheek. "Don't worry. I'll get you a room here for the night."

Her voice was strangled. "You'd do that?"

"Sure. But right now, just try not to be so brave. Try to let it all go, angel," he whispered softly. "Just go ahead and cry for me."

She murmured, "I never could do a darn thing for myself."

He leaned closer, his arm tightening around her, a hand gently stroking her face, urging her cheek against his broad chest. "So, like I said, angel. Cry for *me*."

And so she did.

Sinking against him, Phoebe Rutherford Adair finally quit smiling. And she wept.

Chapter Three

"You're really not going to try to go ahead with the adoptions?"

So many people had asked. And everything was on hold. Grantham watched the woman polish off a last chicken wing from the plate balanced on her lap. Without compunction, she licked her fingers, and he decided he liked the looks of them—sexy and slender, but with short, practical nails, nothing fussy. His chest squeezed tight, and he shook his head. "No. And they'll be fine. They're healthy newborn boys, with a long list of people who want them."

Her voice was soft, low and tentative. "Well, maybe you should think about it. Babies can be so nice. And twins..."

He sighed. "For months, those two boys were all I ever thought about. Celia and I were having so much fun, shopping for them like crazy, and throughout the pregnancy, we were in contact with their birth mother. For a long time, they've been a part of me. But having them now...the daily reminder of Celia would kill me."

"I understand." She gave his hand a quick squeeze. A comfortable silence fell. Grantham watched her, amazed to find himself appreciating the way a woman looked, the way *she* looked. She was a beautiful woman. He could barely keep his eyes off her long, shapely legs. She had wonderful hair, fluffy and airy and cut in fiery, red-gold layers that fell to her shoulders, framing her pale face. She had a ski-jump nose and a small mouth, and she didn't wear much makeup, which was something else he liked. Even her lipstick—just a pale lip gloss—was long lost, nothing more than a cute kiss print firmly affixed to the lip of her drink glass.

"A penny," she finally said.

Grantham leaned back into the cushiony love seat. "I was just thinking of a new house Celia and I were going to move into as soon as the adoptions went through. Now, I figure I'll sell and stay in our apartment." He shrugged. "I guess your eyes reminded me of the house."

"My eyes?"

"They're the color of the ocean out there, in the morning, when there's fog."

"Oh," she said simply.

Those dusky blue eyes were so vulnerable, too. Every time he looked into them, Grantham had to fight the urge to hold her again. When she'd nestled against his chest and cried, her sweet curves had come as a revelation, making something inside him—something he'd thought Celia's death had taken away forever—stir, warm and flicker to life again. Now, past her open suit jacket, he could see hints of her full breasts through a creamy silk blouse, straining her lacy bra cups. She was all womanly curves and soft femininity, and so delicate that she brought out his protective side, reminding him he still had one.

She'd turned out to be every bit as nice as she looked, too.

No doubt that was why they'd passed so many hours together, while the bar lights had dimmed and waiters replaced flowers on the tables with flickering candles in glass globes. Near the bar, musicians were playing old love songs.

In all that time, Grantham hadn't once mentioned the business that had brought him to L.A., and he still hadn't offered the usual information—not his name, job title or address. And yet, for the first time, he'd opened up to someone about Celia's death. He'd spoken about the details—about how a malfunction had caused a cabbie to loose control of his car, while Celia, her head always in the clouds, happened to be calmly walking along the sidewalk. She'd never even known what hit her. That was the only blessing.

"You okay?" she asked gently.

"We've been asking each other that a lot." Grantham smiled. "Yeah, I'm okay."

She smiled. "Full?"

"Couldn't eat another bite." His eyes strayed toward the surprisingly regular, down scale happy-hour buffet where they'd gorged themselves on free vegetables and dip, buffalo wings with blue cheese and nachos with melted Cheddar and green chilies. He raised an eyebrow. "Ready to dance?"

"I..."

Impulsively, Grantham reached out. Twining his fingers persuasively through hers, he didn't let her protest, but urged her from the love seat and onto a small makeshift dance floor. Facing her, he slid his hands beneath her jacket, settling them on her waist. At just the touch of her silk blouse, his palms warmed, dampened. Tentatively, she stretched her arms around his neck.

Grantham's stomach muscles clenched. "I... haven't danced with a woman." *Since Celia.*

"Of course you haven't," she murmured. "And we don't have to."

But he wanted to. He just needed a minute. "I think I do," he said, gazing into her dusky blue eyes. "And with you." He'd told her so much tonight—about how he and Celia had grown up together and been sweethearts for years and how they'd decided to adopt, since there were so many kids in the world without homes. Grantham thought about the twins again and about how badly he and Celia had wanted them.

The woman's voice was a whisper. "You just take your time."

"You're so beautiful, angel."

She tilted her head. "Why do you call me that?"

"What? Angel?"

She nodded.

He shrugged. "Because you look like one. And you act like one. And we're in L.A., the city of angels, so it seems to fit." He reached up and touched her hair. It really was as light as air. "Your husband was a damn fool."

He wasn't sure, but he thought he saw her chin quiver.

Her voice trembled slightly. "Thanks."

Grantham surveyed her. She hadn't said, but he was positive she and her ex had kids. It was in the way her eyes turned sadly soft when he'd talked about the twins, and in how much she seemed to think he should pursue the adoptions. But since she hadn't offered any information, it didn't seem right to press.

They still hadn't moved.

He leaned close again, his hands sliding all the way around her waist, settling at the base of her spine. Realizing he was a perfect head taller, he rested his chin lightly atop her head. Feeling her soft hair, he murmured, "I'm really glad it's you I'm going to dance with."

"I'm glad it's me, too," she whispered, her gentle, slender hands tightening at his nape.

Grantham shut his eyes, feeling the woman's warm body against his. And then, noticing the music, he chuckled softly.

"What?" she said.

"They're actually playing 'Strangers in the Night.'"

"Oh, no." She laughed. "They really are."

As he began leading them in slow circles, he blocked out all his other thoughts—about the twins, about how hard he'd driven himself while he'd tried to get through these past weeks, about the clamoring media in New York. All of it seemed like a play on a stage. And now the curtain fell, and nothing but silence was left inside him, a temporary peace. He'd forgotten how good a woman's hair could smell, how soft the touch of a woman's cheek could feel. Maybe he'd been trying to forget. "You're so different from Celia," he murmured.

She wasn't the least bit offended by the comparison. "How?"

He smiled, his nose crinkling because her hair suddenly tickled it. "Oh, I don't know. More curves. You're taller." The words seemed so trivial. But how could a man sum up his wife?

After a long time, she whispered, "One of these

days, I bet you'll find someone new. Somebody really special.''

"Maybe." But he knew he never would. Not that he didn't love women. He'd always loved the way they looked and moved and smelled. And Celia would want him to find someone. He sighed. "I just can't imagine anyone ever belonging to me like that again." He gave a soft sound that, in other circumstances, might have been a laugh. "Belonging...I guess that sounds sexist."

She shook her head. "Oh, no. People who love each other *do* belong to each other. That's what I think."

"So you think a little possessive jealousy's all right?"

He felt her smile against his chest. "Absolutely."

"Believe in fate?"

"Yeah."

"Me, too."

After a long time, she said, "You really think there'll only be Celia?"

Or you.

The thought came from nowhere. Grantham wasn't sure if it was true, or merely the emotions of the moment, but in another time and another place he knew he would pursue this woman. In these hours with her he'd come to feel something akin to possession. And when something belonged to a Hale, he never let go. But then, Grantham was light-years away from being ready to love again. He guessed there were some possessions fate just never allowed a man to claim.

"All I know," he said, "is that it feels good to be dancing with you." He needed this kind of closeness with a woman, missed it. He wasn't used to being alone.

And so they danced a long time, until their feet slowed, barely moving, and they were merely swaying to the music. And all the while, the warm, fluid stir of Grantham's arousal stole up on him, rolling in like a slow night fog, with just a breath against his cheek, a softly murmured whisper, a brush of her thigh against his.

And when it settled, it surprised him. All at once, his chest squeezed and his breath caught, and he realized that his whole body was aching for her with a deep yearning he knew he could never deny. Her breasts had become a heavy, tantalizing weight against his chest, and her firm curving belly was pressuring his groin, exciting and distracting him. Heat suddenly tightened his loins, and he wanted—no, needed—to take her mouth, to hungrily lick his tongue inside and plunge it deep, losing himself in a kiss. His palms guided the small of her back, dragging her still closer, so she couldn't deny his arousal, so she had to feel it.

She tensed.

But he didn't let go, couldn't. He was shocked at the raggedness of his voice. "Please stay with me tonight."

When she said nothing, Grantham leaned back and gazed into her eyes. They were so beautiful, the color of a steamy, sensual fog. That fog wrapped around him like a dream, like her arms. Under his hair and against his nape, he felt her hands turn damp with desire. His mouth went bone dry. His voice became a rasp. "I know you want to stay with me."

She licked her lips and swallowed hard. "What makes you say that?"

"Because there's such deep longing in your eyes,

angel. You look at me like I'm a distant lighthouse and you're trying to come home."

A soft smile curled her lips. "Maybe that *is* what you have to be...a distant lighthouse."

"No," Grantham whispered, his lips that wanted so much more only brushing her mouth, barely touching. "I'm not distant at all. I'm right here."

She hugged him tight, pressing her cheek to his chest. "I want to. But I can't. I just can't."

"THANKS for the bathrobe." Feeling awkward, Phoebe clutched the slippery chocolate-brown silk. He'd been so incredibly nice. It had gotten too late to call her mother again, and when she couldn't afford the only available room, he'd insisted on paying. Then, from across the hall, he'd brought her his robe. "Well...thanks for absolutely everything."

He nodded. "No problem."

She smiled nervously across the hallway. "I can't believe all they had was this bridal suite." Or that it was on his floor. "Fitting for the night of a divorce, huh?"

He nodded again. "At least the honeymooners finally remembered to call and cancel."

Otherwise, his bed would have been the only one in the hotel, she thought, suddenly remembering how alive he'd made her body feel when they'd danced and how her lips had warmed to the searingly tender brush of his. "Well, it's nice that the couple eloped."

His eyes flickered over her like a flame. "Couldn't even wait for their own wedding night."

"Yep. And so here I am, in a bridal suite."

"Well..."

"Well." Phoebe couldn't think of anything to say.

She guessed he couldn't, either. While her room was being readied, conversation had gotten strained, then all the way up in the elevator, the air had gotten thicker and thicker, until the tension was excruciating.

She tried not to notice how his eyes kept straying from her face to her breasts. Or how the pure, unmasked male longing was making her ache with sensations she didn't fully understand. Somehow— Phoebe would never know how—she managed to shoot him the umpteen-zillionth good-night smile.

He shrugged. "Well, I guess you have everything you need."

Phoebe's heart squeezed. *No, I need so much more. I need to feel like a woman just once in my life. I'm divorced and twenty-six and the mother of four babies, and I still don't really know how to be with a man. If I'd only known, maybe I wouldn't have lost my husband, my kids.* Smiling bravely, she lifted the fistful of silky robe, as if in a toast. "Yep, your robe just about covers it."

She half expected him to grin and make the flirtatious comment that his robe would soon be covering *her.* He didn't even crack a smile. Instead, he lightly licked his parted lips, his gaze communicating undisguised heat. His voice, usually so resonant, sounded hoarse. "Well, then, that'll be just about everything," he said again.

She gave a quick, decisive nod. "Yep."

Still, her lips parted in mute protest when he turned toward his door, and her eyes lingered on his broad back, tracing the angelic golden locks that kissed the collar of the corduroy sport coat. She could imagine those locks licking his bare shoulders, and she could still feel his warm gaze on her breasts, that gentle caress that had teased without meaning to.

She forced herself to turn toward her door. Fumbling in her bag for the room key, she felt as if this special night demanded more for closure. Another kiss...*something.*

Well, Phoebe knew darn good and well what that other something was. And she was having none of *that.* Behind her, his door swung open. But he didn't go inside. He turned around again. She knew because those eyes on her back made a slow shiver wend up her spine. Her hand shook even harder. Oh, maybe he *was* the lighthouse she wanted to bring her home. But she didn't have the nerve to try. Not after Nico.

She imagined herself turning around, crooking her finger and inviting him in. The last time she'd seen her doctor, he'd said she was healed from her C-section and could make love again. Not that Nico had tried. Or that she would have let him after discovering his infidelity...

Her hand suddenly jerked. The rattle of the key was embarrassingly loud, then she dropped the fool thing. Leaning, still clutching his robe, she picked up the key.

Behind her, his voice was gentle. "Angel..."

Phoebe gulped, then she very slowly turned around.

He merely waited, his gaze as tender as it was hot, his head tilted. "You know, you *can* change your mind."

She blushed. She saw his eyes dip and knew he noticed how badly her hands were shaking. She could change her mind, but he wasn't going to push. "I—" *Please, come over here. I can't say what I want, not out loud.*

He didn't move.

She couldn't help it. Her voice shook as badly as her hands. "I just…I don't want to be alone."

"You're not alone," he swiftly assured her. And in a magical instant, his door was shut and he was beside her, his warm, bronzed hand covering hers, guiding her to open the door. Inside, he lowered a dimmer light.

Her voice caught. "It's so beautiful."

The door had opened onto a white airy sitting room, with a fruit basket and fresh white roses, the fragrant scent of which permeated the air. In front of her was a balcony and sliding glass doors. And to her left, the bedroom…

Phoebe's heart suddenly pounded too hard, too fast, especially when his strong fingers caught hers and he led her toward a bed that was huge and canopied, with gauzy white tie-backs at the four posters. Her knees weak, she sank down, perching on the mattress edge, nervously clutching his robe. Next to her, on a table, was another vase of white roses and a complimentary basket, in which she could see oils and foil condom packages tastefully hidden in lace.

When she saw that, her heart started hammering so hard she couldn't even breathe. In one rushed exhalation, she said, "Um, maybe you could just hold me for awhile or something."

Or something. Why couldn't she get that darn *something* off her mind?

She stared at him.

He stared, too. He was so gorgeous, with that bronzed skin sculpted over his high forehead and sharp cheekbones. She longed to trace his thick, golden eyebrows with her fingertips, to sink her thumb into the cleft of his chin.

Wordlessly, he nodded. Gently easing the robe from beneath her frozen hand, he turned soft jazz on the radio, then knelt and slipped off her shoes. He took off his own, shrugged out of his sport coat, tossed it to a chair and slid behind her on the mattress, pulling her down so they spooned together, their knees slightly bent and his arms wrapped around her, drawn up under her breasts.

She didn't know when their lovemaking started.

Maybe it was when their eyes first met in a mirror—as if they were somehow sharing the same reflection. Or maybe it was yesterday or last year—or before they were born. Or a long time ago, in some far-off place where the three Fates decided such things. Or maybe it was when she murmured, "I take it back."

His voice was husky. "What back?"

She flushed bright red in the darkness. "I...I'd like you to do a whole heck of a lot more than just hold me."

The deep groan he released against her neck was like a last unbearable restraint broken free, and it sent a shimmer through her veins. "Ah, angel, I need you so much tonight."

And just how much she realized a second later. Swiftly and deftly, his experienced hands turned her, pulling her against him, crushing her breasts against the hard wall of his chest. He was capable of such tenderness, but his need was so strong now. She hadn't known, but she'd more than rekindled something inside him. For better or for worse, she'd lit a blaze, and now that inner fire was burning bright—making heat seep through his clothes, making his eyes glow. And when his lips suddenly, possessively captured hers, that fire made the spear of his tongue sear her like a brand, claiming and marking her as his own.

He tasted of mints and coffee and straight whiskey, and he smelled of pine and soap. But that fire from within—that wonderful, long-awaited fire—was all his. Instinctively, her hands raked through the strands of his hair, letting it spill through her fingers like threads of spun gold. She'd never known a man could be so immediately hot for a woman. Or that a kiss could be so bold. All those years with Nico, she had certainly never suspected she'd like it this way.

But this man's kiss ignited her. So did the splayed bronzed hands that swept up her body, lifting her skirt without apology, caressing her breasts with unspeakable promises of so much more to come. Like currents in a river of fire, the man left everything he touched awash in ripples of heat.

As his tongue plunged between her lips again, he caught her wrists and raised them over her head on the pillow, winding the long silken tie of his robe around her hands. Not really binding her at all, the chocolate silk was just a gesture, loosely circling her wrists and whispering through her fingers. It was this man's wordless way of saying he wanted her submission.

Leaning back, he crouched above her, those perceptive amber eyes warming her face as he started at the bottom and flicked open the buttons to her white silk blouse. By the time he reached the button at her throat, Phoebe knew it was her, not her blouse, that was about to come undone. Her sharp breath rent the air as the silk finally fell away, and when he flicked open the front catch of her bra, she quit breathing altogether.

Without touching her skin, he gently edged aside the supportive lace cups, moaning as he drank in the sight of her full bare breasts. No man had ever looked at her this way, so tenderly but so on fire and ready to take. Feeling suddenly panicked, she started to explain that sex with Nico would have been long over by now. But she couldn't find her voice. And then she realized his splayed hand was hovering above her chest, mere inches from her skin. Sweet heaven, that hand was shaking. Instinctively reaching out to him, her fingers twined with his.

His voice was low. "I've...never been with a woman other than my wife."

He wasn't having second thoughts. He just needed a minute. So did she. Her throat was so dry it ached. "I've...never been with a man other than my husband."

Seeing the need in his eyes, Phoebe swallowed hard and slowly guided his hand to her breast. At the touch of skin on skin, his breath caught. As she pressed his warm, trembling hand over her heart, she wasn't sure if what she felt was his pulse or her own racing heartbeat.

Her voice caught in a whisper. "Please don't stop touching me."

The corners of his eyes crinkled with his soft smile. "I promise, we're just getting started, angel," he whispered. "And something tells me it's going to be one very long night."

His eyes never leaving hers, he lifted his hand, licked his fingers, then reached out and, in slow, tantalizing circles, began to rub her nipples, making them peak into hard tips, making blood rush through her in surges of heat that tunneled between her legs and promised sweet agony and complete fulfillment. With shaking hands, she fumbled with his shirt buttons, gasping when his chest was bare and his hungry mouth found hers again. With another savage kiss, he laid fully on top of her, his upper body caressing hers, the thatches of gold silken chest hair teasing her aroused breasts, his male nipples pressing, the rest of him all smooth, hard muscles.

Over and over, his lips and tongue slaked his thirst for her until he'd stripped off her blouse and skirt and slip, everything but her panties. And until she felt the urgent length of him through his clothes, pressuring her thigh. Creamy, fluid warmth infused her whole body, and her temperature rose like a fever. Even her breasts felt hot, yearning again for the soothing dampness only his tongue could provide. He gave it, too. That heated spear licked her nipples, his teeth grazing and nipping. When he suckled hard, drawing the unbearably taut peaks deep into his mouth, she fretfully shoved a hand to her mouth, holding back a cry.

"Let yourself go with me, angel," he whispered.

Her voice shook. "Just don't stop. Please. Please…"

"I won't."

And true to his word, he didn't.

On and on, he suckled her, deepening her pleasure, until his hand—shaking hard with excitement—slid between them. Cupping her through her panties, feeling her damp heat, he gasped. Urgently grasping the waistband, he stripped away the silk. Her fingers twined in his hair even as his tangled in her moist curls below. When he dipped inside her and felt her slick readiness, he cried out.

And then her fever broke. Her skin, no longer dry

and hot, was awash in a slick sheen of dew. He was holding her so close to the edge. So close to a place she'd only dreamed about—but had never been in her marriage. She twisted beneath him, her womb aching. She barely even noticed when he stripped off his pants. Because she felt so empty, nothing more than a void waiting to be filled by him.

There were just no words for what he was doing to her.

No words for the salve of his hands on her body. Or for the salve of his love on her soul. All the scattered parts of herself that Nico had broken—mind, body, heart and soul—were slowly being fused together, welded into one again by the sheer heat of this man. She arched toward him with a sob that begged him to hurry and join with her, and take her over the edge.

"Please!" she cried out. "I want—"

His voice was a mere rasp. "I know what you want."

He quickly slid between her legs. She glanced down. Any wind she had left squeezed out of her. Because she saw him, all that hard, manly heat so stark and ready against his golden curls.

"You can touch me," he urged, his voice both ragged and gentle, his eyes capturing hers. When she kept looking, he grasped her hand and guided it to him. The raw open intimacy of his nakedness was nearly too much for her. Her heart hammering, she realized her fingers were still twined with the tie of his robe. The length of dark silk looped around his own silken length, and then it was her hand that circled him. He shuddered, barely able to take the touch, but wanting her to explore her power over a man who wanted her so badly. He made her feel so in control. And yet so weak.

But she knew she had to stop when, with another shudder, he eased her hand away. Reaching into the basket, he got a condom and rolled it on. Then, resting his hands on her drawn-up knees, he slid his palms along her inner thighs, parting her. With a whimper, she relaxed, opening all the way for him.

"Ah, yes," he moaned. "Yes. Yes. Yes."

He needed her so much. And she needed him, this man who called her angel and touched her so thoroughly. She stared at him wide-eyed, her whole body hot and damp and aching. He'd swept away all thoughts of Nico. Of the quick thrusts, of the emptiness that used to follow.

This man touched her face so tenderly.

Then he kissed her. As his body poised to enter her, his tongue began a slow thrusting, creating a rhythm, licking pure fire between her lips. And then it wasn't just his tongue on her mouth. Below, he parted other lips, and with a slow, practiced movement, he penetrated. Thrusting and withdrawing in tandem with his rhythmic kisses, he went deeper and deeper each time, until they were completely joined. Huskily, he whispered, "Now, come with me, angel. No brave faces, just let go."

She could no longer hold back her pleading moan. He made a soft shushing sound. And then his mouth completely covered hers as he started loving her in earnest, driving her toward ecstasy, plunging with her to precarious depths. All the while, his fingers raked through her hair, until she begged him to stop. Until she was clinging to him, mindlessly weeping in gratitude with a first climax that came as a total shock.

The second was electrifying. And then he came—explosively, taking her right off the mattress. After that, they simply hugged each other, not talking for a very long time.

He finally whispered, "Angel?"

"Oh, no," she whispered quickly. "You're the angel."

And he was. Because now Phoebe knew. The problems in her marriage bed hadn't been her own. There wasn't a darn thing wrong with her. There never had been.

Against her cheek, his breath felt soft, like a feather falling on her skin. He found her hand in the darkness, gave it a gentle squeeze and whispered, "That's the way it's always supposed to be between a man and a woman."

Tears stung her eyes, and her voice caught. "I just never knew."

GRANTHAM DRIFTED.

Vaguely, he wondered if he loved her. Probably. If he didn't already, he knew he could. Because they'd loved all night. Ordered food and bathed and spoken in whispers. They'd even laughed. Oh, God, they'd laughed.

Hours had passed, and he still couldn't stop wanting her. She'd touched him so deeply. He wondered if she was aware of the countless times she'd begged him to stop loving her—all as she clung to him, letting him take her over the edge again and again.

And now they lay so still.

A white rose was on her belly. He'd laid it against her pale skin after he'd traced it over her body. Feeling arousal build inside him again, he turned, pressing his

cheek to hers. He'd discovered that he liked to mold
his face to hers. The bump of his eyebrow locked perfectly into the hollow above her cheekbone, just as her
thumb fit into the cleft of his chin.

He leaned back. Gazing at her in the dim light, he
knew he could no longer deny his arousal.

She lifted a hand and stroked his cheek.

Ah, how he needed this intimacy, this closeness. It
was love, pure and simple. A giving that Celia had
taught him all his life. And that he'd shared with this
woman tonight.

"You okay?" she whispered.

His soft chuckle was barely audible. "So much better than okay."

And he was. From the first glance, this woman had
begun dismantling the wall he'd built around his heart
the day Celia died. Like a strong sun, she'd broken
through and given him light. He'd felt lost lately. But
this woman had found him. And over and over tonight,
he'd turned to her like a beacon, and she'd pointed
him in the direction of home. Funny, he mused. He'd
become her angel, and she'd become the lighthouse
that was bringing him home.

Now he turned to her light again. With only a soft
murmured warning, he entered her and she moaned
softly. And as he kissed her, Grantham forgot about
tomorrow. All he needed to know was that a new day
would dawn. And in the morning light, he would go
on. He'd changed his mind. He'd get his twin sons.
He'd raise those boys just as he and Celia had planned.
He couldn't shut himself away, couldn't let himself
die with Celia.

Because Grantham Hale was ready to live again.

And he had a future whose name was still nothing
more than angel.

Chapter Four

Manhattan Family Court
The present

"I repeat," Judge Winslow roared, "I hereby sentence you to be parents together!"

Grantham had barely heard. Everything seemed to disappear—Judge Winslow and the lawyers, the scribble of reporters' pencils, the flash of cameras. Even the babies' noisy chortling and the six bright, curious pairs of eyes that glanced between him and her.

"Angel?" Grantham whispered.

"Mama," announced Kirby wisely.

"Da." Langdon giggled, beating a rattle against the side of the stroller he shared with Nicolas. "Da-da!"

Grantham stared at her from his seat in the front row of the courtroom. She stared back from the lawyer's table in the gated area. Time had stopped. He was afraid if he so much as breathed, she'd vanish right before his eyes, the way she had ten months ago. He'd awakened alone with nothing more than the scent of her—all roses, musk and jasmine—still in the air, on his hands. The white rose he'd trailed over her naked body had been gone. Besides her diamond-studded wedding ring, she'd left nothing behind—except the indelible handprint on Grantham's heart where she'd touched him. He hadn't moved then, no more than he could now.

Thank God he'd finally found her. His mind was reeling with words like fate, kismet, karma and luck. Lifting his hand, he covered his heart and felt her ring beneath, on the gold chain with his cross. *Phoebe,* he thought in shock. *Her name is Phoebe Rutherford.* He'd waited so long to hear that name.

Joyce Moon stared between them. "Do you *know* this man?"

Phoebe was gaping at him, her knuckles white from gripping the back of her chair. Her voice was strained. "No. Of course not."

Joyce Moon scrutinized her. "Are you sure?"

"I swear."

Grantham's lips parted in unspoken protest.

Phoebe stared.

Those dusky blue eyes were utterly spellbinding. They were the color of night smoke floating in thick summer air. Or of a dreamy fog rolling across a calm winter sea. And right now, they were so masked and unreadable that Grantham felt strangely off balance. Surely she hadn't forgotten that night? Surely she wouldn't—couldn't—deny it?

For ten months, he'd searched for her—only to find there wasn't even the slightest hint of recognition in her eyes. He fought the urge to get up, stride across the room and jog her memory with a soul-searing kiss. Instead, he settled for a look, his eyes slowly rediscovering every inch of the body he'd once so passionately possessed, from the collar of her slender black knit tube dress all the way down to her shapely legs and black high heels.

Then his eyes traveled the long way back up again. When they settled on her small, lip-glossed mouth, it was Grantham who was remembering—the heat of those lips, the cries his deepest kisses had torn from between them. He felt the weight of her breasts in his hands, the curve of her waist, her heat below. His mouth went bone dry.

It took all his willpower to stay seated. He had to hold her again—had to know everything about this woman with whom he'd shared that magic night. His eyes fondled and caressed her hair. It was blond now, but the texture was still so airy that he knew it could be stirred by nothing more than his tenderest sweet nothings.

Joyce Moon's screech brought him to reality. "I demand to know what's going on here!"

Phoebe's voice was measured. "Nothing."

Those dusky eyes were so blank that Grantham felt completely taken aback. He hardly expected her to announce their affair in a crowded courtroom, but he expected some small sign, some nonverbal promise of rekindled passion. Together, he and this woman had gone to oblivion and back. Hell, Grantham had *never* come back. He was still regularly torturing himself with memories of how she'd touched him. He'd imagined her living in L.A., in mansions, in ocean apartments, in bungalows, never having the slightest clue who she really was or what kind of life she lived.

But now he'd found her. And *she* was the mother of quadruplets—of the quadruplets *he'd* adopted? And what was that utter nonsense about her having committed criminal acts such as adultery? It hit him all at once. For an instant, he felt breathless again, as if a trapdoor had opened beneath him and he was plunging feet-first into outer space. Grantham was a smart man—Ivy League educated, top of his class. But his mind couldn't even begin to catch up.

He hazarded a glance at the painting of the three Fates. The three angelic ladies, draped in their ethereal white dresses, smiled placidly back. One spun, the second measured, the third snipped the thread of his fate. Grantham decided those ladies were nowhere near as sweet and innocent as they looked.

Neither was Phoebe Rutherford.

Judge Winslow was peering between him and Phoebe, as if sensing some curious energy between them, his thick, ponderous eyebrows knitted. "Mr. Hale," he intoned, "it would please the court, sir, if you could explain why you are ogling Ms. Rutherford."

Because I spent the most amazing night of my life with her. Now it turns out she's the mother of four of my six kids, but she's acting as if she doesn't even remember me. Somehow, Grantham doubted very much that it would really please great-granddaddy and the court, not to mention the New York media, to hear that he'd held Phoebe Rutherford through the longest, hottest night of his life.

"Mr. Hale? If you refuse to respond, I could hold you in contempt."

At Judge Winslow's censure, Grantham could swear a faintly victorious smile ghosted over Phoebe's lips. That, more than anything, pricked his pride. He may have searched ten months for her, but no one ever got the best of a Hale. Grantham let his eyes drift over her as if he'd never seen her before. "Sorry," he murmured. "For a second I thought we'd met. But—" He shot her a quick, apologetic smile. "I was obviously mistaken. She must just have a common face." At that, the first hint of barely discernible anger sparked in her eyes. Her face was anything but common, and she knew it.

Grantham smiled pleasantly.

She scowled.

And Grantham felt tremendously relieved. No, she hadn't forgotten their night together any more than he had. Good. For a minute there, she'd really had him going. Surely, once they were alone, everything would be different.

Judge Winslow cleared his throat. "So there is no sexual attraction felt by either party, then?"

Grantham nearly choked. Had Judge Winslow completely lost his mind? Gripping Langdon and Nicolas's stroller, Grantham held on tight, as if the weight of two babies could anchor him. No doubt, if the judge didn't have a reputation for brilliant unconventionality, a clerk would have run for help long before now. These court proceedings weren't just out of order—they were most certainly illegal.

Judge Winslow looked livid. "Mr. Hale?"

Did the judge really expect him to respond to a question about sex? Grantham dragged a hand through his hair. "Uh, yes?"

Judge Winslow sighed impatiently. "Do you or do you not feel any sexual attraction, Mr. Hale?"

"Oh, I have on occasion, sir," Grantham couldn't help but say dryly. When his glance ascertained that Phoebe was still looking at him as if he was nothing more than a stranger, it rankled. He raised an eyebrow. "But do you mean attraction for Ms. Rutherford?"

"Of course I mean for Ms. Rutherford!" Judge Winslow roared. Grantham loosened his grip on the stroller, then he stared at Phoebe, tilting his head as if considering. Her cheeks turned a bright florid pink under his gaze. "I confess," he finally said, still wondering where the judge was headed with this, "I don't feel even the slightest twinge of attraction." It was, of course, a blatant lie.

Judge Winslow nodded sagely. "In light of her highly questionable history, I most certainly understand that, my poor, dearest Mr. Hale. However, the fact remains that you are a healthy, virile male. And, as such, I must make quite certain you would not feel, er, inhibited by Ms. Rutherford."

Grantham's gaze flicked over her. "I don't think she could ever make me feel...inhibited, Your Honor." That much was the truth.

Judge Winslow intoned, "Ms. Rutherford, have you any...untoward feelings about Mr. Hale that might interfere with your ability to jointly and responsibly parent with him?"

Phoebe had turned beet red. She was glancing between him and the judge. "I don't have any feelings, either!" she exclaimed.

But those dusky eyes said differently. The smoky depths were charged with brilliant fire. Apparently, her palms had turned damp, too. When she slicked them against the sides of her dress, Grantham felt more of his equilibrium return. He flashed her a quick smile. Abruptly whirling and turning her back to him, she seated herself. Frantically she whispered to Joyce Moon.

The lawyer's index finger shot into the air. "Your Honor, at this time, may we please request a sidebar?"

A second later all the lawyers approached the bench. Huddling with Judge Winslow, they began conferring in hushed whispers.

"Da. Da?"

It was Langdon. The white-blond tyke was getting antsy in his stroller, so Grantham lifted him onto his lap. Gently bouncing him, Grantham stared at Phoebe.

She wouldn't even turn around.

Damn. He had been sure they'd meet again. The pull between them was magnetic, so strong it had to be destiny. But he'd always imagined her running into his arms. He'd imagined a quick, hard embrace, thirsty kisses.

Sudden emotion made Grantham's heart swell. Surely, Phoebe was worried because of the babies. But didn't she know everything was different now? They'd found each other. Maybe they could share the kids, raise them together. It could be wonderful.... Of course, she *had* left him in a hotel, without leaving her name or number.

His eyes narrowed. Where had she been between the night they'd shared in the Wilshire Arms and her husband's death last week? Grantham had made love to her, and he knew her soul. He couldn't believe she'd committed the criminal acts mentioned in court. She was no more capable of adultery than he, and she could barely choke down a weak Cape Codder. So why would she claim to have been in some rehabilitation center called A New Leaf?

None of it made sense.

The only certainty was that she hadn't seen her babies for ten months. She'd tried, though, attempting legal appeals and even breaking into her husband's house, defying a restraining order. On the night they'd met she said her husband had taken everything—the house, the money, her car. Apparently, he'd taken away her children, too. Grantham sighed. Should he get up and take the babies to her now?

"What do you think?" he whispered to Langdon.

The little boy peered up, grinning.

When Phoebe half turned, Grantham studied her profile, searching for the soft vulnerability he remembered. Now that he was over some of his shock, he felt worried. Wherever she'd been, he'd bet it was nowhere good. She looked washed out, pale. He felt as if he was looking at her harder, meaner twin sister. Somehow, he had to get her alone. They needed to talk. About them. About the babies. If only she'd turn around...

The lawyers returned to their tables.

Judge Winslow slammed down his gavel. "It is settled. I hereby rule that both Ms. Rutherford and Mr. Hale will reside under the same roof, at Mr. Hale's residence, for the entire duration of their sentence."

Grantham blinked.

Phoebe shot to her feet. "That's impossible! You don't understand!"

Judge Winslow glowered at her from the bench. "You, Phoebe Rutherford, are the one who doesn't understand. You have exactly two options. One—I rule against you and you lose your children this very instant. Or two—you move in with Mr. Hale and attempt to work out a parenting agreement. Which is it?"

Phoebe stared mutely.

A world of emotions whirled within Grantham—wounded pride and anger because she wasn't glad to see him. Curiosity because her relative, the eccentric judge, had apparently decided to play matchmaker. At least that was what Grantham suspected.

As if his ruling was the most conventional in the world, Judge Winslow brought a pocket calendar to the top of his massive scarred desk, then leafed through the pages. "Court will resume in five weeks, on November seventh. In addition to parenting together, Ms. Rutherford and Mr. Hale shall also take evening constitutionals, as well as play sets of tennis—"

Grantham raised an eyebrow. "Tennis?"

"Tennis!" Phoebe gasped.

Judge Winslow glanced up, his expression benign, his voice annoyingly reasonable. "You *do* both play, don't you?"

Phoebe sounded panicked. "Yes, but—"

Judge Winslow thundered, "Do you want to lose your children?"

"Well, no, but—"

"Well, then," he said dismissively.

Speechless, Phoebe implored her dream team with panicked eyes, looking for support. When she got none, she wailed, "I'm paying you lawyers good money! Why aren't you doing something?"

Joyce Moon smiled. "I'm sure what my client means to say is that she would like to thank the court for this momentous—"

"I did *not* say that!"

Joyce Moon didn't miss a beat. "What she means to say is that she's grateful for this chance to prove herself. And I, for one, sincerely promise that she'll be in complete compliance with your generous ruling, Judge Winslow. We also would like to assure Mr. Hale that she'll make no untoward advances—"

"Advances!" Phoebe exploded, sounding so much like her great-grandfather that Grantham winced.

Her three attorneys smiled at her every bit as placidly as the three Fates. Obviously, her lawyers felt this insane ruling to cohabitate for five weeks while caring for the children would strengthen Phoebe's case. On the other hand, James Sanger, the attorney from Big Apple Babies who had spoken on Grantham's behalf, winked as if to say that playing along with Judge Winslow would help Grantham, not Phoebe.

Grantham sighed. He wished he could explain that he didn't want to just win anymore. He wanted Phoebe. It was absolutely fine with him if, on a trial basis, they cohabited and parented together.

Phoebe said, "Please, Granddaddy."

At her pleading tone, Grantham felt a rush of real temper. Now she was begging. Meantime, his hands longed to touch her, his lips to taste. He was all for the idea of having her reside under his rooftop. Maybe if some other biological mom was threatening his complete custody of these babies, he'd fight tooth and nail. But he'd never deprive Phoebe Rutherford of anything. All this time, he'd been searching for her.

But she was objecting to five measly weeks, when *he'd* wanted *her* for eternity. It had never once occurred to Grantham that when he finally found her, his sweet Cinderella would be so reluctant.

Well, the Fates were on his side.

Grantham had lived long enough that he knew never to discount things that came in threes. The Fates had brought him and Phoebe together, they both had claims on a passel of children, and now they'd been legally sentenced to live together.

It had to mean something.

Yeah, it meant hell on earth—at least if Grantham listened to Phoebe's version of it.

Her plea was strained. "I *can't* go home with him!"

Grantham couldn't help but say, "It's not that terrible."

She turned and gaped at him.

Before she looked away again, the hard glint in her eyes gave him pause. Why wasn't she denying the criminal charges against her? Would she continue to deny they'd met? And how were they going to come to terms with their joint claim on the quadruplets if she wouldn't be straight with him?

"Granddaddy," she implored one last time.

Judge Winslow didn't even grace her with a glance. "I'd like to assure Mr. Hale that Ms. Rutherford will earn her keep. She will cook, clean, do laundry and carry out any other household chores he deems appropriate—all as part of her ongoing and obviously very necessary rehabilitation. Are there any objections to that, Mr. Hale?"

"*Laundry!*" Phoebe shrieked.

Grantham sighed again. He already had a housekeeper. What he wanted was a wife.

"Objections?" Judge Winslow queried again.

Yeah, I object to her objecting. All this time, I assumed she'd be glad when I found her. Well, at least Fate and the law were on his side. He had full legal custody of her children. And she'd be staying under his roof. If he wanted to, he could be every bit as cool about this as she was. "No objections."

With a relieved sigh, Judge Winslow brought his gavel crashing down. "I hereby sentence you to be a family. Court will resume in five weeks. May the best parent win!"

"LADIES FIRST."

Phoebe's heart was hammering—she was still reeling from this wild turn of events—and warmth flooded her cheeks. What must Grantham Hale think after hearing about her supposed criminal behavior in court? She swallowed hard. "Uh, thanks."

Taking a deep breath, feeling weak-kneed, she crossed the threshold to his apartment, entering the foyer. *Remember, you're Queen of the Brave Face, Phoebe. Just don't look at the babies or you'll break down. Soon you'll be alone with your kids, and then you can cry your eyes out. After that, you can call and give Granddaddy Winslow a piece of your mind.* She still had no bright ideas about how to deal with Grantham.

He was ushering their large group inside a round, ultramodern living room. Her three lawyers—Joyce Moon, Orsen Daily and Bert Taylor—were behind her, pushing the strollers. His two lawyers—James Sanger and Jake Lucas—juggled the briefcases. Grantham had relieved her of her two vinyl suitcases, leaving her to carry only her well-worn tennis racket and a stack of books she kept tied together with a faded red ribbon. Immediately, Grantham offered the group drinks, then vanished with her bags. Yep. He was still every bit the gentleman she remembered.

Keeping her eyes studiously trained away from the babies, Phoebe tried to take stock of her surroundings. Other than a messy open gym bag near the door, the room was pin-neat, with a white sectional sofa and chrome and glass end tables. Shadow boxes were set into the round walls, and inside hung chrome-framed posters, presumably from his favorite advertising accounts. Three sets of French doors opened from the round room onto hallways.

Grantham breezily reentered the room, crooned to the babies, then rested a hand casually on the stroller nearest her. His resonant voice was too close for comfort. "Think you can stand spending five weeks here?"

She hazarded a glance in his direction—and wound up staring. Yep. He really was everything she remembered. Drop-dead gorgeous and bristling with integrity. With that noble nose and thick, waving golden hair that he wore slicked back from his face. It curled angelically against the collar of a chocolate brown suit that brought out the deep, fiery amber of his eyes. She couldn't help but recall how perfectly her thumb had fit into that sexy cleft in his chin.

When she finally found her voice, it sounded as if it came from somewhere far outside herself. "Your apartment seems very nice."

In court his eyes had burned with intensity. Now they were more guarded, his tone annoyingly unreadable. "Well, why don't I show you around?" Raising his voice, he said, "Please, I hope you'll all excuse us while I show Ms. Adair—"

"Rutherford," Phoebe managed.

He nodded. Lifting his hand from the stroller, he slipped it beneath her elbow. At the mere touch, unwanted memories teased her consciousness. How she'd awakened ten months ago with those same strong fingers curled around the stem of a white rose that lay across her belly.

Concentrate on the matter at hand, Phoebe. Just pretend this is some sort of business arrangement. Keep your emotions under control—and you'll be alone with your kids soon. Surveying him with an expression she hoped was both neutral and interested, she squinted as he explained the layout—which sets of French doors led to which rooms.

He paused. "You know, it's just an apartment, not rocket science."

She blinked. She was still so stunned, she hadn't heard half of what he'd said. "Right."

Somehow she followed him as he began her guided tour. She was in shock. Everything was moving so fast. After Nico died last week, she'd found out her babies had been processed by Big Apple Babies, with two of them winding up at her Granddaddy Winslow's because he was listed as next of kin. As soon as Phoebe had arrived in New York, she'd followed her grandfather's nurse, Dani Newland, trying to catch a glimpse of Lyssa and Kirby. Just last night Phoebe had followed Dani here. Standing outside on the dark, cold sidewalk and staring at this apartment, Phoebe had never imagined that it belonged to Grantham Hale.

Not that she would have recognized the name. She'd never known it. Nor had she guessed she'd ever see him again. That her eccentric Granddaddy Winslow would sentence them to live together and share custody of her babies was unthinkable.

And yet it had just happened.

Warring emotions were tearing her apart. Grantham Hale had reappeared in her life in the most unusual way. But she was going to have to lie to him about what had really happened between her and Nico.

He ushered her from a hallway into the living room. As he guided her toward another set of French doors, Joyce called out, "Don't manhandle my client!"

Grantham's fingers tightened on her arm in a sign

of possessiveness that sent a surge of unwanted warmth through her whole body. He said, "I'm just making sure she's settled."

Phoebe couldn't help but say, "How do you expect me to feel settled when you're gripping me like this?"

He shot her a fleeting smile. "Oh, do I unsettle you?"

"Of course not."

He shrugged as if it were immaterial, leading her past a window with a view of Park and Eightieth streets. He sighed. "Sorry," he murmured. "But somehow I didn't imagine sharing the babies' first night here with five lawyers."

The babies. More than life, Phoebe longed to take a good look at them and hold them close. She reminded herself that she had to ignore her attraction for Grantham for the babies' sakes. Somehow she mustered a dry tone. "Oh, at least you're not all alone with me. Which means your, uh, *inhibitions* are intact and your virtue's still safe."

He didn't miss a beat. "We'll be alone soon enough."

"You make it sound like a threat."

"A promise."

He wasn't nearly as ambivalent as he was pretending. The knowledge should have further unsettled her, but strangely she felt relieved. He hadn't forgotten her. No more than she'd forgotten him. *Phoebe! Keep it businesslike.* She fought the urge to stare toward her babies as a reminder of what she was doing here. She mustered an approving tone. "Everything's baby-proofed."

She realized his devastating eyes had turned watchful. Intense and curious, they were full of questions she could read like a book. *Why did you leave the hotel without leaving a name or number? Didn't my love-making mean anything to you? Aren't you reeling from this crazy turn of events?*

Grantham calmly said, "Someone referred me to a professional baby-proofer. Last night she prepped the apartment for all six babies."

Phoebe made a show of glancing around. The woman *had* done a good job. No door was without a baby gate, no sharp-cornered furniture without plastic buffers. In the kitchen, everything was shipshape. There were six high chairs, six stacks of bibs, six matching plate sets. Grantham led her toward the living room, then down the final hallway.

They went to the end—and Phoebe found herself smiling. "So what's this? An insane asylum for babies?"

Grantham chuckled. The white-tiled playroom was virtually empty. It contained one closed white toy box, a TV, a collection of Barney videotapes on a high shelf, three playpens and six walkers.

He shrugged. "The room's engineered for safety. And according to one psychologist, white is soothing for them."

All at once Phoebe imagined her babies playing in the room, and her nose burned with unshed tears. A second later her eyes blurred and she blinked hard. *Please, just help me hold it together for another few minutes, until I can be alone with them.*

Her throat tightened, aching. "There are six remote controls for the TV?" she managed pleasantly.

"Langdon and Nicolas loved mine," he explained, as they headed toward the living room again, "so I got them each one." Raising his voice, he said, "I think we can show the kids the nursery now."

As Grantham, James and Jake started maneuvering the three strollers, Phoebe's eyes flitted around the room. Tears were pressing her eyelids, making them feel swollen and heavy. She followed the lawyers.

Over his shoulder, Grantham nodded. "That's your room."

She peeked in. It was a small plain room with a single bed, meant for a nanny. Next door, Grantham and the lawyers pushed the strollers inside the nursery. Phoebe followed. As soon as the babies were inside and the lawyers had retreated, Grantham quietly shut the door.

An insistent rap sounded. "What are you doing alone in there with my client!" Joyce demanded.

"Acclimatizing her." Grantham's voice was so unnervingly reasonable that Phoebe suddenly wondered if he really did share her nervousness at this strange reunion. "Since we've been sentenced to be a family," he continued, "I think we all need to bond."

There was a long pause. "Well, uh, I guess you've got a point," Joyce said through the door. "While you bond, we'll all wait in the living room."

As if familial bonding could be accomplished in a matter of mere minutes. Joyce's controlling aggressiveness was starting to bother Phoebe. Outside, footsteps sounded as the five lawyers dutifully trudged away. Below her line of vision, Phoebe could feel the six babies glancing around, curiously studying every detail of their new room. *Just ask. Maybe Grantham will leave for a minute, so you can be alone with them.* She'd hadn't yet glanced at them, not even once. How much had they grown? Did they have hair? What if she couldn't tell them apart from the twins? What if she couldn't even recognize her own babies?

"Well, Phoebe. This is the nursery."

She nodded. Catching a whiff of Grantham's pine and soap scent, she suddenly remembered the smooth, hard muscles of his chest against hers and the silken feel of his golden hair spilling between her fingers. Blinking hard, she forced herself to take in the room. On either side, to her right and left, doors opened to the master bedroom and nanny's room respectively.

Screens and speakers for the high-tech baby monitors were positioned at the bedside tables in both his and what was now her rooms. There were six stainless steel changing tables, six steel wastebaskets, six cribs in a row. Two triplet strollers, to replace the three double strollers the kids were using now. The only spot of color was a wraparound Barney mural and an overstuffed yellow leather armchair. Everything else seemed pristine and ultra-sterile.

It was so…uniform. She couldn't help but wonder if she might add some colorful doodads. She shot him one of her fleeting Queen of the Brave Face smiles. "It's a little like a baby barracks."

Grantham took no offense. "It *is* a little military."

Her straying eyes suddenly riveted on the open door of the master bedroom, taking in the deep rich chocolate carpeting, open master bath and Jacuzzi. When she looked at the king-size platform bed, she blushed. She couldn't think of anything to say.

Suddenly she sensed that all six babies were gazing at her uncertainly. She imagined their plump necks craning, their bright eyes questioning, as if understanding their situation and wondering what in the world their mommy was going to do to fix things. *Phoebe, hang on. Don't be silly. They're probably not even looking at you.*

"Angel," Grantham said. "You okay?"

Something twisted inside her like a knife. She wished he'd said anything but that. The words took her racing back in time to the night he'd made love to her. They must have asked each other that fool question at least a thousand times.

She swallowed hard. "Yeah."

His voice gentled. "Guess you're still the Queen of the Brave Face, huh?"

Her eyes darted to his. Oh, why did those eyes have to be so wonderfully warm? "What's that supposed to mean?"

He surveyed her for a moment, as if debating with himself. "Phoebe," he said carefully, "in all this time, you haven't even once looked at your babies."

She blinked rapidly, fighting the tears. Of course, he'd notice. He noticed everything. She'd found that out ten months ago. As if to prove him wrong, she ventured a quick glance downward—and a soft sob escaped her lips. She was so sure all the white-blond babies were hers. But she hadn't seen them for so long. They had hair, and their eyes were different in color, a deeper blue. She knew the girls were hers— but at this age, girls and boys could look so much alike. Nope, Phoebe wasn't positive. Not a hundred percent. And she couldn't bear to ask Grantham.

But he guessed her dilemma.

"Oh, angel," he said simply. Swiftly he lifted the two white-blond boys from their stroller. Urging her into the yellow armchair, he placed them in her arms. "Here—" He rolled the girls' stroller close, then lifted them out and onto her lap. Phoebe bit her lower lip, but she couldn't mask her emotion. Her eyes blurred so much she could barely see her babies. Another sob escaped her throat. Even worse, one of Grantham's strong bronzed hands she remembered so well squeezed her shoulder.

Softly, so softly she could barely hear, he whispered, "There. Cry for me, angel."

Her voice was strangled. So much had happened between that night they'd shared and now. "Please...could I be alone?"

He didn't hesitate. "Of course." Only when he reached the door did he turn. "I'll be right outside if you need me."

Through tear-filled eyes, she watched him turn. "Grantham." His name was on her lips before she thought it through.

"Hmm?"

Her throat was on fire, aching. "Thank you."

He nodded. And then he was gone. As the door closed quietly, love and relief washed over her. Softly crying, she hugged her babies tightly, then let her greedy eyes rove over them, while her lips brushed their heads. Last time she'd seen them they'd had only downy fuzz for hair, and their delicate bodies were still curled, as if they were still in the womb. Now their eyes were so dark and they were so heavy—as strong as little oxen.

There was no holding back. She cried so long and hard that she was crying for everything that had passed. After all, her night with Grantham had roused her love—*and* her anger. It was his tenderness that taught her how truly abusive Nico was. Her ex had been a sadist. He'd wrapped himself in wealth and possessions to build himself up, and he'd belittled her to hide his inadequacies. He'd made *her* seem unfit because *he* was unfit.

And he hadn't let her go.

Nope. Even after divorcing her and taking the babies, he'd continued to make her life a living hell, destroying her credit and job references so she couldn't get work or find a place to live. Legal-aid lawyers quit believing her. She'd lost all the appeals. Her mother, who'd sublet her mountaintop cabin in Cat's Canyon and left for a dig, was nowhere to be found.

Phoebe had wound up in a shelter for homeless women.

It was a far cry from some nice pristine rehab center called A New Leaf, which, of course, Phoebe had never even seen. Oh, finally she'd been lucky enough to land a cashier's job. And then a small room. By the time her mother came back into town, she was nearly on her feet.

But then, last week, Nico's heart attack had changed everything. He'd never rewritten his will—no doubt having convinced himself he was immortal—and Phoebe had inherited his fortune. By the time she found out, her babies had vanished, headed for New York City and their next of kin. She'd been beside herself with worry, convinced they were lost forever in some huge, bureaucratic system. Immediately she'd hired the best lawyers in the country, determined to find the babies and get them back.

But she sure hadn't counted on Grantham Hale being their adoptive daddy.

What was she going to do? She nestled her cheeks against Lyssa's and Kirby's, then kissed Langdon and Nicolas. All the babies were silent, gazing at her, their eyes—so like her own—touched with concern. Phoebe blew out a shaky sigh. "Yep," she whispered, "your mommy's being a big crybaby, isn't she?" She sniffed, rubbing at her eyes, which felt nearly swollen shut. Sending the twins a quick, fleeting Queen of the Brave Face smile, she crooned, "So far, this isn't very fun, is it? I bet you'd all rather be in your brand new playroom!"

That got them smiling.

Rising, Phoebe put the quadruplets into their cribs, then the twins in theirs, which would at least get the poor things out of the strollers for the moment. When Kirby started to fuss, Phoebe lifted her. Settling her daughter on her hip, she leaned over Langdon's crib, cooed and gave him a toy.

A soft knock sounded at the door. "Angel?"

Phoebe blew out a shaky breath. She could handle this. "C'mon in."

She was almost sorry she'd said it. Grantham edged behind her, and when she turned, bouncing Kirby on her hip, she realized he'd backed her up against Langdon's crib. When Grantham's eyes roved over her, narrowing with concern, she wished she'd at least splashed some cold water on her tearstained cheeks.

He looked as if he was striving for a neutral expression, then he gave up. "Phoebe," he said. "Can you give me some answers now?"

She tried to tell herself that they were on opposite sides of a legal battle. But after all that crying, she felt raw and vulnerable. And the nursery, however sterile in feel, was adorable. He'd built a playroom and made the apartment so safe. "What was the question?" she managed.

"I've got a number of them. I don't believe a word

of what was said in court about your being drunk, disorderly, lewd, bouncing checks..."

Her heart suddenly swelled—or else her chest got too tight. Grantham believed in her. For ten whole months—and even before that—people had been turning on her. But on the strength of one special night, Grantham Hale didn't believe she could commit those crimes.

"Why can't you talk to me?"

Somehow she kept her voice calm. But the pain of the last year was right beneath the surface. All that time she'd been so scared for her babies. Now she wasn't about to let them go. "Grantham—" She clutched Kirby closer. "You're trying to take away my babies."

He shook his head. "Angel, as of two hours ago, I thought the quadruplets were orphans."

Color seeped into her cheeks. "Well, they're not!"

"Phoebe—" He lifted a hand, brushing a strand of hair from her face. "I looked for you. I even hired a PI—"

Her heart hammered. "You hired someone to find me?"

Grantham looked faintly uncomfortable, but he pinned her with a calm amber gaze, looking determined. "I don't know how you feel. But I'll lay it on the line, angel. I never forgot how it felt to hold you. Or how all the walls inside me came tumbling down that night. And now you've erected them again—but this time around yourself." He paused, searching her face for a reaction. "I looked for you as if you were the last living Cinderella."

Phoebe could barely breathe. She could never fight this man—not his romanticism, not what his mere touch aroused in her. Only the weight of Kirby wiggling on her hip served as a reminder of why she was here. Her throat constricted with emotion. She glanced at her black high heels. "No glass slippers here."

Grantham surveyed her for a long moment. Then he glanced at the cribs. "Oh, but there are. Six of them."

"Cinderella's slippers were on her feet."

"They're on yours," he returned. "But I don't understand why you're wearing them to walk away from me." For an instant, something akin to anger flickered in his eyes. "I won't let you go easily," he warned softly. "I'm a tough, ambitious man. And I usually get what I want."

Including my children? The question rocked her. She kept her voice cool. "I can't walk away. Not when the prince has me trapped against a crib."

He didn't budge. Sparks of heat suddenly charged the air around them. Then he sighed. "C'mon, Phoebe. Don't you find this bizarre? I mean, fate's thrown us together in some wild ways. Can't you face what it means?"

She hugged Kirby tighter, smelling her soft baby scent. She'd have to proceed carefully to protect her heart and get custody of her babies. She'd done nothing wrong. She'd never deserved to lose them. From behind her, Langdon toyed with the fabric of her dress through the crib rails. "What?" she finally managed to say. "Do you really think my being here *means* something?"

His eyes were so rock steady that she thought she'd come unhinged. "I sure do, angel. I think it means that heaven and earth and everything in between— including your matchmaking great-grandfather—are conspiring to throw us together. I think it means you belong here."

She couldn't help it. Her voice shook like a leaf. "That's crazy. And don't get so close, Grantham. Nothing's going to happen between us."

He edged an inch closer. "It already happened. In a hotel room in L.A."

Things were spinning out of control. Nervously she turned away and busied herself by nestling Kirby in the crib next to Langdon. Then she turned to face Grantham, crossing her arms protectively over her chest. "Let's get some ground rules straight. The first is that I absolutely, positively do not want to talk about that night."

His voice was heartbreakingly gentle. "Why did you leave?"

She felt the stupid tears again, pressuring her sinuses as if it was the worst hayfever day of the season. How could she explain to Grantham that he'd been her dream lover, her knight in shining armor? She'd wanted the memory to be like the night—absolutely perfect. She didn't want reality to shatter it—not an awkward breakfast with a stranger or a rushed goodbye on the sidewalk in front of the Wilshire Arms while she was still wearing yesterday's clothes. She'd left because the fantasy was over—and in real life she had to lock horns with an abusive ex who'd taken away her kids.

But she couldn't tell Grantham that. Because then he'd know her real feelings, which might jeopardize her ability to get custody of her children.

"Fine," he said. "If you don't want to talk about that night, then let's talk about fairy tales."

That night *was* a fairy tale. "Fairy tales?"

He nodded. "Yeah. Don't you think this is strange? We met once, and now we have children together, not one, not two, not even three—but six."

"Only four are mine."

"Phoebe, this is like magic."

"Funny, I thought it was a custody battle."

Temper flared in his eyes again. "It's that, too. And I have a right to these children."

"Well, I want *my* children back." Her heart thudded against her rib cage. "And I want to know what happened to the money you withdrew from the babies' bank account. A million dollars is a lot of money." Not that he'd understand how much. She thought back to her cot at the homeless shelter, her lower lip quivering.

His parted as if he wanted to say more than he could. "I can't explain. You'll just have to trust me."

Nico used to say that. And Phoebe had learned from hard experience that it was pointless to keep questioning. Besides, Grantham was apparently already richer than Midas. Maybe he'd made an investment he wanted to keep private. She sighed. "Look, I suggest we don't say anything about our past. It's clear your fidelity to Celia's memory helped you get custody, so it would hurt your case if people knew you'd been with someone in the past year. And I…I don't need anything further damaging my reputation."

The blood drained from his face. His tone turned almost regal. "I promise I won't further damage your reputation." He stared at her for a long moment. Then his voice turned deceptively soft. "Please tell me. What's happened to you? What's made you become so guarded? I know every word that came out in court about you was a lie."

Her eyes slunk away, straying over the cribs and babies. She couldn't let him guess the truth, at least not until she discussed it with her lawyers. "I assure you I'm capable of being quite bad."

Grantham sighed. "Is this how you want it?"

Her eyes widened. "What do you mean?"

Before she knew what was happening, he stepped forward, pressing his body against hers. He said, "So, you can be bad?"

She nodded, knowing she wasn't convincing him. "Yep."

"Well," he said simply. "Let's be *quite* bad then."

As she gasped, his mouth covered hers in a kiss that was as she remembered—so hard and hungry, possessive and claiming that she couldn't even begin to fight. She rose to her tiptoes, her heels coming out of her shoes, and her arms circled his neck. Holding on tight, she arched against him, while the honeyed warmth of his tongue plunged between her lips, forcing liquid heat through her body. It was long moments before she thought of the babies and tried to wrench away. He held on for a full extra minute, still licking his tongue into the corners of her mouth, as if with a hunger that could never be appeased. Vaguely, she realized that the babies had gone wild. Giggles sounded, hands clapped and rattles beat madly against the crib rails.

Phoebe leaned back, gasping. "Let me go, Grantham."

That was what her mouth said. But everything else told another story. Her pulse was pounding wildly out of control, throbbing in her wrists and neck. Her voice was a mere croak. "Please. I'd better go see my lawyers. There must be some other solution to this."

His voice was husky. "I'm afraid you're all mine for the next five weeks."

Feeling thoroughly undone, she clutched her throat. The man was right. She was stuck here. Legally. "You probably are going to make me cook."

"In more ways than one," Grantham murmured. Then he squinted. "Oh, please," he said with a sigh. "The way you're vainly clutching at your throat, you could be a virgin in a Gothic romance fleeing from the plundering master of the house."

She swallowed hard. "I guess that would be you."

"Right," Grantham said dryly.

She had no idea what he was thinking, but a decided expression crossed his features. As if completely forgetting he'd just kissed her senseless, he reached past her. Grabbing a stack of diapers, he pressed them against her belly and into her hands. "Diaper duty, Jane Eyre," he said. "Your turn. As you probably recall, there's more to parenting than giving birth."

Still stunned by the kiss, Phoebe glanced around.

"All six, angel."

Somehow, she managed to separate four diapers and hand them back. "You take four. I'll take two." Somehow she mustered a sweet smile. "As you seem to have guessed, I'm out of practice. That means you're probably twice as fast."

He handed her a diaper. "Three each," he bargained.

The man was impossible. She sighed. "Deal."

They set to work, strapping the babies to the changing tables, passing powder and Wet Ones. Kirby shrieked, then suddenly calmed. Langdon squawked. Stanley giggled. As Grantham gripped Lyssa's tiny crossed ankles, lifted her pint-size behind and snuggled a fresh diaper beneath it, he said, "Angel?"

Phoebe stopped in mid-change, pausing to tickle Devin's tummy. "And quit calling me that," she said.

"Why?"

"For the same reason I don't want you kissing me. Because it can't happen again."

He shrugged. "I'll make you a promise. It won't happen again until you want it to." His quick sexy smile made the corners of his eyes crinkle. "But you'll want it to."

She decided to ignore his aggravating self-confidence. "Maybe. But I want my babies back, and I can't afford to get confused about what I'm doing here."

"It's hardly confusing. You're parenting with me." Grantham shrugged. "And, angel?"

Her knight in shining armor definitely had a persistent side. She met his gaze. He looked as if something very serious was on his mind. "What?"

Lifting a hand, Grantham lightly gestured toward her hair. "It looked so natural red," he murmured. "But since the babies have light hair, I guess yours really is blond instead of red. Is that right?"

They were neck deep in a custody battle—and this is what the man wanted to know? Phoebe shifted Devin on her hip. "Why, Grantham," she couldn't help but drawl. "Only my hairdresser knows for sure."

He smiled. "You'll tell me."

As he turned to put Lyssa in a crib, Phoebe surveyed his broad back. Even now she could hear his clear, resonant voice teasing her ears. *Let's talk about fairy tales.*

What if the strange, coincidental way she'd found

Grantham *did* mean something? Could it be a real-life fairy tale coming true? Phoebe did believe in fate. And in God. And in angels in heaven. Oh, Nico had caused her to pour a deep moat around the castle of her heart. But there was still a drawbridge. Because she'd never once stopped believing in the power of love.

Should she go along with Grantham? Get to know him?

She wanted to. But as she watched him tease her babies, tendrils of fear snaked through her. What if she fell in love with Grantham? Married him? What might happen later, if it ended in divorce?

Grantham was even richer and more powerful than Nico.

And like Nico, he could destroy her.

Chapter Five

"Did you miss Mommy?" Phoebe cooed, nestling in an overstuffed red wing chair in Grantham's study, snuggling Lyssa under one arm and Kirby under the other. Langdon was sprawled on her chest. In the living room, the twins and Nicolas were with Grantham. "Did you miss her? Did you? Mommy sure missed every single one of you. Yes, she did."

Joyce Moon stopped pacing long enough to blow out an aggravated sigh. "Phoebe, aren't you listening to a word?"

No, I'm not. Crying had done her a world of good. And now, with the babies in her arms, she was happy for the first time in nearly a year. Yep. The more Phoebe got used to being here, the less horrible all this seemed. No doubt, she'd have to be very careful. She wanted custody of her kids, and Grantham definitely needed to answer for the money that was missing from their bank account. Still, when he'd kissed her in the nursery, memories of the night they'd shared came flooding back. She couldn't pursue a physical relationship right now, not under the circumstances. But she simply had no choice except to get to know the man.

Joyce stamped her foot. "Phoebe!"

Forcibly tearing her gaze from the babies, Phoebe felt as if she'd entered another world. In contrast to Grantham's stark white, ultramodern living room, the study was from another century, with thick red carpeting and floor-to-ceiling shelves full of leatherbound books with gilt-lettered spines. Perched atop a polished wooden table with intricately carved clawed feet was a collection of gargoyles, and on another table, next to some old-fashioned binoculars, was a bronzed Cupid, his bow raised, his arrow just happening to point right at Phoebe. In a corner, a sepia-toned globe turned lazily on its iron stand, where Joyce had absently given it a push.

Watching the world spin, Phoebe realized she still felt completely dizzy. How in all creation had she wound up here, in Grantham Hale's apartment? She hazarded a glance through the closed French doors at Grantham, who was in the living room, seated on the white sofa, with Stanley on one knee, Devin on the other and her own little boy, Nicolas, slung over his shoulder.

"Phoebe?"

This time it was Orsen Daily. The wiry man slung a gray suit jacket around a straight-back chair, the posts of which were every bit as narrow and spindly as his shoulders. Adjusting his scholarly wire-rim glasses on his nose, Orsen smoothed a hand over his graying hair. He was probably forty, but he looked closer to fifty.

"Sorry," Phoebe murmured. Why couldn't her lawyers understand? She hadn't seen her kids for nearly a year. All she wanted to do was snuggle with them. She couldn't wait to do all the simple things—feed them, bathe them, put them to bed. At this particular moment, she didn't care if she had to share them with ten million Grantham Hales.

But Joyce was grilling her again. "You've got to tell us the truth about Grantham Hale."

Phoebe sighed. As far as she was concerned, her past with Grantham should have no bearing on the case. But Joyce was refusing to back down. "Okay, I do know him. We...were lovers. It was—" Phoebe's voice caught. *The most wonderful night of my life.* "Just one night."

Joyce gasped. "What!"

Bert Taylor wolf whistled. He was the youngest of the lawyers—and the epitome of slick. He had dark eyes. Thick, black, carefully barbered hair. And a navy suit, gold watch and alligator shoes—all of which Phoebe thought looked way too expensive.

Orsen pressed his wire rims firmly against the bridge of his nose. "You mean to say you slept with him, and now he's got legal custody of your children? How the hell did *this* happen?"

Phoebe swallowed hard. "I don't know. Uh, it just kind of did."

Orsen stared. "I mean when? Where?"

Phoebe tamped down her blush. "Ten months ago, in L.A. At the Wilshire Arms. Look, it was just one time. I didn't...I didn't even know his name."

Bert shook his head. "I can't believe it. You're from L.A., he's from New York. You meet, have a one-night stand in a hotel and now he's the adoptive father of your kids?"

"Phew!" said Joyce. "We really need to sit down and take a good hard look at the implications!"

Oh, no, we don't. Feeling dizzy again, Phoebe

glanced toward the whirling globe. Then she strained her mental muscles—stirring much unused gray matter, she was sure—trying to shove all the implications to the furthest reaches of her mind. She especially wanted the implications to steer clear of any brain centers dealing with central nervous behaviors and love hormones. Or anything else that might make her wind up kissing him again, the way she had in the nursery. At least until she got to know Grantham Hale. Not the fantasy dream lover and knight in shining armor Grantham Hale. The *real* Grantham Hale. Her chest was heavy from Langdon's weight, so Phoebe resituated him in her lap.

Orsen said, "So, how can we best use this affair thing against him?"

Affair thing?

Phoebe snapped to attention. "No! My past with Grantham can't be a factor here," she protested. "Just now, in the nursery, we agreed not to make an issue of it. Reputation-wise, I don't want to look any worse than I already do. And he doesn't need negative publicity."

Joyce Moon stopped pacing, turned toward Phoebe and crossed her arms. "When you hired us, you said you were willing to go to any lengths to get your children back. This would work in our favor. It'll make him look bad, since his supposed fidelity to his wife's memory was a factor in helping him get custody."

Don't back down, Phoebe. Your lawyers have no right to challenge you. "He was completely faithful to Celia. And I said no," Phoebe returned firmly.

Orsen threw up his hands. "Oh, cripes, Phoebe. Don't get so moral on us. It was just a one-night stand."

Just a one-night stand? Phoebe's heart fluttered. How could Orsen make something tawdry out of that night? She'd use almost anything to get her kids back, but not that. Never that. "I hired all of you to do a job. But I absolutely will not have Grantham Hale's good name dragged through the mud."

The lawyers exchanged glances.

Joyce gave up pacing and plunked herself down opposite Phoebe in an armchair. "But your ex-husband dragged *yours* through the mud."

"Exactly," Phoebe said, trying to remind herself she shouldn't be feeling defensive. After all, the attorneys were her employees—not the other way around. "I don't like cutthroat tactics or lying. And I definitely pride myself on being a better person than my ex-husband. I know I've agreed to act as if all those trumped-up charges against me are true...." Her voice trailed off. "Look, do you all *really* think the only chance I've got of clearing my name is to pretend to reform? Can't you somehow just expose Nico's lies?"

Joyce moaned. "Phoebe, your ex-husband was a professional publicist. He hired other professionals to slander you—and they covered their tracks well. The only possible way out is to pretend you were completely rehabilitated at A New Leaf. C'mon, we've already found a counselor who will swear you were there."

"Sounds like *he's* the one who needs to turn over a new leaf," Phoebe couldn't help but say petulantly.

"Don't worry." Bert slicked back his dark hair. "Everything's going to be fine. Young Confused Mother Reforms for Long-Lost Children. The press will eat it up. They love human interest—and always root for the underdog.''

"But I don't want any media," Phoebe protested.

The lawyers exchanged glances again.

Joyce suddenly gasped. "You didn't tell Grantham Hale what really happened, did you?"

"No, but—"

Joyce heaved a loud sigh of relief. "Good. If you want your kids back, you really can't tell anyone. For the past ten months, you've been trying to convince people Nico slandered you. Well, no one bought it. If anyone—especially Grantham Hale—suspects the truth, you'll lose all your credibility again."

Phoebe's eyes strayed over the babies' heads. She resented having to lie. But even her brilliant great-grandfather had fallen for Nico's scam. "I can't even tell Grantham the truth in private?" she asked slowly.

"No!" Joyce exploded. "Didn't you hear that man in court? He means to keep those kids!"

"But now that he knows it's me, maybe he'd be willing to work something out." The longer Phoebe thought about it, the idea of Grantham Hale seeing her kids a couple times a week didn't seem all that terrible.

Bert leaned forward, his dark eyes imploring. "Phoebe, you've been declared an unfit mother. Even if Grantham Hale wanted to give you joint custody, the court might still decide against you. Don't you understand? He has full legal custody. And we're under time pressure. These five weeks might well be the last you'll ever spend with your children."

Tears suddenly stung her eyes. She whispered, "I know."

Bert nodded, seemingly glad he'd finally gotten through to her. "Meantime, you have a job to do."

She pulled the babies closer. Little Langdon squeezed her thigh and giggled. She smiled at him. They were amazingly good babies, so even-tempered and quiet—at least so far. Swiping at her eyes, she said, "A job?"

Bert nodded again. "To be the best parent ever."

That would be easy. Heaven knew, Phoebe had missed these kids so much. She hugged the babies tighter, smelling their soft powdery baby scent. Kirby yawned. Lyssa played with her dress. Langdon teethed on his hands.

Orsen was all business again. "Well, you looked wan today in court. That's good. We want to pull off a very public transformation for the press, as if your contact with the babies is turning you into a new woman. Over the next five weeks, you might get a new wardrobe, something more maternal and subur-ban, sportier."

"Warmer suits," Joyce said with enthusiasm. "Add some extra moisturizer in the morning, so it'll look like you're simply glowing."

"I can arrange photo ops," said Bert. "Hale's al-ways in the news. We want all of New York to see you doing fun things with the kids. Their birthday's this month, so you could throw a party."

Didn't these people listen? Phoebe wondered un-easily. She'd hired the best attorneys available, and she wanted her children back more than life. But... "I said no press. If I have to, I'll pretend I did all those horrible things Nico said I did. I'll even lie and say I was rehabilitated in A New Leaf. But the focus *has* to be on me looking good, not on Grantham Hale looking bad. Is that understood? I want my children. But I'm not out for blood."

Bert shrugged. "Fine. No press."

Phoebe sighed in relief. When her gaze caught Grantham's again through the French doors, she sucked in a quavering breath and quickly looked at the babies. Soon she'd be all alone in this apartment with him and the babies....

"Phoebe?"

She'd been completely lost in thought. "Hmm?"

"Would you mind asking Grantham for some pens and paper?"

"Sure," Phoebe murmured, wanting the excuse to talk to him, and not wanting it. Which was silly, she decided, since they were trapped under the same roof for five weeks. No doubt, they'd find plenty of opportunities to talk. And to do much more, if Grantham had his way.

Phoebe put the babies on the floor. Lyssa remained seated, still playing with her dress, while Langdon and Kirby immediately turned and used the chair to pull themselves to their feet. "I'll be right back," Phoebe said.

Joyce's easy smile gave Phoebe some relief. At least her lawyers had listened. There was no way Phoebe could allow Grantham's reputation to be tampered with, especially not after the way Nico had tampered with hers.

"CLIENTS LIKE THAT." Orsen pushed his wire rims firmly to the bridge of his nose. "Ya gotta love 'em."

Joyce sighed. "Well, she wants the illusion she's in control. That's part of what she's paying for."

"Ah," Bert sighed. "And for that swanky suite at the Plaza Hotel where she's putting us up for the next five weeks."

Joyce tossed her dark hair over her shoulder, took off her jacket, then rolled up her sleeves. "Well, while she's gone, let's get down to business. She slept with Grantham Hale. How *are* we going to use it?"

Bert flashed her a quick smile. "I'll send someone to the Wilshire Arms for hard proof they were together. Eyewitnesses. Room service receipts. Video from the hotel security cameras. Anything we can blackmail him with."

Joyce squinted. "You want to blackmail Grantham Hale?"

Bert shrugged. "We might as well get someone to approach him with the proof. He'll make the payoff, not wanting to jeopardize his case, especially since the whole city's under the illusion that he's been so faithful to the memory of his wife."

"You think he'll make a payoff?" Joyce asked.

Orsen scoffed. "A guy like that? Sure."

Bert's voice warmed with enthusiasm. "We could even take pictures of the payoff. Five weeks down the road, we can show in court that he had an affair, and that he was so ashamed he was willing to pay to cover it up. If we decide not to use the blackmail angle, we could call the guy to the stand, introduce him as a newspaper stringer or a free-lancer who collects information on newsworthy celebrities. He could offer the proof of the affair. We don't even have to mention that it was with Phoebe."

"That information wouldn't matter," Joyce said. "Given how Nico destroyed her reputation, Grantham's involvement with her would only make him look that much sleazier."

"And what about the money?" said Orsen. "I still can't believe Hale actually withdrew a million dollars from an account for those kids and now he won't say why.''

Joyce frowned. "Unfortunately, I'm sure it's nothing.''

Bert nodded. "In reality, the man seems clean as a whistle.''

Orsen looked glum. "He seems like a saint.''

"Well," Joyce reminded them, "all we really need to do is stir up suspicion in the press." She smiled. "What do you guys think of this headline. Millions Missing! Ad Man A Bad Dad?''

Bert laughed. "Joyce, I swear. Your future was in the tabloids, not in a courtroom. We'll get somebody to run it in the *New York Post*.''

She smiled back. "Okay, so we tail him. Research his finances. Hire a blackmailer. And don't forget. The honest ones always fall the fastest." Joyce leaned back, feeling satisfied. "Phew! I think we're going to win this one, boys.''

"We always do, Joyce," said Orsen. "We always do.''

"WHAT'S THE MATTER?" Grantham crooned. Not that the soothing tone helped. Baby Nicolas glared, his tiny lower lip trembling and tears clinging in his blond eyelashes. Frowning, Grantham wedged the phone receiver between his jaw and shoulder, then he glanced toward the living room where Doc Holiday, the pediatrician from Big Apple Babies, had joined Jake Lucas and James Sanger. "Maybe we should ask Doc about your bad temper. What do you think about that, huh, Nicolas?''

Nicolas tilted his head as if he might be coaxed into

a smile—however small—so Grantham showered his face with kisses and kept bouncing him on his hip.

The line clicked on. "Grantham?"

"Yeah."

"Sorry about that. My wife was on the other line. I swear, all hell broke loose today. I've got a dog at the vet. And my three daughters want to tattoo and pierce every conceivable body part."

Grantham laughed. To hear Cy Lynde talk, you'd never guess he was one of the best PI's in the business. Not to look at him, either. Cy was paunchy, middle-aged and prone to wearing baggy suits that hardly helped his hunched Igor-like posture. Still, it was Cy's mind clients paid top dollar for, and that was razor sharp. He would have found Phoebe ten months ago if there'd been anything more to go on than a grainy picture from the Wilshire Arms video security system. Grantham glanced around. He'd loaded Phoebe up with pencils and paper, and she was conferring with her lawyers again. Good. This was one conversation he definitely didn't want her hearing.

"Do you think you can help me out, Cy?"

"Sure. But I can't believe this. You not only found her, but she's the quadruplets' mother?"

"Yeah." It *was* amazing. Grantham didn't have the least doubt that the Fates were at work. "Well, here's what I've got. She was married to a guy named Nicolas Adair. He was a west-coast image consultant. I want you to find out whatever you can about him. And about a place called A New Leaf. Supposedly, that's where Phoebe was rehabilitated."

"Phoebe," Cy said. "So that's her name."

"And, Cy—"

"Wait a sec. I'm still scribbling all this down."

Grantham took the time to try to amuse Nicolas. Yeah, he was definitely the brooder. Grantham frowned, pondering the fact that Phoebe's ex-husband's namesake just happened to be the worst-tempered of the bunch. Nicolas scowled, as if Grantham were personally responsible for global warming and the destruction of the rain forests.

Cy sniffed. "Okay. So why do you want dope on Nicolas Adair?"

Grantham finished explaining the situation. Then he said, "Phoebe's not capable of doing all those horrible things. I had a drink with her, and she could barely choke down a weak Cape Codder. And an extramarital affair? Forget about it."

"Well, her ex was an image consultant," Cy said. "Maybe he really did tamper with her image, the way she initially claimed."

Grantham nodded. "I'm sure of it. I just don't understand why she's no longer denying the charges."

"I'll see what I can find out. I take it you're still hung up on her?"

For ten months, she was all Grantham thought about. He said, "I...I like her."

Cy hooted with laughter. "Right."

After hanging up, Grantham headed into the living room. "Hey, Doc," he said as he settled on the sofa, bouncing Nicolas on his knee. Stanley and Devin crawled around his shoes, pinching the toes and untying the laces.

Grantham chuckled. "He's licking my shoe." Swiftly, he scooped Devin from the floor, settling him on the knee opposite Nicolas. Devin giggled naughtily, gazing up with huge mischievous sandy eyes.

Grantham squinted with mock censure. "Yuck."

Stanley clapped his hands in delight. "Da-da!"

"Well, Grantham—"

Grantham glanced at Doc. The pediatrician's real name was Winston, but everybody called him Doc. As usual, he wore a thigh-length white lab coat over faded jeans and a denim shirt, a Stetson he didn't bother to take off inside and cowboy boots. A stethoscope was slung around his neck.

"Well, anyhow," Doc said in an accent that placed his origins due south of New York, "I can't stay." He plunked down six fat file folders. "They're the copies of the babies' records you asked for, Grantham. All I can say is look out for that Devin. He's the demon child. Doesn't surprise me the least little bit that he's been lickin' your shoe. Nicolas is the cryer. And to-night, you'll figure out that Stanley's the insomniac. How you're gonna sleep two winks is beyond me."

With that rosy pronouncement, Doc headed toward the door. "Just call me if you've got any questions. I'll go ahead and see myself out."

When he was gone, Jake Lucas laughed, making his dimples show and his green eyes twinkle. The adoption lawyer didn't look like a head executive, but he ran Big Apple Babies like a tight ship. He brushed a hand through his thick raven hair, then gave his black mustache a tweak. "Still sure you want to be a papa, Grantham?"

"After interviewing me for ten months, you guys should know I've done my homework."

James Sanger grunted, shifting his stocky, power-fully built frame in an easy chair. "Well, I'm worried about this Phoebe Rutherford."

Jake said, "She *has* been declared unfit."

Grantham's temper flared. "I...I've met her. And

I'm sure she never could have committed those crimes. I don't know why she was accused of them." And Grantham was definitely going to find out.

Jake sighed. "Still, given her legal standing, we'll need to check in with you periodically." Seeing the look on Grantham's face, he continued, "As a new parent of adoptive children, you know we're obliged to check in with you anyway."

Grantham nodded. He knew. It was just that Phoebe brought out his protective instincts. He kept his voice even. "She's a trusted guest in my home. And she's the mother of four of my six children. As crazy as it is, we've been sentenced to be parents together, and that's exactly what we're going to do." His expression softened. "Look, guys. You've been a great help to me in the last ten months. I assure you, everything here is going to be fine."

Jake unbuttoned his charcoal suit jacket. "You're sure you want to play along with Judge Winslow instead of fighting this utterly insane ruling of his?"

"Yeah." To Grantham, five weeks of enforced parenting with Phoebe Rutherford sounded like a vacation to heaven. Not that she was quite as attuned to all the potential possibilities as he was—yet.

"The way I see it, she's dug her own grave," James said. "The best she'll ever get is shared custody—and Grantham would have to agree."

Jake nodded.

Grantham could merely shake his head. "Don't you guys ever quit? Pardon me for saying so, Jake, but you got *engaged* today." It had happened right outside the courtroom. "Aren't you even the least bit anxious to go home?"

Jake's eyes looked far off for a second. No doubt,

he was thinking of Dani Newland, his bride-to-be. She was a nursing student, previously employed by Judge Winslow. "I just want to make sure you and the kids are settled," Jake murmured, still sounding a little distant.

James continued, "I'll start going over the case files for Phoebe's legal aid appeals. But it seemed pretty obvious in court that the original case against her was clear-cut. She was proven decisively unfit."

"James, I know that stuff's not true. For a number of reasons, I'm not going into my history with her, though. It's just not pertinent here." And Grantham wasn't about to further damage her reputation.

Jake sighed. "Grantham, we're your lawyers and your friends. We may need to know—"

Grantham shook his head.

"I do need to ask what you did with the million dollars you took out of the bank," James said.

Grantham sighed. He should have guessed that was coming. He glanced at Jake, who looked away. "Sorry, James," he said. "But I can't answer that."

James stared at him. "Excuse me?"

"I said I can't answer that."

After a long moment James sighed, accepting it. Grantham gazed at Phoebe through the French doors. He didn't know why these last months had been so hard on her. But he'd find out the truth. And, starting tomorrow, they'd forget all this legal business. For the next five weeks he'd show her what it could be like if they recaptured even a glimpse of the one night they'd shared. Maybe he'd open the house in Genesis, Long Island, so he and Phoebe could head out to the beach with the kids on weekends, make sand castles and collect shells. Halloween was right around the corner, so they could buy costumes for the kids....

"Grantham?"

Roused from his fantasies of domestic bliss, Grantham glanced at Jake. He found himself saying, "One look into that woman's eyes and you can tell she's just not capable of any kind of bad behavior, Jake."

Jake tilted his head, considering. "If you're wrong, the babies could be...at risk."

"I'm not wrong."

James shrugged. "You know, if you're right and if she can prove she was slandered, then chances are she *can* take away the kids."

Grantham's eyes strayed toward Phoebe again. He'd thought of her for ten months. He'd thought of her in his bathtub, in his bed, in his arms. But the very last place he'd ever imagined her was on the opposite side of a court case.

"She'd never do that to me," Grantham finally said. And he could only pray that he was right.

Chapter Six

Little Stanley's deep, melancholy wail of abandonment sounded from the nursery. Again.

Phoebe's aching eyes flew open.

Yep. It was just as she'd thought. She could still see perfectly well in the dark. Her eyes hadn't stayed shut long enough to un-adjust. In fact, her night vision was so good now that she was beginning to think she'd developed X-ray vision, like Superman. Groggily, she imagined herself leaping from bed in her flying bathrobe and being introduced as Super Mom.

She pressed the heels of her palms to her eyes. Sure enough. They were still nearly swollen shut from the lack of sleep and from today's tears—both shed and unshed. Not that she minded as she gazed at the video monitor.

Next door, the pristine nursery gleamed in the semi-darkness. The six baby cribs were in a neat little row. All the babies were adorably curled on their mattresses, dressed in the cute matching mint green sleepers that Grantham had had stitched with their names. Yep, each and every one was still sleeping like a heaven-sent angel.

Except for Stanley.

The poor little thing was standing in his crib, gripping the rails with tight fists, as if he'd been wrongfully imprisoned, and letting loose with a powerful wail.

"Oh, Stanley," Phoebe murmured. Her swollen eyes strayed to the digital clock on the bedside stand, just as they had at midnight. And at one o'clock, two, three, four and now... It really was five o'clock in the morning. Her usual dry sense of humor was starting to return, so she was half tempted to tell Grantham that the tiny, cantankerous insomniac twin was his sole responsibility.

But no self-respecting woman, no matter how dog-tired, could ignore cries like that. They plucked her every last maternal heartstring as surely as they shattered her eardrums. *And if you don't get a move on, Phoebe, the others will be up and at 'em soon and screaming every bit as loud.*

Fourteen hours of parenting, and this was one lesson Phoebe had learned.

Another was that six kids needed diaper changes more often than she'd supposed.

Staggering from the narrow bed in the nanny's quarters, Phoebe swiftly grabbed her robe from the top of the covers and punched her arm through a sleeve. As she stumbled next door, she murmured, "Shoot, that's the wrong arm." She tugged off the robe. As she entered the nursery, she slipped her arm into a sleeve and realized the whole slinky thing was inside out.

"Wardrobe difficulties, angel?"

Phoebe tried to remind herself that Grantham's voice wasn't intentionally sexy, just throaty from the lack of sleep. Nevertheless, it warmed her—from her aching muscles right down to her extremities. In re-flex, her hand shot to her disheveled hair. Her voice was a sleep-creaky croak. "I'm inside out," she managed to explain, feeling suddenly flustered.

"Well, you look just right-side-in to me."

Phoebe smiled as she leaned past Grantham and lifted Stanley from the crib with a softly whispered, "C'mere, kid." As she began bouncing the baby on her hip, she cleared her throat. "I guess I look as good as a woman can look at five in the morning." *Why did I say that?* She could have kicked herself. Did it sound as if she was asking for compliments? *Was* she asking?

Stanley suddenly wiggled like a wet fish in her arms, drew in another deep breath and loosed a wail that could wake the dead. Then his bony little sleeper-clad shoulders started hitching with pathetic sobs.

Grantham groaned with humor. "C'mon, Stanley. The first couple of times it was kind of cute..." Grantham moved closer, and because he seemed so anxious to hold the baby, Phoebe carefully transferred Stanley to his father's arms.

"Why won't he stop?" she whispered, staring worriedly into Stanley's squinched-up face and following Grantham as he turned and padded barefoot toward the master bedroom, so Stanley's sobs wouldn't wake the other babies.

"I don't know." Grantham bounced Stanley on his hip, trying to calm him. "But Doc said he was the insomniac of the bunch."

"Guess it didn't take ten years of medical school to figure that one out," Phoebe murmured, her eyes inadvertently dipping over Grantham. He'd slung on his robe over his boxer shorts. It was the very same chocolate brown robe he'd lent her ten months ago in L.A., the tie to which had wound up loosely binding her hands....

She quickly glanced away, but her eyes only strayed right back to Grantham. The tie was looped around his waist, but the robe was gaping open, so the weeping Stanley was cradled against Grantham's naked chest. She saw the hard, smooth muscles, and her fingers suddenly itched to twine in the golden chest hairs that she knew were the texture of silk.

Her heart skipped a beat. Feeling breathless and dry-mouthed, she could merely stare. Her wedding ring was hung around Grantham's neck on a gold chain, next to a gold cross. She'd forgotten the ring in the hotel, and once she'd gotten to her mother's in Cat's Canyon, it was too late to get it back. If she'd had it, she would have pawned it. Had Grantham really been wearing it all this time? Instinctively she knew the answer was yes.

Standing there watching him in the dim light, she was sure she'd never felt so moved. This man hadn't forgotten her. He'd hired a PI to search for her. He'd kept her ring. She could almost hear Joyce Moon say, *We really need to sit down and take a good hard look at the implications.* Not that Phoebe was about to.

Especially not at five o'clock in the morning.

Seemingly oblivious of her train of thought, Grantham sat on the edge of the king-size platform bed. Phoebe suddenly frowned at father and son. "Do you think Stanley's sick or something?" she asked, taking a tentative step toward the bed. "Maybe he has bad dreams. Or night terrors."

"Night terrors?"

"They're like bad dreams. Except that they seem particularly real."

"Just like our situation, huh?" As Stanley loosed another loud howl, Grantham shot her a wry smile over the top of the baby's head.

Phoebe glanced around with mock hopefulness. "You mean there's still a possibility that none of this is real?"

Grantham chuckled. "Are fairy tales ever real, angel?"

Phoebe put her hands on her hips and stared archly. "You really think our situation is just peachy?"

He wrestled with the squirming, squalling Stanley. "Now, now," he returned lightly, "don't be such a spoilsport. I bet we wind up having fun."

Phoebe glanced from his bedside clock to the weeping baby. "Yep. So far, it's a real blast."

Grantham shot her a smile, one that said he knew she didn't really mind getting out of a warm bed to attend to Stanley. One that said he'd like nothing more than to keep her up late nights for altogether different reasons. Feeling herself blush, Phoebe was glad for the dark.

"Night terrors, huh?" Grantham said.

Relieved at the change of subject, she nodded. "He could even still be in a dream state."

Grantham shrugged. "Looks wide awake to me."

Phoebe stared at Stanley. "True. And he sure *sounds* awake." Suddenly feeling groggy, she swayed on her feet.

"Why don't you sit down?"

She glanced at the bed. Then at Grantham in the bed. And then she started to say she could think of a whole lot of reasons she shouldn't sit down. Nevertheless, she was awfully tired. After edging toward the mattress, Phoebe eased onto it. The second she did, Stanley stopped crying—right in mid-wail.

The room fell dead silent.

Except for Grantham's breathing. Suddenly Phoebe felt uncomfortably aware of his presence on the other side of the bed. Feeling his eyes drift over her, she couldn't help but pull her robe closer around herself. Heavens, if she'd had any idea she'd be bunking within miles of Grantham Hale, she probably would have packed something other than her oversize T-shirts and the short, lacy silk hand-me-down robe her mother had given her.

Or maybe not, Phoebe amended, her eyes straying to Grantham's chest again. When she lifted her gaze, she realized his sleepy eyes had settled on her exposed thigh—and she jumped from the bed as if he'd just reached out and pinched her. Stanley drew in a deep quavering breath of protest, his lower lip quivering, then he opened his mouth wide and exhaled another ear-piercing wail.

Grantham groaned. "Oh, no."

Phoebe sighed. "Yep."

She sank onto the mattress again. And then she frowned. The instant she was seated, Stanley quit crying.

"Just sit here for a minute," Grantham whispered.

"Okay," Phoebe whispered back, already feeling every second as pure torture. She was awake enough to notice that the bed smelled of Grantham. And that he had silk sheets, printed in a masculine navy and brown plaid, which were rumpled. The imprint of his head was visible on one of his four pillows. She couldn't believe he'd been wearing her ring all these months—and even to bed. As her eyes drifted to his chest, she had the fleeting, tantalizing thought that the master bed felt a whole lot more comfortable than her narrow little cot in the nanny's quarters.

"You know, Phoebe," Grantham said in a low, conversational tone, "the way we've been flung together *is* really strange."

Oh, no, not this again. Feeling congested from the lack of sleep, she sniffed and dug her knuckles into the corners of her eyes. Her voice was scratchy. "Haven't we already discussed this?"

"Have we?"

"Uh-huh." *When you kissed me in the nursery.* Phoebe scooted back against the headboard, suddenly feeling too darn tired to care whether Grantham Hale's impertinent eyes happened to stray to her thighs. She yawned. "Earlier I think you may have mentioned fate and fairy tales. But you know what? Stranger things than this *have* happened, Grantham."

He raised an eyebrow. "Like what?"

She watched Stanley curl against Grantham... against the thatch of curly golden-blond chest hairs. One of Grantham's hands nearly covered the baby's back, and the sight was so heavenly and peaceful that if Stanley had been anywhere other than pressed against Grantham's chest, Phoebe would have kissed the baby. But as things stood—or sat on the bed, as it were—Phoebe didn't dare.

"Stranger things like what?" Grantham asked.

Realizing she was staring at the space where her ring hung between his pectorals, Phoebe slowly blinked and lifted her gaze. "Oh, I don't know," she said vaguely. "Alien visitations. Cows jumping over the moon. That the world turned out to be round instead of flat."

His soft chuckle, throaty with sleep, teased her ears. "Battling poltergeists," he continued amiably. "Charging admission to your own out-of-body experiences. Seeing Elvis."

She nodded. He was getting the point. "Exactly."

He rolled his eyes. "C'mon. Didn't you notice that picture of the three Fates in the courtroom today?"

Phoebe had, but something told her not to admit it. "The Fates?"

"I could almost swear they were looking at me."

Phoebe pressed the heels of her palms to her eyes again and groaned. "It was a painting, Grantham," she said flatly.

His mouth quirked. "Ha! Caught you. I knew you saw it."

She squinted at him. Was this really the same man who looked so commanding in a suit and tie? Who kissed her like nobody's business? "I don't think the Fates in the painting were looking at you specifically, Grantham."

He shot her a long, assessing look. "I think they were."

Her lips twitched with a smile, then her shoulders started to shake with barely suppressed laughter. "Well, maybe they thought you were cute."

"Somehow, Phoebe, I think that's projection." Grantham laughed softly. "So, *do* you think I'm cute?"

She felt another telltale flush warm her cheeks. *Cute* hardly described Grantham Hale—even if he was turning out to be far more flirtatious than Phoebe would have guessed. Still, he had a proud warrior's face and a noble nose that eternally banished him from the realm of fuzzy kittens, eager puppy dogs and anything else even vaguely resembling cute. She kept her voice steady. "I think we'd both be cuter with more sleep."

He chuckled. "What? You're not going to tell me whether I'm cute?"

She scoffed. "You have mirrors!" And plenty more, she thought, feeling uneasy. Grantham's apartment wasn't ostentatious, but he was obviously wealthy. And, like Nico, he could so easily use his money and power against her....

Becoming serious, Grantham nodded. "Well, I was hoping to take tomorrow off, but I've got a big account pending, so I'm going to have to go into the office, at least for a while."

The lawyers had stayed so late that she and Grantham hadn't begun to work out the logistics of child care. And six babies would be too many for just one pair of hands. Well, Grantham had so clearly thought of everything.... "I'm sure you've got some help coming in, right?"

"Uh, no."

Her eyes widened. She woke up just a little more. "No?"

Grantham sighed. "Well, I did start interviewing nannies, but...well, no one seemed good enough. There's a nanny service, though—Nine to Five Nannies—so we can call in the morning. They'll send one or two people for the day, whatever you think you need. With luck, I can take some time off. I really want to be at home with the kids."

Especially for the next five weeks. Phoebe was sure that was what he was thinking. Grantham wanted every chance to make sure the kids stayed with him.

"You have your own advertising business, right?"

Grantham nodded. "Built it from the ground up."

After a moment, he added, "Without a dime of my inheritance."

Phoebe's respect for him rose another notch. Her eyes strayed toward the grainy black-and-white video monitor. All five babies were still sleeping like angels. They were so adorable. Together, she and Grantham had bathed them and put them to bed. Then, for a while, they'd simply stood there, watching them sleep. She could barely stand to tear her eyes away. "I can handle things tomorrow," she said confidently. "Especially if someone from the nanny agency shows."

Grantham nodded again. "Tomorrow night we'll go through the files Doc left and get a handle on the medical histories for each of the kids. And it would be great if you could help sort through the nanny résumés, too. I know Jake Lucas's fiancée, Dani Newland, is looking for a job. She's a nursing student. She was taking care of your great-grandfather when he had his cast."

Phoebe gasped. "Granddaddy Winslow had a cast?"

"He's recovering from a broken leg."

Phoebe squinted at Grantham. "So you know my great-grandfather, right?"

"Yeah. We've...done some business together." Grantham looked down, gently rocking Stanley in his arms. "Hmm. Looks like we can put him in his crib."

Phoebe stood.

Stanley reacted to the slight rocking on the mattress as if it was movement of a world order. He squirmed and shrieked, his tiny shoulders wrenching.

"Sit down," Grantham whispered.

She did.

Stanley drew a quivering gasp and fell silent.

"Let's try an experiment," said Grantham. He laid Stanley in the middle of the bed. Phoebe frowned at the baby. He looked so tiny and fragile all nestled in Grantham's mussed covers. She really hoped bad dreams weren't keeping him awake. "What in the world do you think babies dream about, anyway?"

Grantham didn't answer. When she glanced up, she found him watching her, his amber eyes looking almost black in the dim light. Shadows played on his cheeks. He shook his head. "I don't have a clue, angel. But I sure like it that you ask crazy questions like that."

Her lips quirked, and she glanced at Stanley again. "I'm sure this was a very good experiment, Grantham," she finally said. "But what *was* the experiment?"

Grantham laughed, sounding a little punch-drunk from lack of sleep. "I don't know, but it proves that the only way we're going to get any sleep is if you stay in here with me and Stanley tonight."

Phoebe sent him a long, level, sleepy-eyed stare. "You've got to be kissing."

"Kissing?" said Grantham.

Phoebe groaned. She was sitting on the bed. He was sitting on the bed. And it was very definitely the wrong time for this kind of Freudian slip. "I said kidding," she ventured.

"Beg to differ."

"Beg all you want."

He chuckled. "It's clear you intend to make me." His slow, seductive grin made the toes of her bare feet curl. Even in the dark, she could tell he was waking up, too.

"The devil himself couldn't make me sleep in here," Phoebe announced, quickly standing.

Stanley's fists crashed downward in protest. He beat on the mattress, loosening another one of his mournful wails—this one followed by a series of hysterical, gasping pants.

"Maybe not the devil himself," said Grantham, "but what about a one-year-old?"

Telling herself the very last place she wanted to be was in bed with Grantham Hale, she mustered what she hoped was a businesslike tone. "Well, I guess we *do* have to get some sleep tonight." Then she sank gratefully onto the bed again. Slipping her feet between the covers, she pulled the bedspread to her hunched shoulders—and tried not to be too infuriated by the annoying sound of Grantham's soft teasing chuckle.

"I figured you'd find your way back to my bed, angel," he whispered. "But I didn't think it would be on your very first night."

Phoebe mustered a mock grumpy harrumph. Lifting her head, she gazed lovingly at her babies in the monitor. Then she gave Stanley a quick kiss good-night—and the pillow a good solid punch. Nestling her face into the cool silk pillowcase, she tried not to notice the movement on the mattress as Grantham slid beneath the covers—way on the other side of the big bed—leaving nothing more than the baby between them.

Okay, now sleep, Phoebe commanded herself. Unfortunately, now that she was lying prone in the same bed as Grantham Hale, her body was racing with adrenaline. Her heart was hammering so loud in the silence that she started praying he wouldn't hear it.

She felt Stanley wiggle between them, getting comfortable.

Grantham finally said, "Hey, Phoebe, doesn't this remind you of those old farmer's daughter jokes?"

She blinked her eyes open and squinted into the dark. Yep. There was something truly impossible about this man. She thought back to the day they'd met, when he'd raised his hand and said, "How. I guess that's Indian for hello."

How could such an austere, classically handsome suit-and-tie type guy say such occasionally absurd things? She blew out a quavering breath. Trouble was, his brand of sexy offbeat sincerity would be so easy to fall for. And she already knew firsthand that he could be in total command when he wanted to be. Especially romantically speaking.

"Phoebe?" he whispered.

She suddenly felt a little breathless. "Hmm?"

"Are you asleep?"

Obviously not. "Almost," she lied. "I guess you mean those old jokes where the farmer's daughter has to sleep with some guy, and the farmer keeps putting stuff between them to keep them from having sex? Like eggs and boards and babies?"

"Yeah."

Phoebe sighed. "Okay," she admitted. "This kind of reminds me of that."

"I knew it would." Grantham sounded incredibly pleased, as if this somehow proved they were on the same wavelength.

Phoebe blew out one last exaggerated sigh. But no matter how much she pretended annoyance, Grantham Hale did excite her like no other man ever had. And nothing could put a damper on the joy she felt at being reunited with the babies. Not even that day one of parenting with Grantham was ending in this very long night.

Phoebe let her aching eyes drift shut—only to have them blink open at the shrill sound of Grantham's alarm clock, which started to ring.

Chapter Seven

"Phoebe Rutherford is on line one again, sir."

As usual, Grantham studiously bit back the urge to ask his matronly assistant, Caroline Dapinsky, to please feel free to call him Grantham instead of sir. He'd been asking her to do so for five years, right up until last week—when she had marched into his office, high color staining her papery cheeks, and stiffly exclaimed, "Sir, you simply cannot teach this old dog new tricks! If you should like to hire a young, untrained puppy who would be comfortable addressing you by your Christian name, then *you* please feel free!"

The last thing Grantham wanted around his shipshape office was a young puppy, so, feeling a little in the doghouse, he'd quickly whisked Mrs. Dapinsky out to lunch and assured her that she was the best dog he'd ever worked with, young *or* old. Not that Caroline Dapinsky had exactly lapped up the compliments. She wasn't the type. But with her sharp mind and clockwork efficiency, she was irreplaceable.

Maybe the best thing about the lunch was that Phoebe had called while Grantham was gone. When he'd gotten home, she'd had countless seemingly casual questions prepared. Oh, so where did you and Caroline go for lunch today, Grantham? Is Caroline a client? What's this Caroline person like?

This Caroline person. Grantham loved how Phoebe's jealousy had tinged her phrasing. Somehow, he still hadn't bothered to let it slip that "this Caroline person" was gray-haired, sixty-two and happily married with four grown kids, all of whom were older than Grantham.

"Mr. Hale, sir?"

Well, Grantham thought with a sigh, today he *felt* like a sir. The lack of sleep over this past week had aged him considerably. He didn't know which was worse, poor Stanley's all-night crying jags or the frustrating fact that Phoebe kept winding up sleeping on the opposite side of Grantham's big bed. She wasn't even wearing the sexy robe anymore. She'd switched to sweat pants. "Thanks, Caroline," he said.

As he picked up line one, Grantham decided he and Phoebe were going to have to take the bull by the horns—or the child by the diaper pin—and isolate Stanley. They'd just have to let the baby cry himself to sleep in some far corner of the apartment, if for no other reason than Grantham couldn't continue to trust himself with Phoebe. Besides, Doc Holiday had suggested they let Stanley cry it out. So far, Grantham and Phoebe hadn't had the heart.

He frowned. "Phoebe?"

She still hadn't said a word. In the background, he heard a faint roaring, as if she was phoning from a subway station. Then he thought he heard crying, probably Nicolas. It definitely wouldn't be Stanley. No, Grantham thought with a wry smile, after his fitful nights, the little insomniac slept peacefully all day, leaving everybody else to suffer. Well, Grantham just hoped things were okay. This was the fourth time Phoebe had called, and he was starting to worry.

"Phoebe?" he ventured again.

Probably she and the nanny were attending to one of the kids. While he waited, Grantham wedged the phone receiver between his shoulder and jaw. His eyes strayed over his desk, settling on various headlines in the latest issues of the *Post*. Ad Man A Bad Dad? Millionaire Babies Cry Foul Play! Shame On You, Daddy, Say Untrusting Tykes! Hale-Storm Of Controversy Surrounds Missing Million!

Grantham winced. He'd known the newspapers were going to crucify him. Not that he could do anything about it. He couldn't replace the money in the kids' account for another five weeks, and even then, he couldn't divulge why he'd taken it. Even worse, just reading the fool headlines reminded him of what he kept trying to forget—that if this kept up, Phoebe really could take away four of his kids. At least if her reputation was cleared.

But she would never really take them away from me.

In fact, Phoebe got more enraged than Grantham about his treatment in the press. He loved seeing her mad, too. Each new headline made her more livid than the last. She would pace the floor with stormy, agitated strides, usually bouncing a baby on her hip and stepping right over the crawling ones, her whole body coming vibrantly alive, bristling with energy over the injustice, her eyes turning the bright burning blue of raging gaslit fires. "It's not right, Grantham!" she would exclaim over and over. "It's just not right!"

Somehow these scenes of fury made Grantham feel

as if he was plucking daisies that kept landing on "she loves me."

Grantham sighed. Right or not, he was still getting crucified. He loosened his tie, then dug his fingers into his aching shoulders. He couldn't help but wish the hands were Phoebe's. He could almost feel her strong, slender fingers stimulating his muscles through his button-down shirt.

He really was tired. He'd had meetings all week, which meant he hadn't yet been able to take time off to be with Phoebe and the kids, except last weekend when they'd opened his beach house on the shore of Genesis, Long Island. He had another meeting this afternoon that would determine whether he'd gotten the New York Retro account.

Items manufactured by the young, hip downtown firm were neatly arranged next to the open pages of the *Post,* mostly trendy clothes made from recyclables—license plate handbags and rubber skirts from car tires. The company was launching housewares, whimsical clocks that had faces set in everything from old pay phones to junk-yard motors. Grantham had fallen in love with the clocks—he'd even bought one. He just hoped he landed the account. He had so many great, splashy ideas about how to market recyclables.

He had to remember to take the phones home. The six standard-issue black push-button telephones, which he'd bought after Caroline Dapinsky's lunch, were lined up on his desk. He figured the kids might like them, since they kept playing with the real ones, instead of their plastic Fisher Price versions. Grantham and Phoebe were repeatedly missing calls—only to discover that one of the kids, usually devilish Devin, had unplugged the jacks again. Or taken the phones off the hook, hiding the portable handsets.

"Oh, Grantham!"

His heart skipped a beat when he heard Phoebe. Not that she'd really voiced a greeting. It was more an exclamation. Listening to her breathless panting, he smiled. The kids must really be running her ragged. "I wondered what happened to you," he said pleasantly.

"Oh, no!" she shrieked. "Oh, *no!*"

The phone clunked down. Footsteps pounded.

Grantham flinched from the phone receiver, then he squinted briefly toward the mouthpiece, as if he could see right down the phone wire to what was happening on the other end.

It was absolutely nothing, he tried to assure himself, determined not to jump to conclusions. At least not yet. He'd learned he could be overly emotional when it came to Phoebe and the babies. He eased into one of the earth-tone ergonomic chairs he'd recently ordered for himself and his staff. Then he unbuttoned the top button of his shirt, shut his eyes, sighed and thought about Phoebe. She was still trying to pretend that the night they'd shared ten months ago was nothing more than a fading memory. A door that had closed firmly behind them. Significant, yes, but definitely a thing of the past.

But the more Grantham got to know her, the more he wanted her to stay with him—and for a whole lot longer than five weeks. What had started out as true love ten months ago had turned into an all-consuming and maybe even unhealthy obsession. Grantham could admit that now. Most men, even very rich men, wouldn't hire a top-dollar detective such as Cy Lynde for ten full months in hopes of finding a woman with whom the man had only slept once.

But then, Phoebe Rutherford wasn't most women. And that one night *was* more than special. Which was why Grantham had started out loving Phoebe, right off the bat. After that, for ten months, he'd been obsessed with finding her. Now, he'd discovered he plain old *liked* her. And liking Phoebe Rutherford was the very best emotion of all.

Every day Phoebe's presence reminded him of what it could mean to have a woman in his life again. He'd catch her wistful, smoky blue eyes drinking in the babies as she cradled them. Or surreptitiously drifting over *him* as they jointly bathed and dressed them. He'd found himself listening for her soft voice. Waiting for the touch of their brushing bodies as they made morning coffee or fed the babies breakfast or cleaned up together after meals.

They didn't share a bathroom—Grantham used the one in his bedroom—but he liked glancing into hers, seeing her footprints in the powder dust on the floor or her hand-washed stockings slung over the shower rail. He liked how she arranged her toiletries at the sink with military precision, the small matching red jars of face creams looking like able-bodied warrior chiefs ready to charge into a war zone.

Often, he'd think of Phoebe's nickname—Queen of the Brave Face—and imagine those face creams as her front lines of military defense.

Then he'd make a renewed vow to infiltrate the ranks. He meant to get past every last one of Phoebe's defenses. To bury himself deep inside her. And to share what they had that one glorious night ten months ago.

Phoebe was just so…well, womanly. Like Celia, she always thought of the little things. When they'd stayed up late to read the babies' medical files, she'd baked cookies—then sent a plate to Granddaddy Winslow as a peace offering, which had, in turn, gotten them an invitation to dinner with the kids. She'd made plaster of Paris pie molds for the babies' footprints, too. And one night, while Grantham dutifully held the wiggling, uncooperative babies, she'd taped paper to the wall and somehow managed to make perfect shadow drawings of each pint-size profile. Finding some woodworking tools he hadn't used in years, Grantham carefully built simple oak frames and hung the six silhouettes in a neat, even row in the apartment's foyer.

And then, standing back to admire their handiwork, he and Phoebe had laughed themselves silly. Because, while expending all that creative energy, they hadn't realized that the tiny portraits were indistinguishable from each other. Which, of course, they *would* be—since four of the babies were quadruplets and the other two were identical twins. As she'd glanced down the long row of identical pictures, Phoebe had swiped tears of laughter from her eyes, saying, "Yep, they have so much individual personality that you completely forget they do *look* alike. Don't you, Grantham?"

Somehow, moments such as that had made Grantham sweet on Phoebe Rutherford.

Another such moment had come when Grantham casually glanced over the personal items lying around her room. Her books, which were tied in a red ribbon, turned out to be a Rutherford family bible and four identical baby books titled *Baby's First Year*, which had spaces where a parent could write in particulars, such as the baby's height and weight each month. Inside each of the four books, Phoebe had carefully written one of the quadruplet's names. But, because Phoebe had been separated from her babies for so long, the rest of the pages remained totally, heartbreakingly blank. She didn't even know when the walking babies—which meant all of them but Lyssa—had taken their first steps.

Grantham had decided to fill in the blanks for Phoebe, of course. And then he'd opened her Bible. Inside, carefully pressed in waxed paper between the pages, he'd found a single white rose. Instinctively, he'd known it was the one he'd trailed over her flushed, naked body the night they'd made such tender love. His chest had squeezed tight. She might be trying to keep some distance between them. But all this time, Phoebe had kept that rose, just as he'd kept her ring.

He sighed. After he'd kissed her in the nursery, he'd been trying to give her plenty of space. He'd been so sure she'd quickly change her mind and get a little more inviting. But she hadn't. On the other hand, she hadn't made the least effort to have her lawyers block Granddaddy Winslow's ruling and move out of the apartment. Meantime, Grantham had come to like so many things about her. Even how she was managing her inheritance from Nicolas Adair. She'd set up college and trust funds for the kids, then made a large donation to charity.

"Where *is* she?" he murmured.

As if reading his thoughts, Phoebe came onto the line. She sucked in a gasping breath, then exhaled a series of quick pants. She sounded as if she was still in labor in the delivery room, instead of mothering toddlers. With a smile, Grantham decided that delivery-room breathlessness probably wouldn't stop until their kids toppled from the nest and flew into college. If then. "Are you okay?" he said.

"Uh, Grantham, would it, uh, be possibly possible for you to send a limo?"

"Possibly possible?" he repeated. Why did she sound so nervous? "A limo?" He guessed he could, but...

"A stretch limo," she qualified.

Her voice sounded so strained. "Pardon me for saying so, angel, but if you need to go out...well, isn't a stretch limo a little extravagant?" Grantham bit back a sigh. He was an advocate of public transportation and took a bus to work. Not that he was holier-than-thou, but every time he drove unnecessarily he couldn't shake the notion that his personal car exhaust was directly responsible for global warming and the ever-widening hole in the ozone layer. He'd start imagining melting glaciers in Alaska and Micronesian islands that would one day vanish beneath the resulting rising sea level....

"C'mon, Phoebe," Grantham continued reasonably. "I'm sure something smaller would do. What about a cab or even a town car? I mean, I *have* access to stretch limousines through our corporate account, but I feel—"

"I *need* a stretch limo!"

"Look, angel, I just think a cab—"

"But you're rich!" she burst out. "You can afford it!"

He felt taken aback. As usual, Phoebe seemed to have temporarily forgotten that *she* was rich. That she'd inherited Nicolas Adair's fortune hadn't yet sunk in. "True," he said, gripping the phone tighter than he had to. "But..." Grantham started to say his family had become wealthy by being downright tight with money, but then he changed his mind. If there was one thing Celia had taught him, it was that people born with the shopping gene—meaning all women—never wanted to hear his penny-saved-penny-earned axiom at moments such as this one. Phoebe would probably never want to hear it. She did have the shopping gene, at least judging from the bags that kept appearing from the Baby Gap store.

"Grantham."

It was a plea. He told himself to stay calm. This was the one thing he'd forgotten about women—their changeable and often volatile moods. Celia had certainly had hers. Of course, she'd always appreciated his patience. She'd said he was like a rock. Well, he'd be a rock for Phoebe, too.

"Angel," he said gently, "are you sure everything is all right?" Grantham tilted his head, listening hard past her labored breathing. What was that ungodly roar? He thought he heard crying, maybe music. Maybe the TV. Something banging. "Phoebe?"

Her voice was no-nonsense. "Don't be ridiculous, Grantham. Everything is fine."

He wasn't trying to be ridiculous. He was trying to help. He sighed again. "What exactly is going on there?"

"Nothing. Well, okay. There was this weird guy who called. He said he needed to talk to you, and he sounded very mysterious, but he wouldn't leave a message."

Grantham nodded without concern. He did have secret, under-the-table business pending. That—and the fact that he was suffering a cash-flow problem—was why he'd withdrawn the babies' money from the bank. The people he was dealing with wouldn't want to leave names. "What about the babies? Are they really all right?"

"Absolutely. I would just…like a limo."

He frowned. "Is the Nine to Five Nanny still there?"

"Uh, yep. Yep, as a matter of fact, she is, Grantham." Phoebe's tone was brisk.

To her credit, she didn't seem to be a very good liar. Grantham glanced at the new clock from New York Retro. According to the face, which was set in the innards of a motor painted in green and pink neons, his meeting was in ten minutes. "I'm coming home."

"No!" Phoebe said quickly. "Oh, no! Please, Grantham. Don't come home!"

"Phoebe," he said cautiously. "This is the fourth time you've called."

"I'm sorry," she apologized in a rush. "I really am! I couldn't be sorrier. I just— Look, could you please simply trust me and hurry up and send that limo?"

He started to say he'd didn't trust her as far as he could throw her at the moment—but he thought better of it. Instead, he simply said, "I'm on my way."

And then, before Phoebe could utter another protest, he hung up the phone. Standing, he quickly snagged his suit jacket from the back of the chair.

His phone buzzed. "Sir?"

It was probably Phoebe again. "Yes?"

Caroline sounded worried. "There's a man on line three. He's refusing to give his name, but I…I just don't know. I think you'd better speak with him, sir."

He frowned. If Phoebe's face creams were her first line of defense, Caroline Dapinsky was his. And it was hardly like his assistant to let an unidentified caller through to Grantham's inner sanctum. Maybe the man who'd failed to leave a message at the apartment was someone other than Grantham had thought. Maybe this had nothing to do with his million-dollar expenditure. "Thanks, Caroline," Grantham said thoughtfully. And then he picked up the blinking line. "Grantham Hale speaking. Who's calling please?"

"You don't need to know *that* information." The man's voice was gruff—angry and muffled. "You just gotta meet me."

Grantham's blood chilled, and his senses went on alert. He kept his voice even. "Why?"

"I've got some pictures you'll want to see. Bring five thousand bucks if you don't wanna lose those quadruplet kids."

Grantham hadn't moved a muscle. Realizing he was holding his breath, he very quietly exhaled. His voice was dead calm. "Are you threatening to kidnap my children?"

"No. Just a little matter of blackmail. If you lose those kids, it'll be in court, not because I'm gonna take them. When these pictures get out, you'll lose your case for sure. Kidnapping's got nothing to do with it."

At least that was a relief. The Hale family had been worth a fortune for a century, so this was hardly the first time some joker had tried blackmail. Not that a Hale had ever paid. Hales were honest, forthright and above reproach. It was the only safeguard against strong-arm tactics such as this. With nothing to hide, Hales could never be strung up with a price tag. There had been one kidnapping—but Grantham's cousin had been returned, no ransom paid.

Grantham's voice was ice-cold. "What pictures do you think you have?"

"Pictures of you sleeping around with Phoebe Rutherford at the Wilshire Arms in L.A. If it gets out you weren't faithful to your wife's memory, it could cause you some real trouble."

Ah, damn. Grantham swallowed hard. Leaning his hip against the desk, he crossed his arms and considered the options. The pictures probably weren't graphic. And it wasn't an illicit affair. He'd been with Phoebe after Celia had died. Besides, in spite of this week's headlines in the *Post*, Grantham had maintained a solid personal and professional reputation in the New York community for years. He was sure that his sleeping with Phoebe Rutherford ten months ago wouldn't really hurt him, as the blackmailer seemed to think—at least not that much.

On the other hand, Phoebe had lost custody of her kids because of crimes Grantham was sure she hadn't committed, among them adultery. Her reputation definitely couldn't take any more disparagement. And he wanted to protect her.

Not that the blackmailer would stop with this one phone call. Grantham knew better. Nevertheless, if he paid, it would protect Phoebe until their case was decided. She'd already been declared an unfit mother. Having slept with him the day of her divorce might further endanger her chances of having that ridiculous legal decision reversed.

"I'll pay," Grantham said. His father, Jonathan Hale, was no doubt turning over in his grave. "But only after you give me the proof. Just say where and when.''

''Right now. Over by your place. At the Pat Hoffman Friedman playground for kids in Central Park. It's at Seventy-ninth and Fifth. Bring the money in a brown paper bag, like it's your lunch. Don't look for me. I'll find you.''

Grantham's blood suddenly boiled. His apartment was around the corner, on Park and Eightieth. The guy even knew where he lived. ''I'm heading into a meeting right now, so it isn't a good time,'' he calmly said. He hoped Cy Lynde would be available to watch the drop and then tail the guy. ''I'm sorry, but we'll need to meet later this afternoon.''

The man snorted cynically, as if reading Grantham's mind. ''No way. It's now or never. I know you have plenty of money in the bank. If you don't come right now, I'm gonna give all my information about you and Phoebe Rutherford to the *Post.* Everybody knows what kind of a woman *she* is—now they'll know what kind of women you like to secretly fool around with.''

Yeah, Grantham had slept with Phoebe Rutherford. And if Phoebe would let him, Grantham would be the very first to shout it from the rooftops. But he wasn't about to let her reputation suffer. ''I'll be there.''

The phone went dead.

Grantham got a new line and punched in Cy Lynde's number. ''Oh, Phoebe,'' he said simply, hoping he could reach Cy and stop this guy from hurting her. And then wondering, for the umpteenth time, what in the world was going on with her and the kids at the apartment.

"LADY, you're gonna have to move."

Through the rolled-down window of her illegally parked Lexus, Joyce Moon watched the off-duty detective pocket the badge that had identified him as Sean McSween. He looked vaguely familiar. Had she seen his picture in the New York newspapers? Hadn't he gotten a special commendation or something? Joyce couldn't remember. All she knew for certain was that this was the absolute worst time for some conscientious off-duty detective to tell her she couldn't park.

In her rearview mirror, Joyce could already see Grantham Hale. Dressed in a coffee-and-cream-colored business suit and a wide dark tie, he was striding purposefully through the crowds in front of the Metropolitan Museum. Clutched in one hand was a sandwich-size brown paper bag. In the other was a shopping bag.

From the opposite direction, walking north on Fifth Avenue, came an equally purposeful stocky figure in a dark windbreaker and a black cap. His name was Cappy Nelson, and he was the blackmailer. Or at least he was pretending to be one, since Joyce, Orsen and Bert had hired him for that purpose.

Joyce's gaze settled on the detective again. Sizing him up, she tried to decide how to proceed. The man had short raven hair and bottle-green eyes. His pregnant wife—a tall woman with honey hair that feathered around her shoulders—was waiting for him on the sidewalk. Next to her, tucked in a stroller, was a raven-haired boy wearing a Giants shirt and a baseball cap. He was carrying a green toy dragon. Apparently, the family was visiting the museum.

"Is everything all right, McSween?" the wife called.

He waved. "Coming, Britt."

Leaning in Joyce's window, Detective McSween glanced around, scowling as if expecting to see something suspicious. Like live hand grenades, Joyce thought with irony, or machine guns.

"Please, Detective—" As Joyce reached past her camera, her fingers skated over the zoom lens, then she dug into her purse for her wallet. She withdrew a handful of cards. "I'm a lawyer. I work for the prosecutor's office," Joyce lied. As a defense attorney, she wouldn't have a prayer. She'd be pegged as a bleeding-heart liberal who devoted her life to getting criminals off the hook—the very ones this detective risked his life daily to catch. But cops loved prosecutors. And Joyce couldn't afford to lose this parking spot at the entrance to the Pat Hoffman Friedman playground in Central Park. No more than she could bear to lose a court case.

"You say you're a lawyer?" Detective McSween asked.

Joyce watched Cappy Nelson enter Central Park. On the steering wheel, her hands started to sweat. She lifted one and nervously tucked a lock of dark hair behind an ear. "Yes, for the DA's office."

Detective McSween handed Joyce her cards, then glanced at her camera. "You wouldn't happen to be taking pictures for the prosecutor's office right now, would you?"

The detective was sharp. He'd nearly guessed right. She glanced anxiously toward the park. Grantham was entering the playground. Cappy Nelson was a mere fifty feet away. "We got a tip on a meeting between two men," Joyce lied quickly, "one of whom we're trying to take to trial. I volunteered to bring my camera over here and take some shots.'' She swallowed hard, knowing the detective would recognize Grantham Hale if he looked, since Grantham was a known New York City mover and shaker. Grantham's agency had done free-of-charge public service announcements for the NYPD's war on crime.

He nodded. "Is there anything I can do?"

She shook her head. "Actually, if these guys think they see someone who even vaguely resembles a detective in the vicinity, they might not approach each other." Through the windshield, her gaze riveted on Cappy. He wasn't but ten feet behind Grantham Hale.

"Well, I'll leave you to it," Detective McSween said simply.

A second later, the detective was gone, walking with his family in the direction of the museum steps. Joyce sighed in relief.

Cappy Nelson was an arm's length from Grantham.

Joyce grabbed the camera, focused the zoom and started shooting.

Chapter Eight

Something was terribly wrong.

Grantham stopped in the apartment foyer, cautiously setting down the new neon clock and the shopping bag in which Caroline Dapinsky had kindly packed the six black telephones. A shudder had just gone down his spine.

For a second, Grantham thought it was because of the unsavory character he'd met in Central Park. At least the pictures he'd been shown weren't graphic, just videotape stills from the hotel lobby, but everything else had gone awry. Cy Lynde was unavailable, and because Grantham was cash poor, he'd had to pull the five thousand dollars from his ad agency's account. Every dime was his, of course, but before today, Grantham had always kept the accounts separate.

But something else was wrong. Where were Phoebe and the babies? "Phoebe?"

The roaring he'd heard on the phone was louder. Was it the vacuum cleaner? He grimaced. He'd begged Phoebe not to bother with housework, but she kept insisting. Trouble was, Grantham's longtime housekeeper had arrived last Wednesday—and become furious because the apartment was so clean. She was convinced Phoebe was after her job.

As he glanced at the neon-motor clock, Grantham's muscles tensed in warning. Forty-five minutes had passed since he'd talked to Phoebe. Why would she keep a vacuum cleaner running that long? Between her and the housekeeper—who thought she was having a cleaning competition—the apartment was spotless. Frowning, Grantham glanced around. Nothing in the living room seemed out of place.

You're just on overdrive because of that guy in the park. Stay calm. He raised his voice to be heard over the drone. "Phoebe?"

There was no answer.

Noiselessly, Grantham headed in the direction of the sound—down the center hallway and toward the kitchen. Yeah, the roar was definitely coming from there. Cautiously, Grantham knocked. Then, pushing open the kitchen door, he glanced inside—and drew a sharp breath.

Countless impressions assaulted him. The room was wrecked. Bibs and clothes were on the floor. Two of the six high chairs were overturned. The trays were filthy, the floor strewn with food. Two bowls of Cream of Wheat had rolled to the door, trailing milk. Beneath the oven, he spied a plastic cup. And the baby books, usually neatly arranged on the shelves, had been tossed to the floor, as if an intruder had been searching for something.

Terror struck through Grantham's soul.

He could merely stare at the red vacuum cleaner. Phoebe hadn't been using it to clean at all. It was sitting dead center in the middle of the gray marbled kitchen table, its long red cord stretching through the air to a countertop wall outlet. The kitchen wall phone was gone.

Stay calm.

But his heart was pounding, his mind running through scenarios with lightning speed. Was the drone of the vacuum supposed to mask cries for help? Had the kitchen wall phone been removed so Phoebe couldn't call for rescue? Had the blackmailer lied? Was the meeting a lure to make sure Grantham wouldn't head home for lunch while the blackmailer's cohorts came for Phoebe and the babies?

Grantham moved quickly and silently. If anyone was here, he could only hope he hadn't alerted them to his presence. Letting the vacuum run, he backed from the kitchen. Fully alert, his ears strained to hear anything unusual. His eyes darted right and left. The hall phone was gone, too. Swiftly, he unplugged a lamp. Silently, he removed the shade, then slung the heavy base over his shoulder.

He was in great shape. He worked out. Played tennis three times a week on the rooftop courts. More now, since he'd been sentenced to do so with Phoebe. He figured he could take on at least three guys. With the lamp, he could inflict serious damage.

Even if they were gone, there was still a chance. Grantham's cousin Eloise Carrington Hale had once been held for ransom. Not only had she been returned unharmed, but Uncle Norman still bragged that he hadn't paid a red cent to get her back. Grantham shuddered to think of how long Uncle Norm would have held out before the kidnappers were stuck with Eloise.

He paused in the living room. No phone. Should he plug in one of the phones he'd brought home and call the cops? *No, keep checking for Phoebe and the kids.*

Cocking his head, he heard more sounds. Oh, no, was that screaming? Adjusting the lamp on his shoulder, he headed in the direction of the noise.

Without stopping, he saw that Phoebe's bedding had been tossed to the floor.

Next door, the nursery was as bad as the kitchen.

So was his room. And the playroom.

Grantham sighed in relief. Whoever had ransacked the place hadn't taken the kids. They were screaming and crying, running wildly through the wrecked playroom, but otherwise, they looked unharmed. He did a swift head count. Six. Good.

He suddenly realized his heart was hammering hard, his mouth dry with anticipation of a rumble. He was angry, too. If one hair on Phoebe and the kids had been touched, he'd be out for blood.

And then he saw Phoebe.

His heart lurched. She was sitting in an empty corner of the all-white playroom, her knees drawn up against her chest and her short silk robe open over the sweat suit she'd worn to bed last night. Her expression was...vulnerable. Or was it blank? Yes, she was staring into space, her eyes glazed.

He quickly crossed the room, stepping around the toys strewn across the floor. He crouched in front of Phoebe. She didn't seem to see him. Gently, he gripped her shoulder with his lamp-free hand, squeezing reassuringly as he peered into her eyes. He didn't even want to think about what must have happened in the kitchen.

She blinked.

Her pupils seemed dilated, he decided. Was she in shock? Should he haul off and slap her? Grantham winced. Probably—but he couldn't bring himself to do it. Besides, no matter how deep her shock, he was fairly sure Phoebe wouldn't forgive him for hitting her—at least not in this lifetime.

He mustered his most soothing tone. "Phoebe? It's me, Grantham. Tell me everything you can. I have to call the police now."

"The police?" Phoebe echoed, sounding stunned.

She really looked far gone. Suddenly, using his shoulders for leverage, she heaved herself to her feet. Her cheeks were chalky pale and she clearly needed his help. Grantham wanted nothing more than to grab her and hold her tight. But he'd sworn he wouldn't, not even in comfort. So, instead of crushing her against his chest, he peered deeply into her bloodshot eyes. "Did he hurt you?"

Phoebe squinted. "Hurt me?" she repeated.

"Yes, angel. Did whoever's responsible for this..." Grantham glanced over his shoulder at the pandemonium. The kids appeared unharmed, but only two wore diapers. The rest were naked. Nicolas was bawling his eyes out. Langdon was screaming like a maniac. Kirby was running wild, tripping and falling over toys. Unperturbed, Lyssa was beating on a xylophone with a toy truck. The TV blared.

The only thing peaceful was Stanley. He was curled up, in a diaper-clad ball, in front of the television, sleeping—as it were—like a baby.

Grantham frowned. Devilish Devin was alone in an opposite corner, crouched down, surrounded by telephones that had come from the far corners of the apartment. Apparently, intruders hadn't taken the phones.

He realized Phoebe was smiling at him—however weakly. "Oh, Grantham," she said breathlessly, dragging her hand through her hair and glancing at the lamp. "You were going to defend us. You thought we were being robbed."

Or worse. "You weren't?"

She stared at the lamp again, color tinging her cheeks a rosy pink. Her voice caught. "Uh, nope."

Feeling faintly idiotic, Grantham put down the lamp. Phoebe's sudden look of gushing, unmitigated adoration hardly helped. Maybe he would kill anyone who tried to lay a hand on her or the babies, but he hardly wanted her to know it. After all, she kept professing she didn't even want a relationship with him. Still, what had happened here?

Grantham cleared his throat. "Well, it looked like..." Like she'd sustained a visit from an organized crime family. Or an *unorganized* crime family, he amended, glancing around. Or poltergeists.

"You really didn't have to come home," Phoebe said in a quick rush. "Everything's fine. We were just..." She gestured vaguely toward the kitchen. "Having so much fun! We...ate breakfast, lunch..." Her voice trailed off. The glazed look returned to her eyes.

His eyes narrowed. "Where's the nanny, Phoebe?"

She squinted in a perplexed way, as if the nanny weren't a person, but one of many stray items she'd somehow misplaced. When she finally spoke, she sounded a little distant. "Well, that's a long story." After a pause, she added, "The agency finally did send someone. But by then...well, the woman just took one look around the apartment and left."

Phoebe had been trying to handle all six babies by herself? Grantham could merely stare. Had the babies really done all this damage? "Why's the vacuum running?"

Phoebe flashed him one of her fleeting Queen of the Brave Face smiles. "Nicolas liked the sound. It made him quit screaming."

Grantham glanced at Nicolas. Hardly. The kid was sitting naked on the floor, shrieking, with tears running down his face. "I can see that," Grantham said dryly.

"It worked for a while," Phoebe said weakly.

Lithely, Grantham leaned, snagged a videotape from the floor, then headed for the TV. "You know, he always quits crying when we put in the Barney live in New York City tape." And with some peace and quiet, Grantham could start doing what he was supposed to—parenting with Phoebe. He felt terrible about not being here.

He was about to shove the tape into the VCR when Phoebe loosed a blood-curdling cry. He wrenched around in time to see her lunge at him. Her fist closed over his upper arm in an attempt to restrain him bodily.

"No, Grantham! You'll ruin the tape!"

He calmly unpried her fingers. "Phoebe," he said reasonably, "we play this tape all the time." In fact, Grantham had heard it so often that the theme song was imbedded in his mind. Once, he'd caught himself humming it in a public elevator. Fortunately, he'd been the only person on board.

"Oh, Grantham," Phoebe said, wringing her hands, "after I fed them lunch, I made myself a peanut butter sandwich."

Grantham nodded. Then he patiently waited, trying to remind himself that he was a rock. And that women liked rocks. But when Phoebe didn't continue, he finally prompted, "And?"

She heaved her own sigh—a greater, wearier one.

"Well, then Devin took my peanut butter sandwich and stuffed it in the VCR. Because it was square, maybe he thought it was a videotape. You know how obsessed he is with those toys where you match up the square blocks to the square holes, and the round blocks to the round…" As if realizing Grantham had got the point, Phoebe's voice trailed off again.

Grantham squinted, wondering where to begin. Then he hit the off button on the TV. With a blip, the screen went blank. Giving Phoebe's shoulder a squeeze, he said, "Wait right here."

After he'd turned off the vacuum cleaner in the kitchen, Grantham returned. Pulling Phoebe into the hallway, he cupped her chin, lifting her face. "Looks like they gave you a hard time, angel."

"I love them so much." Her lower lip quivered. "Every minute is worth it. But…" She swallowed hard and flashed another one of those fleeting smiles. She shrugged. "The Nine-to-Five Nanny left. Then Nicolas started crying. And then Langdon started beating his head against the side of his crib."

Grantham's heart stilled. "Beating his head against the crib?" That sounded serious. "Did you call Doc Holiday?"

Phoebe nodded. Because her pupils still looked dilated, Grantham had a half a mind to call Doc to treat *her*. On the other hand, he was sure the glaze in her eyes was probably from unshed tears. She finally said, "Yes, I called."

When she didn't elaborate, he prodded, "You called Doc?"

"Eleven times today!" Phoebe burst out. "Langdon was beating his head, I thought Lyssa might be choking, then Nicolas had a fever—"

"Okay, angel," Grantham said gently, even though the mere thought of such things was making him feel a little anxious. "What did Doc say about Langdon?"

Tears of pure righteous indignation shimmered in her eyes. "He said it was nothing to worry about," she said with barely controlled fury that made her voice snap and come alive. "He laughed, and in that casual drawl of his he said it's just Langdon discovering that he has rhythm. *Rhythm!* Can you believe Doc said that!"

No, Grantham couldn't.

"Well—" Another wave of color flooded her cheeks, this time of guilt. "When I turned off the music, Langdon *did* quit. So maybe Doc was right."

Grantham sure hoped so. Sighing, he couldn't help but reach out and trail a finger down her cheek. Her skin was amazing. It was like the softest silk whispering against his fingertips. "Why didn't you tell me what was happening here? We're supposed to be parenting together. I want you know you can rely on me, Phoebe."

She cast her eyes downward.

"Why?" he asked.

"Oh, Grantham." She glanced up, and her voice caught. "I know your meetings for the New York Retro account were today. If you lost that account just because I couldn't take care of the babies by myself—"

His heart wrenched. Hadn't she realized he'd always put people before his work? "Oh, Phoebe."

And then the last thing he expected happened. She suddenly lunged, flinging herself against his chest. For a second, he was so stunned he stood there, staring down. Then he got hold of his senses and embraced his good fortune—and Phoebe. Wrapping his arms around her, he hugged her as if he'd never let her go. Her arms tightened around his waist, the way a little girl's might around a teddy bear.

But she was all woman. Every inch of her made Grantham's body warm. Shutting his eyes, he nuzzled the top of her head, sighing into her cloud of fluffy blond hair. He reveled in all the sensations—the soft swell of her breasts against his shirtfront, the heat that seeped from her body to his.

He'd fantasized about holding her so often that there was no holding back his immediate response. He felt a sharp, undeniable tug at his groin, the quickening of his pulse. The acceleration of his heart as she burrowed her face into his shoulder. He had to fight to keep his hands on her back instead of letting them drift over her backside. It was an excruciating show of restraint that he knew she'd never fully appreciate. But he wanted her emotionally, too. "Angel," he assured her gently, "nobody can take care of six babies alone."

"Well, I tried."

"And you get big points for trying," he whispered. "I would never have made it through this week without you."

Her voice caught. "Really?"

"Really."

All week she'd been such a help. She was creative and really understood what he was trying to do with the Retro account. Because he had to work, she kept insisting that she—not he—get up in the night to attend to the babies. Not that he always let her. Still, as tired as he was, he knew she'd had much less sleep.

"I bet you could use a good cry, angel," he coaxed softly.

"But I—" A tiny dry sob escaped. "I don't have time to cry." She glanced up. Being so close to her, holding her so tightly in his arms while she gazed at him with those heavenly smoky blue eyes nearly did him in. He was glad she seemed perfectly content right where she was. She belonged here, fitting to him like a hand in a glove.

"But the press is coming, Grantham."

He raised an eyebrow. *Great.* "The press?"

She shrugged helplessly. "I kept telling them no. And I told the lawyers. But the *Times* wouldn't take no for an answer. They said they want photographs of the babies. And then I thought maybe…" She flushed. "Maybe they'd give you better coverage than the *Post.*"

Grantham bit back a sigh. It was sweet of her, but the last people in the world he wanted in his apartment were reporters, he didn't care from which paper. This case might be unusual, but he didn't want his family put on display. He didn't want to defend himself, either. He didn't need to. He'd done nothing wrong.

"So, then," Phoebe continued, "I thought if I just called and got a limo…"

Grantham surveyed her. She was starting to ramble again. She didn't need a photo op, she needed a good night's sleep. Tonight, he told himself, he'd turn off the baby monitors in the master bedroom and give her his bed. He'd watch the kids from the nanny's room.

Her eyes were fixed on his. "One of the books in the kitchen said kids calm down if you take them for a drive. But I didn't have a car. And I couldn't get six babies in a cab. So I thought if I got a stretch limousine, they'd all fit and—'' In midsentence, she stopped and drew in a sharp breath.

Grantham swayed, rocking her in his arms. "C'mon, angel," he found himself murmuring. "From now on you're going to tell me if a situation like this arises. For now, just take a two-minute vacation from all your parental anxieties. Just forget everything."

She glanced toward the pandemonium in the playroom. "Oh, Grantham," she said with a sigh. "Only you would say something like that."

He smiled. "C'mon."

Her eyes looked positively mesmerized by his, and she was still swaying in his arms. Her small mouth looked so soft and inviting that he drew in a deep breath, lowering his hand on her back.

"But Grantham," she suddenly protested, her voice sharply rising. "There's a peanut butter sandwich in the VCR. The vacuum cleaner probably has a burned-out motor. There's food slung from one end of the kitchen to the other. Four of the babies are stark naked—"

Grantham nodded, not having the heart to tell her that while they'd been standing here, Stanley had awakened and somehow managed to disrobe himself.

Phoebe pressed a finger to her throbbing temple. Then she stared helplessly at Grantham. "How in the world do you expect me to forget?"

For a minute he could merely stare into the depths of those beautiful eyes. And then he whispered, "Here's how."

His mouth settled over her lips. They were so soft and warm and moist that he was immediately lost. He'd dreamed of this kiss. Waited for it. And he took his time, wanting to rekindle memories of the passion they'd shared. Against all her softness, his body was so hard—his muscles tensed with wanting, his arms circling her in a display of pure masculine strength while his tongue explored her. Lazily, he licked between her lips, tasting and testing.

His foot settled between her feet, gently forcing her legs apart. Instead of protesting, she opened for him— ever so slightly—and her delicate back arched over his arm. At her response, he flooded with heat. Desire for her sung through him, dancing in his veins, sparking along his nerves. Deepening the kiss, his tongue thrust. His hands dropped, molding over her backside, lightly squeezing the flesh, pulling her flush against his arousal. The pressure was sheer agony.

"Phoebe," he murmured.

She gazed at him through lazy, unfocused eyes. Her voice was husky. "I'm taking a vacation."

"Maui," he murmured against her lips.

"Cancún," she whispered.

"Oh," he said with a sigh, then he kissed her again.

Everything about the way she was kissing him said she wanted him. Only fools thought sex and love were separate. And Grantham was no fool. Desiring what he didn't love was completely out of the realm of his experience. It wasn't in Phoebe's, either. No, she wanted him. It was in the pliant way she molded against him, how her soft, womanly body leaned into his strength. And for her, wanting him would mean deepening their relationship. He moaned softly against her lips. He was just about to turn, to coax her toward the bedroom, when the doorbell rang.

He groaned. And this time not from desire. She

turned in his arms, but he held fast, unable to let her go.

"Some vacation from my anxieties," she purred. Then reality seemed to return full force. Her eyes widened. "The press! They weren't supposed to come for another hour!" Her eyes darted wildly around as if she'd landed on Earth after vacationing on another planet. He took in her wet, well-kissed lips and flushed cheeks. He could see her mind starting to work again—imagining the wrecked kitchen, remembering she was wearing sweatpants, registering the naked babies.

He lightly kissed her forehead. "It's not the press, Phoebe. It's the limo."

Looking flabbergasted, she licked her lips, as if still tasting the kiss. Her voice was raspy. "You really got a limo? I thought you didn't believe in extravagance."

"For you, angel?" His eyes flicked over her. "I made an exception."

She let that sink in. Then a slow smile curled her lips. "You weren't supposed to kiss me like that, you know."

"You were kissing me, too."

The color of her cheeks deepened. "Yep. So I was."

"You have to admit—" he glanced pointedly toward the playroom "—these are extreme circumstances."

The throatiness of Phoebe's sexy chuckle warmed him right through to the bone. She said, "I guess extreme circumstances do call for extreme measures."

"Does that mean you want me to keep kissing you?"

Her eyes were lit up like Christmas. "If circumstances arise."

"They'll arise, all right." Morning, noon and night. Grantham would make sure of it. Suddenly he felt uneasy. It was just too bad so many negative things were happening. The lousy press and the suspicions surrounding his financial decisions. The blackmailer. Such things could sure put a damper on a fairy tale. Gazing into Phoebe's eyes, Grantham decided not to mention the blackmailer. She was under enough pressure. He'd rather protect her in silence. Soon it would all be over.

The doorbell rang again.

Grantham grabbed her hand and gave it a quick squeeze. "It's a driver I know and trust. A young guy named Gary Trent. So why don't we pack up the babies? We'll have them chauffeur-driven up and down the FDR Drive until they decide to nap. By the time they get back, I bet we can have the apartment clean. Since neither of us really wants the press around, I'll send them packing, and then we can spend the afternoon together, having fun with six well-rested kids. What do you say, angel?"

She didn't say a word, but the look in her eyes and the smile on her lips said he was the greatest guy in the world. Feeling like a million bucks, Grantham turned and headed toward the front door.

Softly, just as he reached it, she said, "Grantham?"

He turned.

"Blond," Phoebe said on a sigh. "My hair really is blond."

He grinned. The breathless way she announced her hair color, he could almost swear she'd said, "I'm falling in love with you, Grantham Hale."

Chapter Nine

Shooting her a quick glance, Grantham raked a hand through his sun-kissed golden hair. "Do me a favor and take a breather, angel. You've been at it all day."

Phoebe nodded absently, then she frowned. "Now," she murmured to herself, as she looped a clean chef's apron around her neck, then tied the sash over her sweat suit and drummed her fingertips against the kitchen countertop, "if I can just do the stuffed mushrooms, cupcakes and sheet cakes this week. These hors d'oeuvres will all freeze. And right before the party starts, Dani will help me heat up everything in the employee kitchen at Big Apple Babies."

"Just looking at you heats me up."

Phoebe continued staring at the various cookie sheets of spinach cakes, stuffed mushrooms and sausage balls. The two quiches were ready to go. "Oh, please, Grantham," she chided absently. "You're not even looking at me."

If he was, Phoebe would have felt the heat of his eyes. Heaven knew, half the time he gazed at her, she felt as if her very clothes had started to smoke. But Grantham was wheeling up and down the row of six high chairs on an ergonomic roller stool he'd bought just for the purpose. As he glided from baby to baby, he pretended to play basketball, tapping a spoon against the plastic bowls in a dribble, then slam-dunking each tiny mouth with a spoonful of pastina and crushed carrots. If he hadn't insisted on feeding the babies alone tonight, she'd never have gotten all this cooking done.

"No, Devin," he said, chuckling softly as he wiped Devin's mouth with a damp hand towel, "the basket-ball's supposed to dribble, not you."

Two more minutes until those spinach cakes come out. Phoebe forced herself to lean against the counter and wait, ignoring everything behind her—the flour-dusted, dough-spotted Formica, dirty pots and pans and countless rumpled pot holders and dish towels. She adjusted her sloppy loose ponytail—it was more practical than pretty—and then put her hands on her hips and blew out a self-satisfied sigh.

"We could have had it catered, you know," Grantham said without turning around.

Phoebe couldn't imagine such a thing. "You know how much I wanted to cook. It's the kids' first birthday party." Even though Stanley and Devin wouldn't technically turn one year old for another month, she and Grantham had decided to throw a huge party on the quadruplets' birthday for all six.

"As soon as I'm through feeding, I'll give you a hand."

"Nope. Take a breather yourself."

The babies were at their most adorable, she decided. Already bathed and in their sleepers, they showed no signs of getting filthy again, even though they were eating. Phoebe's eyes settled on her little girls. Wiggling her eyebrows, she flashed them a smile. Kirby and Lyssa grinned, their bright blue eyes sparkling.

"Bar! Bar-bar!" Stanley called, excited by her attention.

"You do like Barney, don't you?" Phoebe crooned.

Grantham grimaced. "I wish I could get that theme song out of my head."

Phoebe chuckled. "I wish you could, too." She'd had to elbow him in the line at the grocery store this week to get him to stop humming. The look of mortification on his handsome face had been priceless.

Grantham's mouth quirked. "At least I didn't burst into song during the most boring sermon in history."

Sending him a look of mock censure, Phoebe tried and failed to bite back a smile. Last weekend, in Genesis, Long Island, they'd taken the kids to Sunday services for the first time. As much as they'd tried to muster enthusiasm, both she and Grantham had finally agreed that the minister wasn't exactly the most energetic. "Well, it's a good church," she offered.

Grantham's lips twisted in a wry smile that deepened the cleft in his chin. "Maybe. But with a sermon that slow and you sitting next to me, my mind sure started taking devilish turns." He glanced up, his eyes warm and twinkling, and shot Phoebe a grin so seductive that her knees got weak. She sighed wistfully. Just looking at him, she found herself doubting the wisdom of having this birthday party at all. Every day she and Grantham continued to share lives with all six babies, they became more like a family. Stanley and Devin were even calling her Mama. *But this family comes without sex and marriage. Big difference, Phoebe. And don't forget it.*

"What are you thinking, angel?"

Phoebe smiled. "Don't you know better than to flirt with me when I'm cooking?" she shot back, fluttering her eyelashes.

"I thought the whole point of flirting was to make a woman *start* cooking."

"Why, Grantham, you make me lose all my concentration."

"It's not lost." He gently dabbed at Nicolas's mouth with the cloth. "Just think of it as wealth that's been redistributed."

Peeking toward the glass window of the oven, she squinted, wondering whether to take out her spinach cakes. "Redistributed?"

Grantham's low, resonant laughter teased her ears. "Yeah. Reallocated, so your focus is where it should be—entirely on me."

Phoebe smirked playfully. "Reallocations and wealth. Spoken like a true businessman."

Not that Grantham was wearing one of the suits that made him look so smart and commanding. He was in his stocking feet, clad in red sweatpants and a cream colored V-neck T-shirt. Phoebe's eyes drifted, settling on the thick thatch of golden chest hairs that were visible in the deep V of the shirt. The crest of each curl glistened as if sun-kissed, and nestled among them, his gold chain sparkled.

Even lifting so little as a baby spoon made Grantham's taut biceps and pectorals flex, and beneath his shirt Phoebe could detect her ring and the darker color of his nipples. Riding just below the navel of his washboard flat tummy, the red sweats rippled with folds and yet molded to his hips, shaping each blessed contour so there was no mistaking the outline of his maleness when he got up and moved around the kitchen.

Grantham chuckled. "Keep looking at me like that and I'll lose *my* concentration, Phoebe—or else burn to a crisp. Like your spinach cakes."

Flushing a deep pink, she started—and whirled toward the oven. Yep. If she'd taken another minute to peruse Grantham, her hors d'oeuvres would have burned. She grabbed a pot holder, pulled them out, then slid in two more trays. "Well, before I make you melt," she said, sliding a small, steaming cake onto a plate, "why don't you try one of these and tell me if they're all right?"

Grantham squinted. "Looks hot."

She arched an eyebrow. "Well, then, let's let it cool."

The remark hung in the air—and suddenly, it didn't seem to be about the temperature of the hors d'oeuvres at all. Heaven knew, she and Grantham had been smoking all week. Especially after the ball they'd attended for a special children's charity to which she'd contributed. Dani Newland Lucas, who'd married Jake just days after their engagement and who'd begun helping with the babies during the day, had baby-sat that night with Jake and their six-year-old son, Tyler.

For Phoebe, the night of the charity ball had been a dream, a far cry from the nights with Nico, where she'd played the trophy wife. During a fancy dinner at the Waldorf Astoria, Grantham—who'd looked devastating in his tux—had eyes only for her. Later, they'd danced until her mind was flooded with memories of their very first dance and their lovemaking in the Wilshire Arms.

Afterward, in the hallway outside the apartment, Grantham had thanked her for the night with a kiss so deep, wet and thorough that just remembering it sent shivers of awareness through Phoebe and left her aching for him. She watched Grantham blow on his spinach cake.

He winked as he chewed, then pronounced, "Excellent."

Smiling, she started puttering around the kitchen again. "I'm so glad Dani suggested we have the kids' party in the Big Apple Babies' nursery," she said conversationally.

From the first day Dani came to help with the kids, she and Phoebe had been fast friends. And, as the head executive at Big Apple Babies, Dani's husband had gotten to known Grantham while he'd been trying to adopt. The Lucases were Phoebe and Grantham's first couple friends.

"Oh, I was supposed to tell you," Grantham suddenly said. "Gary says he'll swing by with the limo to help transport the hors d'oeuvres."

Phoebe grinned. The limousine chauffeur had become a daily fixture, too, taking the babies for a drive every afternoon, so Phoebe and Dani—or Grantham, if he was home—could take a break. A West Coast transplant like Phoebe, Gary was a student, and he was using his time off from the limo service to study for night classes. "What? Is Gary trying to weasel out of baby duty again?"

Grantham chuckled. Even though Gary obviously loved the kids, he said, "Probably."

"Oh!" Phoebe exclaimed. "Before *I* forget, Jake says there are folding tables in the basement at Big Apple Babies. You're going to have to take them up to the fifth-floor nursery. Jake said Doc and James will help."

"We're not inviting your lawyers?"

Phoebe shot him a fleeting glance. "No," she said.

It was a sticky subject. An unstated agreement seemed to have been forged between her and Grantham, where they steadfastly avoided talking about the upcoming court date, even during the weekly Thursday night dinners they were having at Granddaddy Winslow's.

She sighed, wishing her matchmaking relative would quit grilling her and Grantham about their lives together. Just for Granddaddy Winslow, they'd made sure they always played tennis on the rooftop courts. Fortunately, he was leaving the day after the birthday party for a week's vacation. Phoebe was doing her best not to be short-tempered, but she hadn't quite forgiven him for believing all Nico's lies. Well, when it came to matchmaking, Jake and James Sanger, who stopped by regularly to check on the babies, could be even worse than Granddaddy Winslow.

Grantham was still watching her.

She said, "I thought we'd just invite...friends. Right?" Everyone at Big Apple Babies had become that to Grantham over the last year as he'd prepared to get the twins, and now they were all quickly becoming Phoebe's friends, too.

Grantham nodded, looking faintly relieved.

Not wanting him to worry and having no idea how to resolve their situation, she said, "We still have to decide what kind of Halloween costumes to get."

"I thought you wanted to make them."

Phoebe shrugged. "Well, I guess it depends on what we decide to do. Dani's got a sewing machine she said I can use."

Grantham glanced at her again, his eyes flickering appreciatively over her in a way that made her pulse accelerate—especially when the unapologetic gaze lingered on her chest. Beneath her apron and loose top, the tips of her breasts suddenly constricted, and she felt her cheeks warm.

"You know," he said, "you're a very enthusiastic, creative person."

Somehow, because of the way he was looking at her, she half expected him to refer to some of the more enthusiastically inventive things they'd done together in bed ten months ago. Instead, he said, "You really helped me get the New York Retro account. And you know how to sew?"

She blew out another wistful sigh, suddenly wishing Grantham would train his unsettling gaze elsewhere and let those lazy eyes, which were leaving shivers in their wake, do all their casual strolling somewhere other than across her anatomy. What woman could ever get used to being looked at like this?

She swallowed against the dryness of her throat. "Well, learning to sew was the upside of having a hippie mother and living in an uneventful place like Cat's Canyon." Phoebe smiled at the memories. "We made skirts out of mens' ties. Ruffly patchwork insets for our jeans. Embroidered canvas pocketbooks." She broke off pensively. "Hmm. For the kids, I've been trying to think of things that come in dozens or half dozens, Grantham. I mean, maybe we could attach the strollers, somehow, and make a mini parade float out of them that looks like an egg carton."

Grantham hooted. "And dress them up like eggs?"

"Yeah." Phoebe nodded, warming to the topic. "Maybe they could wear white body suits with stuffed egg-shaped padding for their middles. What do you think?"

Grantham laughed. Then he leaned close to Kirby and Lyssa, piercing each girl in turn with a serious amber-eyed stare. "If you're eggs," he warned, "we'll have to be very careful with you, young ladies."

The girls giggled appreciatively, as if at an inside joke. Grantham turned to the boys. "And we wouldn't want you guys cracking up on us."

Phoebe's cheeks got a degree hotter—and she realized she was positively beaming at the guy. How could he be so commanding in his tux and business suits, then so downright goofy around the kids? Suddenly, she frowned and started to pace in front of the kitchen counter. She crossed her arms, which always seemed to help her think better. "But, you know, Grantham," she continued, "the eggs would be so...colorless. Unless we dressed them as decorated *Easter* eggs. But then, isn't that mixing the holidays?"

After long moments, she looked up.

Grantham was watching her with a bemused expression.

"What?" she said as she paced past him.

He grinned. "I love it when you pace like that. You get so involved with your projects. You're so passionate." Without another word he reached out and grabbed her in mid pace. When his arm wrapped around her waist and he squeezed her hard against his side, her hip wedged perfectly into the crook of his shoulder. "Though maybe you think too much."

She stared at him, smirking. "What? I guess you like women who don't think?"

"Sure I like women who think. But only about certain subjects."

Their eyes met and held. His chest and shoulder

warmed her side, his smile warmed her soul, and she fought the sudden urge to lean down and kiss him. "Like what?"

He shot her a wicked smile. "Sex."

She made a show of trying to weasel from his grasp, not that he let her go. Playfully, she dipped her thumb into the cleft in his chin. "Sorry I asked."

His chuckle rumbled in his chest, vibrating against her, sending ripples of awareness right through her skin to her blood. "No, you're not."

She exhaled a mock-huffy sigh, squirmed away and headed for the oven again. "If you don't watch it," she warned, "the babies will mimic you. They're at that age. Now, how would you like them to talk about—" she shot the babies an arch glance "—s-e-x at their second week of Sunday services?" She stared at the babies inquiringly. "Minister Banks wouldn't like that one bit, now would he?"

Kirby's eyes got wide. She shook her blond ringlets, looking positively scandalized. Lyssa giggled naughtily, and Langdon's mouth made a round little O. The other boys stared at Grantham as if sensing that maybe they should side with Daddy on this one.

Smiling, Phoebe shook her head. "Hey," she said with renewed enthusiasm, "maybe we could somehow turn the strollers into an Easter basket on rollers. Or it could be a country-style basket full of apples or oranges."

"Or just a basketful of babies," Grantham said. "And you and I will dress up as two giant storks and push them around."

Phoebe cracked up. "I love that! I really *love* that! They could wear spring bonnets!"

Grantham's lips twitched. "I was joking, Phoebe.

I'm not putting a diaper in my mouth like those baby-bringing storks—no matter how clean it is." He watched her, looking bemused again. Then he said, "Oh, pea pods."

Phoebe peered at him. "Excuse me?"

He chuckled. "Things that come in sixes. I could get two strollers, take them apart, line up the seats so they're in one long row. Then I'll build a wire frame around the stroller, cover it with papier-mâché and paint it bright green for the pod."

"Yep!" Phoebe enthused. "It's perfect. They'd wear matching green body suits, with round, pea-shaped stuffed middles and little caps, maybe with brown beanie stems." She squinted. "Do peas have stems, Grantham?"

He shrugged. "No clue, angel. In the ten months before you came, I was eating take-out."

She winced. "I'm not sure your diet's much improved."

"Oh, I don't know. That beef and gravy TV dinner with the side dish of—" he sent her a teasing frown "—what *were* those green things?"

She rolled her eyes. "Lima beans," she said flatly.

He grinned. "I kept trying to give them to the kids under the table, but they wouldn't take them." He shot her a playful smirk. "Do you think we could get a dog?"

Grabbing a dish towel and snapping it playfully against one of Grantham's powerful shoulders, she chuckled. By the time they dealt with the kids' necessities, then shared quality time with them, she and Grantham were lucky to find time to eat at all. And Grantham knew it. Making a show of defending himself against the dish towel, Grantham reached forward, grabbed the tie of Phoebe's apron and pulled.

She retied the strings. "Hands off."

"I didn't touch a thing."

"You did, too," she shot back. "Every chance you get."

And she kept letting him. It was impossible not to. She sidled close and helped with the babies, mashing the people food she and Grantham were introducing, grabbing another cloth and wiping up spills. She found herself smiling at him again. Every time he passed the babies, they giggled or beamed at him with pure adoration. He was so good with them. In the evenings, after he changed out of his suit, he'd fling himself on the playroom floor, then let all six kids crawl over his strong muscular frame, swinging on his limbs as if he were a living jungle gym.

Not that Phoebe was any less necessary. Oh, she played with them. But she was the one they turned to with their tears and scrapes. The one they expected to make everything all right. She did, too. And it was making her feel more useful and needed than she'd ever imagined possible. Grantham seemed to need her, too. They complemented each other. And the kids needed a mother *and* a father....

Langdon started tapping his hands against his high chair tray. "He really does have rhythm," she murmured, leaning and planting a kiss on top of Langdon's head. Then, not wanting to appear partial, she continued down the row, kissing all the babies one by one.

"A natural-born musician," Grantham said agreeably as she returned to the countertop.

Phoebe placed a cooling spinach cake on Gran-

tham's empty plate, then slid the plate onto the table.
"Have another."

Grantham smiled. "Thanks, angel."

The man definitely had an appetite. At the house in
Genesis, Long Island, where they were spending
weekends, Grantham always grilled steaks outdoors.
They'd been taking the kids to the beach, too, and
building sand castles and collecting shells.

"Are we going to Genesis this weekend?"

Grantham turned and surveyed her. "You really like
it out there, don't you?"

"Yep. Sure do." He'd bought the house with Celia,
though it never had been fixed up or furnished. Now
it was half-empty, with little more than beds. Dani
Lucas's parents, Thurman and Kate Newland, had a
home nearby, the first house ever built in the community. And while it was a huge structure of chrome
and steel, with glass walkways that connected various
cylindrical outbuildings, Grantham's place was a
homey east-coast farmhouse. It had white siding, a
white picket fence and door frames and windows
painted a crisp forest green. The ocean could be seen
from the wide, wraparound porch, as well as from the
master bedroom, which had an old stone fireplace.

"Hmm. So you like the house...."

Now that the babies were settled, picking at their
carrots, Grantham got up and headed toward her. Before Phoebe knew what was happening, he'd playfully
backed her against the countertop, setting his hands on
either side of her. Reaching around her waist with a
sly, sexy smile, he tugged her apron tie again.

"Quit!" Phoebe tried to ignore that the air circu-
lating between her and Grantham—scant as it was—
was starting to come alive with red-hot energy. She

made a show of retying her apron. "How old are you? Ten?"

"You think that's juvenile?" His wicked smile made her heart hammer. "It's not my fault you bring out the teenager in me."

Her eyes drifted over his face—those sculpted bones, his perennially bronzed skin. "How's that?"

Grantham leaned so close that his breath made pinpricks tingle on her neck. His voice was low, teasing. "Oh, you know. Loss of control. Raging hormones. The works."

Feeling her cheeks flood with heat, she glanced away—only to gaze into those seductive eyes again. "I may think too much, Grantham. But did anybody ever tell you that you have total tunnel vision?"

He chuckled throatily. "Angel, I just keep hoping that you're what's at the other end of that tunnel." His eyes never leaving hers, he reached around and tugged her apron tie again.

"Grantham!"

His eyes were full of heat. "One of these days I'm going to keep going, angel, and you're not going to find the breath to stop me."

"Ah," she returned. "You're so confident of yourself."

He nodded. "Patient, too."

Phoebe surveyed him—the handsome, sculpted face, those sparkling amber eyes, the body that just wouldn't quit. He edged closer, his chest hard, her breasts pressing against the solid wall of muscle. His arms circled her. Managing to wiggle her arms free from where he'd pinned them at her sides, she wrapped them around his neck. Leaning back in his embrace, she smiled into his eyes.

"C'mon, Phoebe," he said simply.

There was no doubt what he was asking—her into his bed. "I..." Her voice trailed off. It always started like this. They'd be having fun with the kids, going about their domestic chores, then they'd start flirting—and wind up in the position they were in now. Her throat, suddenly dry and tight, seemed to close up completely. She was overly conscious of her crazy respiration, the pulse pounding in her throat, her hammering heart, her breathlessness. She managed a wry smile. "Why is it you always make me feel like I'm having an anxiety attack?"

Grantham laughed. "You mean, panicky? With fight or flight symptoms?"

She nodded.

He shook his head. "Who knows? But you make me feel the same way. Think we ought to call Doc?"

"Or a fire truck."

His eyes narrowed to sexy slits. "So you're feeling warm?"

More like she was ablaze. "A little. Maybe you should back up." She playfully poked his chest.

Clearly enjoying himself, he didn't move a muscle. "Keep dreaming, Phoebe."

Suddenly, a quick bittersweet sadness twisted inside her.

Because these weeks with Grantham *had* been a dream. They'd settled into a domestic routine of the sort Phoebe had always imagined. And all the while, the man kept wreaking havoc with her insides. Her outsides weren't faring much better. At least a thousand times she'd dreamed of making love to him again. Now that she was getting to know the real Grantham Hale, not the one-night dream lover Grantham

Hale, she wanted him more than ever. Or maybe not more, but in a different way. A more permanent way. But they were still involved in this custody case. And there were other problems.

Reading the change in her mood, he said, "Angel?"

Her open palms slid up his chest, then stopped, feeling her ring beneath the fabric of his shirt. She'd never acknowledged that she'd noticed it before. Now her hand stilled, and she toyed with the ring through the fabric.

His voice was low. "I've worn it since that night. It was the only thing I had of yours."

Emotion twisted inside her. He was so romantic. Her eyes never leaving his, she sighed. "Oh, Grantham, I just don't know what I want." But it was a lie. She knew she wanted him. But she couldn't trust him, couldn't trust herself.

"I know what you want," he countered softly. "You want to be safe and sound and loved. You want a man. You want a family. You want those babies, all of them."

"Yes," she admitted. "But it's not that easy."

His eyes had taken on a slightly feral glint, hungry and a little predatory. They dropped over her now, glowing with gold fire, seemingly burning everywhere they touched. "Phoebe," he said. "We're not kids. And I'm not Nico. I'm a one-woman man. And you're the woman I want."

Her heart fluttered, and a forced, fleeting smile crossed her lips. Lord, he was leaning so hard against her—all six-plus feet of uncompromising, one-hundred-percent male strength and heat. His mouth had turned hard, determined. She couldn't help but say, "You *are* definitely a man."

"You got that right, angel."

Without another word, his mouth locked over hers in a hard kiss, and Phoebe was whisked away. She was someplace else altogether, swept out to sea on an overpowering wave of sensation. There was hot, wet pressure. Two sharp tugs at her breasts—just the tips quickly peaking—then her heightened awareness of the lace of her bra, its nubby texture, its roughness. Then she was aware of his tongue again. Repeatedly diving between her lips, it pushed surges of heat through her entire system. That heat spiraled down and down in a vortex that swirled at the juncture of her thighs. She felt pure longing. A needy ache she couldn't deny. Then the hard male part of him swept into the vortex, too, the loose folds of his sweatpants leaving no room for denial about his aroused state.

As he angled his hips closer, Phoebe somehow dragged her lips away. "What if we tried," she said with a gasp, no longer able to hide part of what was on her mind. "Grantham, what if we did become lovers again? What if everything worked out and we wound up getting married and we raised the kids together…"

Her voice trailed off. Grantham was watching her, his body as unnervingly still as a coiled snake. Absently he licked his lips, still tasting her flavor. His voice, usually so clear, was deep and husky with raw desire and emotion. "I don't get it, Phoebe. You think that would be a problem?"

She thought of Nico. Then she blew out a ragged sigh, from worry or arousal, she had no idea which. "I know you're not Nico. But you're rich and powerful, the way he was. If we ever got a divorce, I could lose the babies all over again." Was it her imagination or was anger sparking in his eyes? "Sorry," she murmured quickly. "But I want you to know what I'm thinking. I could lose everything."

His lips compressed in a hard line. His words were laced with carefully restrained temper. "I guess you'd have to learn to trust me." Rather than back away, Grantham leaned harder against her, the pressure of his lower body making her shudder. He seemed unforgiving and relentless. There were so many sides to this proud man, but one thing remained—he didn't ever take lightly to hearing the word no.

Grantham stared at her for a long time, the gaze almost cool, assessing. Was this really the same man who, only moments before, had been chuckling with the kids? "I'm not backing off, Phoebe," he said calmly. "When I want something, I get it. Call it anger or arrogance or anything you damn well please, but ever since we made love, I've meant to pursue you until you're mine again."

He waited for her to say something. She couldn't think of a darn thing. After a moment he nodded as if her silence was answer enough for now. Then he kissed her again. It was a strange kiss—punishing in its intensity and yet so tender she could almost cry from it. And it was long and deep enough that she was powerless to do anything other than arch against him in need while all the memories flooded her—of him tonguing her bare skin and stroking her intimately with leisurely, maddening caresses. Even as she kissed him, she told herself she had to back away.

Because she had other fears. Oh, she'd asked him about the missing million dollars. But she knew better than to press too hard. If he'd really done something wrong, he'd probably lie like Nico. She wanted to believe Grantham. But he got so many mysterious calls. Sometimes they came at odd hours and he talked in whispers. Sometimes, immediately following the calls, he'd leave unexpectedly. When she asked why, he said it was business. After such calls, she'd always try the automatic redial on the phone, but the parties had their numbers blocked.

Yep. Her heart desperately wanted to ignore the warning signs. And heaven knew, so did her body. But she didn't really trust him. And yet, here she was, letting him kiss her. The touch of his lips aroused her as she'd never been aroused before, until she was sinking against the kitchen countertop, her body flooded with wanting him, her knees weak. A soft moan escaped her. He dragged his lips across her mouth, his hands slipping between her apron and top, cupping her breasts.

"Need me again," he said raggedly, the words a hot, insistent murmuring against her mouth.

Somehow, she leaned away. Her lips couldn't form the word no, but it was in her eyes.

"Oh, angel," Grantham whispered, not bothering to hide his frustration. "I want it to be like before. For you to call out to me. To let me hold you and love you. I'm not Nico. I don't know what he did to you, but if he wasn't dead, I think I could kill him. I looked for you all year, Phoebe. I never stopped thinking about you. And now you've been in my apartment for weeks, in my life..."

Her voice was a croak. "And you're not going to give up until I'm in your bed."

"That's right." Grantham backed a fraction away, just enough to serve as the admission that he'd let her go—if only for now. But everything in his eyes said he'd never let go.

For a long moment they gazed at each other. There seemed to be nothing more to say, so she stood there, feeling her need for him buffet against her like a gale-force wind. His body heat had seeped all the way through her, making her want to sag, as if her bones had melted together. And yet the sheer hardness of his body seemed to keep her upright. She sighed again, with growing love and longing.

Suddenly, he wrenched in her arms.

Just as she gasped from the abrupt movement, he caught a plastic cup in midair.

"Oh, no!" she exclaimed.

While their backs were turned, all hell had broken loose. Little plates, and bowls and cups had been dumped unceremoniously onto trays. Faces and hands and clean sleepers were besmeared with mashed carrots and juice.

In a second flat, she and Grantham were a flurry of parental motion, grabbing cloths and wiping up the spills. At one point, they met under the kitchen table, on their hands and knees. He was going at a clump of carrots with a cloth. She was sponging a puddle of juice. Their eyes met.

"Phoebe?"

"Hmm?"

"This conversation's not over."

She nodded. If the man had his way, they'd be in bed in a second flat. He'd probably have her walking toward an altar, too. After all, Grantham Hale wasn't exactly the easy-lovin' type.

But Phoebe wasn't going anywhere yet.

She had far too many unanswered questions. First,

she wanted a full accounting of Grantham's secret business meetings and his strange phone calls from gruff-voiced strangers who refused to leave names. And then she wanted to know the exact whereabouts of her babies' mysterious missing million.

Chapter Ten

Dani Lucas leaned against the counter in the fifth-floor kitchen at Big Apple Babies and peered through the doorway at the nursery. "I put out more hors d'oeuvres, Phoebe. Everybody's finished with their cake."

Phoebe nodded. Less than an hour ago, she and Grantham had helped the babies blow out their first candles. Now she inventoried the messy countertop, her eyes skating over some cupcakes and settling on a headline in the *Times*. Investigation Into Hale's Finances Requested. The headline wasn't as lurid as those in the *Post*, but it had been no less disturbing to her this morning when she'd first read it. Some attorney for a citizen's action group was now demanding that Grantham explain for the missing money from the babies' account. And Grantham, darn him, was still refusing.

"If you've done nothing wrong," Phoebe had prodded for the first time this morning, "why can't you respond?"

"Trade secret," Grantham had said lightly. But there was worry in his eyes.

Now Phoebe sighed and leaned next to Dani, thinking how good it was to finally have a girlfriend with whom she could talk. "I want to thank you and Jake for all your help with the party," she said, her eyes flickering over her new friend. "And did I tell you I absolutely love that dress?" The belted jumper, which Dani was wearing over a simple black turtleneck and tights, was of narrow pin-stripes in rainbow colors.

Dani laughed. "Thanks. But it won't fit much longer."

Phoebe felt a rush of warmth. "I'm so happy for you." Dani and Jake had just gotten the news that she was pregnant.

"Can you believe it? I was engaged for all of a week. Then I got married. And now..." Dani's laughter tempered to a satisfied grin. She leaned and pinched the fabric of Phoebe's wraparound skirt. "Well, this sure came out well."

Phoebe had found the birthday-cake print fabric when she and Grantham were shopping for materials for the babies' Halloween costumes. Beneath the simple wraparound skirt, Phoebe wore a lacy black body-suit and tights. "Thanks for lending me the sewing machine. I think I may have gotten the hem a little short." Phoebe laughed. "Well, it could have been a lot shorter. Grantham kept offering to hem it."

Dani chuckled. "Well, the man *is* creative."

"I love the things he's done for Big Apple Babies."

The adoption agency was on Waverly Place, a triangular wedge of street between Sixth and Seventh avenues in Greenwich Village, and over the last year, Grantham had offered his advertising talents, designing a catchy new sign that now graced the front entrance. An exact replica of an oversize diaper pin, it hung over the sidewalk, parallel to the ground. Skewered through the bottom metal rod was a white banner, fashioned to look like a diaper cloth, that bore the agency's name. Inside, the place was homey; painted murals depicted assorted apples of gold, red and green—some with crisp white bites missing, others with cute, wiggly, smiling worms. Beneath the murals ran the agency motto in bold script: Big Apple Babies are babies of all kinds!

Phoebe stared through the kitchen doorway. Playpens had been rearranged to make room for foldout tables that held food and presents. Colorful Mylar balloons swayed overhead and, from a big screen TV in a corner, Barney tapes played. A professional clown worked the room, chatting with adults and amusing babies. The babies—there were about forty in the nursery waiting to be adopted—were outnumbered, mostly by the staff who had turned out in droves with their significant others.

Phoebe's Granddaddy Winslow gripped his cane, slowly making his way through the crowd, shaking hands and kissing babies as if he'd decided to campaign for the presidency.

"I'm glad his leg's healing," Dani said, following her gaze.

Phoebe chuckled, taking in her cantankerous eighty-five-year-old relative. Poor Dani had been his nurse while he'd been wheelchair bound and in a cast. "For his sake or yours?"

Dani drew a deep breath. Imitating the judge's thunderous voice, she intoned, "For mine, Ms. Rutherford, I do assure you."

Phoebe giggled. "Well, right after the party, he's leaving for a week-long vacation, so we'll be spared his overwhelming presence for a few days." In fact,

Phoebe suddenly thought uneasily, her Granddaddy Winslow wouldn't be back until she and Grantham were supposed to square off in court.

Her eyes drifted to Grantham. He was seated in a grouping of metal chairs, easily talking to Jake while the kids wiggled in his lap and crawled around his feet. Grantham was such a natural-born family man. *Why don't you just give in? Become his lover, Phoebe. See where this takes you.* That was one part of their relationship she was absolutely sure would work.

And the rest? They were getting so close. Each night, after they put the babies down, they'd collapse together, exhaling sighs of accomplishment. They'd shared plenty of kisses, too. Not to mention increasingly intimate caresses. And long hours of talk. She'd regaled Grantham with colorful stories about the ever-feuding Rutherford-Winslow clan, and she'd told him about her parents. She loved them but they had free and easy life-styles that had made her long for the kind of stability she was feeling now.

Grantham had told her how the stiff reserve of the upper-crust Hales had made him crave a big rowdy brood of his own, especially since he was an only child of parents who'd had him later in life. As sole heir to his father's fortune, he'd felt pressured and overly protected, and then, in his early teens, he'd lost his mother to breast cancer. His father, many years her senior, had passed on when Grantham was in college. Later, of course, Grantham lost his wife.

Something twisted inside Phoebe now, as if that pain were her own. Grantham was still so young—and yet he'd experienced so much tragedy. So had she. They deserved joy. And they were both finding it—in each other, and in the arms of the babies who were crawling all over him. *Four of whom you're trying to take away.* More and more, Phoebe was considering withdrawing her lawyers from the case. How could she deprive Grantham access to children he loved so much? Assuming that she could really do so. Besides, if the truth be known, she wasn't the least bit eager to move out of his apartment.

Phoebe sighed, now watching Doc Holiday and his brother, Shane, pull chairs next to Jake and Grantham. The two urban cowboys were quite a pair—with honeyed drawls calculated to make any woman's knees weak and broad shoulders that said they took their myriad responsibilities seriously. She suddenly realized Dani was watching her. "Hmm?"

"I said, have you slept with him yet?"

Phoebe colored slightly. "Grantham?"

Dani smirked. "Who else?"

"No," Phoebe said, deciding not to mention her and Grantham's past. She wanted to say more, especially since Dani was always so open. Phoebe's heart still warmed at all she'd heard about Dani and Jake's romance, and how they'd come together, to parent the six-year-old Tyler. It seemed so easy for Dani to share things the Lucases were going through—her new pregnancy, the fact that Jake, who was adopted, had just initiated the search to find his birth parents.

Phoebe had talked about Nico, of course—if only enough to let her new friend know the marriage had ended badly. But when Dani had asked about her presumably criminal past, Phoebe had kept quiet, following her lawyers' orders. Now, she felt a wave of guilt. The newspapers had reported all her supposed wrongdoings—the bounced checks and alleged adultery, the fact that she'd been declared an unfit mother. Still, she

kept looking sympathetic—as if she were the prover-
bial fallen woman now making good. Oh, she knew
her lawyers had wanted that, but the coverage of Grantham was making him look worse and worse. Phoebe
desperately wished there was something she could do.

She shot Dani a fleeting smile. "Oh, Dani, I...I do
want to sleep with Grantham."

Dani's expression clouded as she reached and
squeezed Phoebe's hand. "Is the trouble in the newspapers bothering you?"

"Partly," Phoebe said. "I've asked him about it,
but I don't want to pry."

She wanted to tell Dani about the mysterious phone
calls Grantham received, including those from the
gruff-voiced man who wouldn't identify himself. After
the calls, Grantham would leave the apartment, and
she'd run guiltily to the windows to spy. Once, she'd
seen a white stretch limousine pick up Grantham at
the curb, and her mind had run wild. Illogically, she'd
wondered if he was involved in dirty city politics or
the mob. Of course, she felt too much loyalty to Grantham to share such unfounded, crazy fears with Dani.
Surely, it was nothing.

Dani weighed her words carefully. "Grantham's a
great guy, Phoebe. But the more the newspapers keep
writing about his finances, and the more he refuses to
speak out, the worse he looks."

Phoebe felt as if lead had settled in her stomach.
Her eyes slid toward Grantham, and she was suddenly
gripped by raw-boned terror. In a flash, she imagined
herself discovering that he'd squandered the babies'
money. *Please, God. Oh, please don't let him turn out
to be like Nico.*

"Phoebe?"

Phoebe glanced at Dani.

"I think you're falling in love with him," Dani said softly.

Phoebe mustered a weak smile. "I think so, too." *I know so. I just can't make myself trust.* "I'm…so scared things will end badly." *Again.*

Dani nodded. "Maybe you can talk to Grantham, make him speak out. He's got to put these charges to rest. I know Jake's concerned. So is James."

Phoebe could read between the lines. Grantham's own friends were starting to doubt him. She felt positively ill. *But I've tried to talk to him.* She merely nodded.

Suddenly small footsteps pounded—and Ty Lucas bounded into the kitchen. He stopped breathlessly, tossing his head and shaking his shaggy blond bangs from his dark eyes. "Daddy wants you, Mommy." Tyler glanced at Phoebe. "My mom's gonna have a baby," he continued matter-of-factly.

Phoebe shrugged off her worries and chuckled. "I heard!"

Ty grinned, then made a show of putting his hands on his hips and glaring at his mother's still-flat belly. "And it better be a *brother*."

Dani swatted him playfully. "Well, if it's not, I promise your Daddy and I will keep trying."

Ty stuck out a petulant lip. "You'd better!"

Phoebe glanced toward Grantham again. In a cluster of chairs near him were Jake, and Doc and Shane Holiday. Now her Granddaddy Winslow pulled up a seat. "Well, I guess we'd better go check on the babies and menfolk."

Dani grabbed an organic, juice-sweetened cupcake from the counter and nodded. "C'mon, Ty-ger."

"Jake, you're pulling my leg," Shane Holiday was saying in a deep, throaty drawl as they reached the group. "You swear you just got a letter in the mail, with an anonymous check and directions to open Big Apple Babies?"

Phoebe seated herself next to Grantham. He sent her a slow smile that made her insides feel as warm and runny as molasses, then he resituated Kirby and Devin in his lap and draped his arm across her shoulders. Lyssa tugged Phoebe's leg, and Phoebe immediately lifted her.

Shane said, "Phoebe, darlin', have you heard this hogwash?"

Phoebe laughed, slipping off her earrings and pocketing them to protect her ears from Lyssa's exploring hands. "Yep. But it's not hogwash." Dani had told her the Big Apple Babies story shortly after they met. A few years back, Jake really had received an anonymous letter, and the start-up capital for the agency. "I'd say it's more like a modern fairy tale."

"A fairy tale!" Judge Winslow snorted, sourly pursing his lips and further hunching his corpulent frame into the much smaller confines of the metal chair. "This is New York City! What is all this nonsense about fairy tales?"

"It is a fairy tale, Granddaddy Winslow," Phoebe said, feeling a rush of temper. "Whether you like it or not."

"I, for one, prefer to deal in reality."

"Oh, Granddaddy," Phoebe returned, "you always want to believe the worst about everything and everybody." She still couldn't entirely forgive him for actually believing she was a law-breaking adulteress. Maybe she never would.

Judge Winslow sulked—at least until little Lyssa pointed at him with a short, chubby index finger and giggled. After a moment, the old judge's lips twitched and he wound up smiling at the baby. "All bark and zero bite," Phoebe quipped under her breath.

"I heard that, young lady," said the judge.

Shane was still probing Jake about Big Apple Babies. "C'mon. You really think you can pull the wool over this ole southern boy's eyes?" Shane tipped back his Stetson a fraction. "I just don't believe this."

"Yeah." Doc chuckled. "Jake's probably telling tall tales, Shane." He winked at his brother. "You gotta watch out for Jake."

Dani looped her arms around her husband's neck. "I'll second that motion. This man got me pregnant just by looking at me."

Tyler glanced up from his spot on the floor. "Did not. You and Daddy told me what happened."

"Immaculate conception," Dani deadpanned to the group.

Tyler rolled his eyes and sighed as if to say adults certainly could be juvenile. "Talk about telling tall tales, Mommy!"

Phoebe laughed. Grantham began toying with her hair as he often did, fluffing it and raking his fingers through the strands. "It *is* true, Shane," Phoebe found herself saying. "The letter's right downstairs, framed in Jake's office."

Shane leaned forward. "And the letter was from some secret philanthropist?"

Judge Winslow scoffed. "A secret philanthropist! Whoever heard of such silliness!"

"It is *not* silly, Granddaddy Winslow," Phoebe protested, more huffily than she intended. "The letter he wrote is right downstairs!"

Judge Winslow merely rolled his eyes. Deciding he was just about the most cynical person she'd ever encountered, Phoebe blew out a peeved sigh. How she'd managed to enjoy his company during their dinners together these past few weeks, she'd never know. Especially since he still seemed to think she was such a bad person.

"And you *swear* you don't know who sent the money?" Shane asked.

There was a slightly skipped beat, just quick enough that Phoebe's eyes shot to Jake. For a second, she was sure he *did* know more about Big Apple Babies secret backer or backers than he was letting on. Suddenly, Grantham's strong, muscled hand cupped her shoulder and squeezed, distracting her thoughts.

Jake shook his head. "No clue. But a couple of days ago, I received another check."

Everybody gasped.

Dani said, "And you didn't even tell me?"

Jake grinned. "I was waiting for the right moment. Besides, I wanted the check to clear, which it did this morning. Apparently, our…secret philanthropist wants to see the opening of a Big Apple facility for placing teenagers."

"Wonderful!" Dani hugged Jake hard, giving him a solid kiss on the cheek. He responded by hauling his pregnant wife into his lap.

Phoebe's chuckle tempered to a soft smile when she felt Grantham's voice sound next to her ear. "I sent Tyler to get Dani," he whispered, "but you were supposed to stay in the kitchen."

Phoebe frowned. "I thought Jake sent Ty—"

Grantham's sly smile interrupted her train of thought. So, getting Dani out of the kitchen had been Grantham's ploy. No doubt, he'd wanted to steal a moment from the crowd for a private kiss. Phoebe set Lyssa on the floor again, then raised her voice. "You know, I just got the worst craving for another one of those cupcakes. I think I'll just run to the kitchen…"

With a saucy wink in Grantham's direction, Phoebe rose and headed for the other room. Knowing he was watching, she made her hips swish more than was necessary to get from point A to point B. In the kitchen, she leaned against the counter and crossed her arms.

She didn't have to wait long. He came sauntering in, his eyes sparkling. "Hey, lady," he said, not stopping until he was pressed against her with his arms around her waist. "Looks like you're waiting for a man."

Phoebe lifted her chin and craned her neck around, making a show of looking. Her eyes landed on his again. "Well, not just *any* old man."

Grantham chuckled. "What? You wanted an *old* man?"

"No," Phoebe said with a laugh. "Any man."

"Hmm. If you're looking for any man, then I guess I'll do."

She tilted her head back, giving him the once-over. "Do for what exactly?"

He smiled. "For what I want to do."

"Then I guess."

Grantham shook his head. "Not good enough."

"You will *definitely* do," Phoebe corrected.

His lips came a fraction closer. "Do for what?"

"For what *I* want to do."

His breath now teased her cheek. "And what's that, Phoebe?"

"Oh," she teased throatily, "everything a woman can possibly do for a man, I suppose."

"Such as?"

Her whole body was warming with his proximity and the flirtation. She shrugged. "Oh, excite and distract him. Drive him crazy."

"You're sure doing that to me," Grantham said.

He sighed as his lips parted hers in a kiss that was as slow as a month of Sundays. It felt both familiar and new, and its relaxed, lazy warmth made Phoebe feel as if a summer breeze was wafting right through her. Each time he kissed her like this, it got easier. She felt more open to him, physically and emotionally. A murmur sounded deep in Grantham's throat, and he deepened the kiss, his lips pressing harder, his tongue starting to stretch languorously as if after a long, satisfying nap. She became thoroughly conscious of where their thighs touched, of where her breasts brushed his chest. When he finally drew away, he left her whole body aching.

"Oh, Grantham," she managed wistfully.

His voice was a whisper. "Too bad we're in public."

If they weren't, Phoebe wasn't sure what she'd have said right now. Maybe she'd ask him to make love. "But we are." She gazed into the depths of his eyes, noticing tiny flecks in the irises.

"Oh, I almost forgot—" Grantham's slow smile said whatever it was, he hadn't forgotten at all. It was really uppermost on his mind.

Her eyes narrowed playfully. "You mean, you didn't pull me in here just to kiss me?"

He drew away, then headed for the other side of the room. "No."

"Then I'm sorely offended."

He shot her a playful glance over his shoulder. "Don't forget, you lured me in here."

"You came easily enough." She watched in surprise as he opened a cabinet, then pulled out a medium size blue-and-pink gift-wrapped box. Returning, he caught her hand and guided her to a chair. Pulling one beside her, he handed her the box. She glanced at him, her eyes questioning. Was it something else for the kids?

Lifting a hand, he brushed the hair from her face. "One year ago," he said, "you gave birth to four babies. So, happy birthday, angel."

He'd gotten *her* a present on the babies' birthday? The gift was so unexpected and she was so touched that tears stung her eyes. Reaching out, she placed a hand on Grantham's knee and squeezed. Her voice caught with emotion. "Thank you."

He smiled warmly. "C'mon, open it."

Her fingers trembled on the baby blue bow. Carefully, she removed it and then unwrapped, folding the paper, which she wanted to save. Removing the box lid, she saw the four books she kept in her room titled *Baby's First Year.* In addition to the four, Grantham had nestled two new books for Stanley and Devin in the layers of pink and blue tissue paper.

Opening the first book, she saw where she'd written Kirby's name. Then, as she turned the next page, she realized that Grantham had filled this book and all the others. He must have done it during his lunch hours at work, and the project must have taken him days. On page after page, he'd neatly, painstakingly written in all the information for each baby—the weight and height for every new month, the date when they'd eaten their first solid foods or drunk from a cup, or when they'd taken the first steps.

Emotion squeezed her heart again. It was as if Grantham was trying to restore for her those horrible lost months, when she'd been without the children. Her vision blurred.

"I got most of the information from the files Doc gave us," Grantham explained. "Their previous physician took great notes on their progress, too. What I couldn't find, Doc provided me with."

"Oh, Grantham," Phoebe whispered, her nose burning with the unshed tears. "This is so sweet."

"And there's something else."

Phoebe glanced down. Yep. Sure enough, there was an individually wrapped square present. Taking off the paper, she saw that in the outer box was a frame. Surely, Grantham had fixed up a snapshot of himself and the kids. He was so thoughtful. She drew out the picture—and her heart lurched.

It wasn't a picture of the kids.

The frame was of ornately wrought silver, and of an easel-style, so she could set it on her nightstand. And in it, arranged on black velvet, was the white rose she'd taken away from the Wilshire Arms hotel that long-ago night ten months earlier. She could barely find her voice. "You must have found the rose pressed in my Bible..." Her eyes flitted to his.

His voice was husky. "It's the same one, isn't it, Phoebe?"

Her throat felt raw, dry. "Yes."

The shared memories swirled between them. How the fingers of his large bronzed hands had been curled around that stem. With tantalizing slowness, he'd traced the soft bud over her body. Beauty touching beauty, he'd said. She could still feel the velvet petals trailing over her breasts, across her belly, between her thighs...

Her heart pounded. Her breath felt cut off, her head dizzy. Gazing deeply into Grantham's eyes, she could barely believe the way he was pursuing her and wooing her. Her voice cracked. "Thank you so much."

He was still smiling, the glow of his eyes warming her. Reaching beneath her hair, his palm cupped the nape of her neck. Leaning, his mouth settled over hers with soft pressure. Only after a long moment did he start brushing his lips back and forth across her mouth.

"You're welcome, angel," he whispered.

Her lips sought his again, and she kissed him, gently and tenderly, still feeling stunned and holding the framed rose.

She no longer doubted it. She was falling in love with Grantham. The man was everything she'd ever wanted. Funny and romantic. Creative and tender. Patient. A loving father. And, she already knew, a remarkable lover.

If only I could trust him, she thought. But as he deepened the kiss that no longer seemed to matter. Her earlier conversation with Dani seemed years in the past. Right now, everything seemed so perfect. Like a fairy tale. Somewhere out there was a secret philanthropist who wanted people's heartfelt dreams to come true. Closer still, were her babies. And beside her, kissing her, was Grantham.

No, she thought. Nothing else mattered at all.

Chapter Eleven

"I do assure you," Judge Winslow thundered indignantly, "I knew my ruling requiring Grantham Hale and Phoebe Rutherford to parent together would cause press scrutiny—but not *negative* press scrutiny!" Hunched in his favorite red velvet armchair, Judge Winslow angrily clutched a phone in one hand and his cane in the other.

He was on a six-way conference call, which meant not all the secret Big Apple Babies backers were present. Now, in five well-appointed rooms around Manhattan, there was a long silence while all considered the matter at hand.

"We could wind up being exposed," someone offered nervously.

"It's a real possibility," agreed a deep, reasonable baritone from the Wall Street area. There were two light taps as the man put his wingtip shoes on his desk. "So, I am deeply concerned. My son must never guess I'm a contributor."

"You are all still perfectly anonymous!" Judge Winslow roared. This was an outrage! Ever since last month, when Dani Newland—now Dani Lucas—and Jake Lucas had discovered that he was a secret backer

for Big Apple Babies, Judge Winslow felt as if his
fellow secret backers didn't trust him anymore. Could
he help it if Dani had recognized his handwriting in
the framed letter in Jake's office? Besides, Dani and
Jake had been sworn to absolute secrecy.

"I'm the only one who's been exposed," he huffed.

"Now, now, Tilford," crooned the most secretive
of the backers, the only one whom he'd never met
face-to-face. The youthful, soothing female voice was
mysterious and smoky, with the faintest hint of what
Judge Winslow guessed was a Louisiana accent. "We
trust you implicitly."

"I didn't know sentencing them to be parents together would cause problems," Judge Winslow repeated angrily.

"Oh, Winslow," a shaking, elderly male voice suddenly chortled. "That *had* to be a legal first!"

"It most certainly was," said another aged voice.
This, from one of the judge's oldest cronies who'd
made his contributions to the city years before, back
when people slept safely on fire escapes in the summer
and walked alone at night in shadowy public parks
without feeling fear.

Now, at ninety years old, the judge's oldest, dearest
friend was ill, and because he couldn't bear to think
about it, Judge Winslow suddenly sobered. He sighed
heavily. "With the sentence, if anything I intended to
draw negative press attention *away* from Grantham
Hale."

"Well, it's only made it worse," said the nervous
ninny.

"I know!" And Judge Winslow sorely wished his
esteemed colleagues were less inclined to keep men-
tioning it. "However, if it were not for me," he re-

minded them loftily, "Dani Lucas's father, Thurman Newland—who is the city's most successful banker— never would have agreed to help fund our new teen facility."

"Tilford, you're positively brilliant, and we all know it," crooned the soft-spoken young woman.

He *was* brilliant, the judge thought defensively. However, he *had* made a small error in judgment. He could admit that now—if only to himself. Not that he knew what to do with his great-granddaughter, Phoebe Rutherford. Indeed, she might well be beyond hope, he decided, gripping his cane. After all, he'd done her the supreme favor of sentencing her to be parents with the wealthiest, handsomest, most well-connected bachelor in all of New York City. Last year, the *New York Post* had named Grantham the sexiest man in Manhattan. What more could a young woman want?

In court, it had been obvious that Mr. Sexy was smitten at first sight, too. But once again—probably due to her inferior Rutherford genes—Phoebe was managing to make a muddle of her life. Where Grantham was apparently willing to look beyond her sordid record, Phoebe had not yet even solicited one marriage proposal from the man!

Judge Winslow's blood started to boil. Phoebe was being positively ungrateful. The only thing more he could have done for the girl was arrange her fool marriage. But they hardly lived in feudal Japan where such things were commonplace, Judge Winslow ruminated. No, in the United States of America in the twentieth century, the law—however unfortunately—did have its damnable limitations.

"Tilford? Are you still there, Tilford?"

"Of course!" he snapped.

"Well, I hope this latest investment will be wrapped up before our cover is blown sky-high," said the reasonable Wall Street baritone. "I do want to make sure my son doesn't find out."

Judge Winslow was not going to lose his temper again. He sniffed. "I, for one, intend to leave for vacation this very afternoon," he announced coolly.

"And you deserve it, Tilford," crooned the woman.

"You really do, Tilford," said the shaking elderly voice.

The reasonable baritone said, "Well, should we contact Grantham Hale and speak to him about this bad press?"

"Heavens, no," chided the soft-spoken woman. "He has enough on his mind."

"So we ride out the storm?"

There was more discussion.

Judge Winslow sighed. He felt much worse about all this terrible business than he let on. Oh, why had he attempted to play matchmaker? He supposed it was because of his success last month, when he'd forced Dani Newland to admit on the witness stand that she was in love with Jake Lucas. Now, *that* had been very dramatic. But this...

"So we're all agreed? Tilford?"

"I *am* terribly sorry!" Judge Winslow suddenly burst out. "I'll set this right!"

"We know you will," crooned the female voice.

"I vote that the secret backers for Big Apple Babies—at least those represented here—ride out the storm," said the shaking elderly voice. "We'll reconvene if things get any worse."

As he hung up, the Honorable Judge Tilford Winslow, charter member and secret backer for Big Apple

Babies and secret old softie, felt marginally better. But he was still bound and determined to fix this terrible situation he'd so shortsightedly caused.

Because Grantham Hale, he well knew, deserved many things. And not one of them was negative publicity.

CY LYNDE MOTIONED for Grantham to take a seat. Where, Grantham wasn't exactly sure. He stared at Cy for confirmation, but Cy didn't notice. His elbows were on his metal desk, his back was hunched, and he was clutching a telephone.

"I don't care," Cy was saying. "You *can't* have a tattoo. Miriam, please. I have a client in my office." He shook his head. "Look, if everybody jumped off the Brooklyn Bridge, would *you* jump?"

Grantham bit back a smile.

A moment later Cy hung up, clearly defeated. He looked at Grantham, his shoulders starting to shake with mirth. "I can't believe I said that. My father always said that. I swore I never would."

Grantham chuckled. "Look at the bright side," he said. "At least yours are potty trained."

Cy burst out laughing. "You got a point. Guess you *are* changing a few diapers with six in the house. They running you ragged?"

Grantham nodded. "And I'm loving every minute of it," he admitted.

Cy smiled. His eyes said he loved parenting, too, but he wagged a finger in Grantham's direction. "I want to hear you say that when yours are all in their teens."

Even though he was here on business, Grantham suddenly felt good. When he'd gotten the kids, he'd become a member of a special group—parents. Somehow, it made him feel so...*normal.* He had a family. His whole life seemed to be clicking into place—except for Phoebe, and she was coming around. And now there was this. "So you've got good news," Grantham said.

Cy nodded. "Sure do."

"I came right over."

"Good. Has your blackmailer called again?"

Grantham nodded. "He told me to get twenty-five-hundred more dollars. That he had new pictures he hadn't shown me of Phoebe. He told me to keep it ready at all times, in a brown paper bag. He said he'd contact me again when I'm supposed to meet him."

Cy blew out a frustrated sigh. "He's trying to make sure you don't have him followed when you make the drop. The first time he called, he wouldn't have guessed you had a PI on retainer. Now he's assuming you've hired someone. By instructing you to have the money ready, he can have you meet him on short notice, reducing his chance of getting caught."

Grantham sighed. "So what's the good news?"

Cy set a file on the desk. "Well, as we knew, Nicolas Adair was kind of like a West Coast you."

"Meaning?"

Cy shrugged. "You know. One of those rich, silver-spoon types."

Grantham shot Cy a long, sideways glance. "Gee, thanks."

Cy smiled. "No offense. It just happens to be the truth. Anyway, at first he seemed to be a real golden boy. But people are starting to say he wasn't particularly scrupulous. Now that he's dead, people are willing to talk."

Grantham shrugged. "Well, we knew his clients were usually mega corps." It had turned out that Adair dealt with those who had bottomless pockets and things to hide. He'd been the kind of image consultant who helped gloss over oil dumps in oceans and toxic chemical wastes in small communities. Nicolas Adair had taken on causes that were strictly against Grantham's politics—if not his religion.

"Well," Cy said, "at this point, I can prove Adair continued to promote clients even when he knew they were breaking laws. Also, a credit service employee hinted to me on the phone that Adair paid him to wreck Phoebe's credit rating. It may not pan out, but the guy agreed to meet me."

"That's a start."

"There's more. I went to A New Leaf. The man who previously swore Phoebe was enrolled in their rehabilitation program now admits she wasn't. He was paid to lie."

Grantham nodded. "By whom?"

"He won't say, and I can't prove it, but I'm sure it was one of Phoebe's lawyers. Grantham, you'd better watch out for them. Those three play hardball—and play to win. Anyway, it's becoming clearer that Adair really slandered Phoebe so he could take custody of the kids. After that, it looks as if he kept at it, too."

Grantham frowned. "You mean he kept slandering her *after* I met her in L.A.?"

"I think so. Maybe because he was angry about the divorce. Anyway, the lawyers can't find enough evidence to reverse the damage, so I guess they're trying this new tack, making her look rehabilitated."

Grantham shrugged. "Cy, we figured that all along."

"But now we're really getting somewhere, Grantham. The counselor feels guilty. He'll talk."

Grantham sighed. He desperately wanted to clear Phoebe's name. He wanted her to know he believed in her. Even more, he wanted to undo every single bad thing that bastard Adair had ever done to her. "Even if we get testimony that Phoebe was never rehabilitated, that can't repair the damage Adair has done to her reputation."

"True." Cy shoved a picture across the desk. "But I got a lead on this guy."

Grantham stared at the picture. The man was in his thirties, a blond, blue-eyed, suntanned surfer type. "Who is he?"

"Sven Nordstrom. The guy she was allegedly sleeping with."

Grantham did a double take. He knew the man had probably never laid eyes on Phoebe except when he'd disparaged her in court. Nevertheless, a shiver of cold-blooded emotion went through him. Grantham hadn't felt the feeling for so long that it took him a full minute to identify it as jealousy.

He felt a rush of other emotions, too—the need to love and to protect. Not to mention to soothe his wounded pride. After all, he was a Hale. And no man, especially a dead one, was going to get the best of him. His lips were in a thin, determined line. Somehow Grantham was going to right every past wrong and keep all six of his babies.

And then, by damn, he was going to get the girl.

"Whatever it takes," Grantham said. "You make this guy talk. I want Phoebe's name cleared."

THEY'D GONE with the pea pod.

As Grantham and Phoebe jointly pushed the long green pod containing the babies through the streets of Genesis, Long Island, Grantham took a deep breath. Somehow the city and its troubles seemed very far away. This was heaven, he decided—a tree-lined street in the breezy, warm, autumn twilight, with Phoebe at his side and the kids in front.

All around them, bright orange, yellow and red leaves rustled, shimmering in the branches overhead, blowing onto the pavement, crisply crunching underfoot. In yards, the green grass, combed smooth by the tines of metal rakes, looked like strands of hair. Grantham took another deep breath, pulling in scents of salt and sand from the nearby ocean. Smoke, too. Somewhere upwind, a bonfire had been lit on the beach.

Nearer, he could smell Phoebe. And he wondered if he'd be sharing fires with her this winter, if the life they'd started to build would continue. He could so easily imagine her curled up naked in a blanket after the kids were down for the night, sipping something hot from a steaming mug, while he threw another log onto the andirons. He glanced at her.

"Ready to try another house?" she said.

The kids craned their necks, as if to say it was about time.

"Yeah." He nodded, following Phoebe's gaze around the neighborhood again, taking in the decorations, the plump pumpkins that had been carved into menacing, candle-lit jack-o'-lanterns that glowered from windows and porches. Doors were hung with Halloween fare—posterboard witches on broomsticks, friendly ghosts, glow-in-the-dark skeletons.

Phoebe laughed. Lifting a hand from the stroller, she pointed. "Isn't he adorable?"

Grantham chuckled. Across the street was a pint-size hobo who looked dangerously like the real thing—except for the fact that three ballerinas in pink tutus, presumably his sisters, kept pirouetting around him.

Phoebe sighed. "I still think ours are the cutest."

Ours. Grantham's breath caught. It was the first time she'd referred to the kids as belonging to both of them. For a month, he'd listened to her juggle pronouns with the dexterity of a linguistic scholar, studiously avoiding words such as *yours, mine* and *ours.*

"Well," Grantham murmured, lifting a hand from the stroller bar and casually draping it across Phoebe's shoulder. "We are biased."

"True. Besides," she conceded, her voice faintly tinged with guilt, "Halloween isn't a contest."

He laughed. "Oh, but they're still the cutest, Phoebe."

Her lips twitched. "I know." Her voice rose with her usual enthusiasm and maternal pride. "I really think they *are* the cutest, don't you, Grantham?"

Grantham chuckled. It had taken him all week to build the six-seat stroller and cover it with wire and papier-mâché. He'd built hooks next to each seat for the pumpkin baskets to hold the babies' treats. While he had painted the stroller green, Phoebe had finished sewing the costumes. Their six adorable peas were snuggly fitted inside the green pea pod. The quads and twins wore green body suits, fitted with round, stuffed middles monogrammed with their names and green knit skull caps.

He and Phoebe never had found out if peas had stems.

Of course, Grantham had drawn the line at letting Phoebe dress him as the Jolly Green Giant. In compromise, he'd worn a green shirt and knit hat with his jeans. Phoebe, of course, had gone the whole nine yards and dressed herself as the giant mother pea.

She looked impossibly adorable, too, he decided with another smile. While the costume obscured most of her more womanly curves, her long, slender legs, which were encased in green tights, were almost entirely exposed. Just looking at the shape of them, Grantham found himself sighing. Her fluffy hair peeked from beneath her green knit cap.

"If I slept with you," she teased, lightly picking up an earlier flirtation, "It would be, like, uh, just for sex, right?"

Grantham sent her a long sideways glance. "If you sleep with me," he returned, "you can tell yourself it's for anything you like, Phoebe." Not that it was strictly true. He wanted her—and he wanted her in love with him.

She nodded sagely. "So it wouldn't *mean* anything."

"Coyly fishing for my real feelings again?" In midstep he stopped. He drew her closer—or at least as close as he could, given her outfit. Her soft green middle was cushioned against his belly. Suddenly, he didn't want to joke around anymore. His voice grew husky. "Phoebe, you know, if you slept with me, it would mean the world."

Her dusky blue eyes softened, looking as dreamy as the twilight. "Really?"

"Especially if it meant the world to you."

"Really?" she said again, this time the word a mere whisper on the autumn air. He could tell from her eyes that she desperately wanted to give him her complete trust. And he wished there was something he could do to help her.

He cupped her chin. "Really, angel."

Standing on tiptoes, she clung around his neck and delivered a sweet kiss to his lips that left him wanting more. He imagined her naked in his Jacuzzi, wrapped in his arms with her long legs locked around his back. But of course, they were really with the kids, on a public street. As they started pushing the stroller again, her eyes swiftly checked the babies as they so often did, maternally, automatically.

Suddenly Phoebe's lips twitched. "You'd take me even if I was dressed like *this*, Grantham?"

He couldn't help it. He burst out laughing. God, they had fun bantering together. He shook his head. "You just don't quit, angel. Okay, it is a little difficult to take you seriously in that pea outfit."

Phoebe grinned saucily. "Takes one to know one."

Grantham glanced at his green shirt. "True." His eyes drifted over her. "But I doubt pea outfits are on anybody's top-ten list of how to dress for a man."

"Oh, c'mon," she shot back. "Yep. I'm sure this is right up there with stiletto heels and those black stockings with the seams. You know the kind?"

Somehow, Grantham doubted it. "I know the kind," he assured her dryly. "But I confess, I'd rather make love to you bare-skinned."

Her eyes narrowed playfully. "But you would take me as a pea?"

"I'd take you in any kind of package, sweet pea."

The flirtation was so silly and sweet that Phoebe

grinned lopsidedly. Then she pointed. "Let's try that house."

Together, they wrestled the unwieldy stroller onto a brick sidewalk, then wheeled it to the porch and lifted it, so the kids were in a long row facing the door.

"Get ready, kids," Phoebe crooned, circling the stroller. Gazing inside the pod, Grantham helped her take inventory. While he tried to find Kirby's missing green bootie, Phoebe straightened both Lyssa's and Stanley's green knit hats. "Now, Nicolas, please don't cry, sweetie," Phoebe admonished, when his lower lip started to tremble. "And, Devin, get your hand out of your pumpkin." When everyone was in order, she said, "Let's have our practice run. Can you say, 'Trick or treat?'"

"Tree! Tree!" the kids said agreeably. They really were catching on, Grantham thought proudly.

Circling the stroller again, he and Phoebe gripped the handle. "Want to ring the bell?" he asked.

"Yep." Phoebe grinned at him. Their eyes met and held. Just looking at her, his chest got tight. And then, abruptly, something in her expression changed. Her smile vanished, and her eyes filled with emotion that turned them the same dark blue as the ocean at midnight. All at once, she looked so heartbreakingly, crushingly vulnerable that it took his breath away. He could see the pulse ticking in her throat, and he watched her swallow, as if around a huge lump.

"Phoebe?"

She gulped and sent him one of those fleeting Queen of the Brave Face smiles.

"Angel?" he said.

"Grantham, I know this is a real funny time to say it—" Her voice was suddenly so devoid of humor that it almost scared him, and as if sensing that, she reached out, settling her hand loosely on his arm. She blinked, and tears suddenly shimmered in her eyes. He turned to face her, his hands grasping her forearms.

He peered into her eyes. "Phoebe, what is it?"

"Grantham," she said, "we have so much fun. I...I *like* our, uh, family so much. I'd really like to see it work. I...I *like* everything we do." She paused, looking a little helpless. "What I mean to say is that I...well, I just *like* the kids and you and...I really *like* you and..."

She was in love with him.

That was what Phoebe was trying to say. He was so stunned, he couldn't talk. So he did the only thing he could—circled her with his arms and hugged the mother of his children tight. "Ah, Phoebe," he whispered before his lips crushed down hard on hers, "you know I *like* you, too."

Hell, Grantham had been completely in love since he'd first laid eyes on her. And at the first touch of her lips he completely forgot they were on a stranger's porch and that their six little peas were craning in their pea pod to see what was going on. Pulling Phoebe against him, he delivered his softest, warmest, sweetest, most soul-searing kiss, one that made his body tighten with arousal as he plunged his tongue deep, communicating all his promises to her—the shared hopes and dreams, the long nights of loving passion to come.

"Now, there's a trick I'd just about forgotten!"

Phoebe drew away, gasping. Feeling shell-shocked—had he heard Phoebe right? Was she trying to say she loved him and wanted to make this family work?—Grantham turned to find a spry elderly lady staring at him. She adjusted her round, wire-frame glasses on her nose, then grinned. Lifting a basket of treats, she flung open the door. One by one, she read off the babies' names. Then she glanced over the six little peas until they were all giggling with delight.

"Now that Mommy and Daddy are done with the tricks," the woman crooned, "wouldn't you six like a treat?"

Chapter Twelve

At least she'd tried to tell him how she felt, even if it had come out a little awkwardly. Phoebe wished Grantham had had time to say something. But right after he'd kissed her, the babies had gotten cranky, so she and Grantham had to rush home. *Home,* she thought. *To this beach house you've already come to think of as yours and Grantham's, Phoebe.* As soon as they got inside, they'd changed the kids, then put them down for the night.

Grantham's low voice broke the silence. "They asleep?"

Phoebe glanced along the row of cribs, then stared into Lyssa's again, her hands tightening on the wooden rail. Her daughter was so gorgeously angelic. They all were. "Yep," she said softly without turning. "Even Stanley."

Grantham had been lounging in the doorway behind her. The fabric of his jeans whispered and his soft steps sounded as he came up behind her, easily sandwiching her between his body and the crib. She sank against him. Not that his body yielded. It was so enticingly hard, the solid muscles of his chest alive and flexing against her back, his strong, corded forearms wrapping under her breasts, his powerful shoulders curving around hers.

When he leaned, resting his chin on her shoulder and nuzzling his cheek next to hers, she became conscious of her scant attire—nothing more than green tights beneath a one-piece dance leotard. Because her outfit had been so bulky, she'd forgone a bra. From the second she and Grantham had come indoors, the kids had needed attention, so she'd had no choice but to discard the middle part of her costume.

"Do you really want this family to work?"

Grantham's soft whisper was strangely neutral, as if he half expected her to retract the words. Phoebe's heart hammered, her throat feeling dry. "Yep," she whispered. "I really do."

"Do you trust me, angel?"

She swallowed against the dryness of her throat. Right now love seemed easy, but trust seemed so hard. Nico had sadistically, systematically destroyed her life. And Grantham hadn't offered explanations for some of his behavior. And yet, she did trust him, didn't she? "Yes," she found herself murmuring.

"I...know there are things you're wondering about, including the babies' money. But I really can't talk about it right now."

Her heart hammered. Her voice caught. "I trust you."

When Grantham shifted his upper body against her back, she was flooded with an almost uncomfortable awareness of the aching tips of her breasts, the dewy warmth already gathering between her thighs. She swallowed hard in nervousness and anticipation, and in fear because she didn't know if she was doing the

right thing. All she really knew was that she was falling in love.

"Aren't the kids the most perfect things you've ever
seen?" she murmured, not really expecting a response,
her throat dry and tight.

Leaning back a fraction, Grantham fluffed her disheveled hair, then brushed it to the side with his long,
strong fingers. He settled his chin on her shoulder, his
breath stirring against her neck, tingling.

He chuckled softly. "Cold?"

Her voice was husky, an invitation. "Maybe I'm
shivering with anticipation."

He smiled against her neck. "The answer's yes,"
he murmured. "Our babies are the most perfect things
I've ever seen, Phoebe."

Our babies.

They'd become that. Somehow, she and Grantham
had started to build a life full of its own rhythms and
systems, complete with friends held in common,
church affiliations, parent groups. In smaller ways,
they worked together. He usually distracted the babies
while she bathed and fed them. She made morning
coffee while he got the newspapers. He could temper
her impulsive urges. If he got too serious, she could
make him laugh. They were right for each other. And
their lives had become inseparable, bound together by
the threads of the Fates. Together, she and Grantham
had laid a strong foundation.

Playfully, he tugged her earlobe with his teeth. Then
with warm, wet, fluttering butterfly kisses, his lips
trailed down her neck. His tongue followed, until the
kisses deepened, becoming hotter and more languid,
drawing in skin. Slipping a finger beneath the stretchy

neck of her leotard, Grantham pushed it aside enough to lick at her collarbone.

Dropping her hands from the crib rail, she started to turn in his embrace, wanting that meandering mouth to settle on one place alone—her mouth. But he held her fast, leaving her splayed hands nowhere to go but behind her, on his thighs. Through his jeans, his leg muscles tensed, bracing. Her pulse raced at his reaction, and she slid her hands up, her thumbs stopping only inches from that part of him she most wanted to touch.

The room was so silent.

There was no music. The babies were asleep. Out here, so far from Manhattan, the city sounds—sirens and horns—had ceased. In the windowless room not even the ocean could be heard.

Just silence.

And so she heard each nuance of Grantham's breath, how it quickened with his desire. And she heard the whisper of fabric as his excruciatingly slow splayed palms slid upward over her ribs, and how his breath caught sharply as he cupped her breasts from below, raising them. Then his fingers closed, squeezing around the mounds with heavenly pressure—not hard enough to hurt, just enough that she knew his intentions were serious.

So were hers.

There was a heartbeat. A still second where everything seemed suspended.

And then his tongue was delving lower on her skin, his hands curving around her breasts, his thumbs and fingers tugging the taut peaks through her leotard, his breath, ragged and excited, teasing the tender skin of her throat that he'd already tongued so mercilessly.

She loosed a hoarse sob, gasping out his name. She tried to turn in his arms again, but his were wrapped so tight around her she couldn't move. And then she felt his arousal against her, already full, heavy, insistent.

"Don't move," he whispered hoarsely. His voice lowered another husky notch, becoming almost rough as one hand slid from her breast down her belly. "Oh, Phoebe."

Reflexively, she squeezed her shaking thighs together. She didn't know why, since she craved his touch so desperately. Not that it mattered. Wordlessly, he parted her, cupping her. In the dark, her cheeks flamed. She'd forgotten how boldly Grantham's hands touched. And how completely she responded.

"Phoebe," he groaned against her neck, stroking her, feeling the dampness she couldn't control seep through her clothes. "I've thought about this so many times. Remembered it. Imagined it. Did you think about us together?"

A low moan escaped her. She whispered, "All the time." Even as his slow hand threatened to shatter her, the memories flooded her consciousness—of what had really happened, of the fantasies she'd had ever since. "Oh, Grantham," she managed to say shakily, "I thought about it. I dreamed. I—"

Swiftly, he turned her in his arms. Capturing her mouth, he crushed her lips with his, taking her by storm, his tongue invading in a sweet, savage plundering. He was a man too long in a desert without water. Too long imprisoned without food. A man in total touch with a carnal, animal side that was suddenly hellbent on satisfaction, both hers and his.

"Phoebe." Her name came as a soft pant, the voice

urgent. "I never wanted anything as bad as you." In a lithe movement, Grantham gripped her waist and lifted her off the floor, saying, "Lock your legs around me tight."

They circled around him, her ankles crossing at the small of his back, and her arms wreathed his neck as his lips parted hers again. Kissing her, he strode to the master bedroom. He set her on the bed, then crossed the room. As he went, he grabbed his shirt by the hem and ripped it off, tossing it to the floor. With single-minded purpose that made tremors ripple through her, Grantham drew back the curtains and opened the sliding glass doors that looked out onto the sea.

Her heart nearly stopped. Outside was a gorgeous sunset of purples, oranges and reds. She could hear the tide's powerful roar, the breaking waves. Grantham turned, bare-chested, his arousal obvious through his jeans. The sea was behind him, and there was fire in his eyes. The searing heat never left his gaze as he approached the bed unbuckling his belt, unzipping his pants.

Just the look in his eyes made everything inside Phoebe feel both loose and tight, weak and in a swoon. By the time he'd reached her, he'd stripped for her completely. And her whole body was shaking as he let her eyes take their fill.

Wordlessly, he pulled away her clothes, then he lay next to her, kissing her, moaning against her mouth, as his hands slid down and his fingers tangled in her moist, warm curls. She clutched helplessly at his shoulders as his fingers parted her, and she sobbed against his shoulder as he slid a finger inside, then two. Withdrawing them, honeyed and warm, he circled the turgid nub of her desire, rubbing with her own slickness, until she begged him to stop.

"You don't really want me to stop," Grantham said, his rough, breathless whisper coaxing her toward oblivion. "You really don't want me to."

And she didn't. She came right off the mattress, convulsing in his arms.

"Yes," he whispered raggedly, turning and kneeling between her legs, parting them with his knees. "Ah, yes."

She gasped. She wanted to tell him she couldn't take any more. But she couldn't talk. Reaching for a drawer, he got a foil packet, ripped it open with his teeth, then rolled on a condom. He slid between her legs again, wasting no time. She felt him hard and hot, right at the opening. Leaning, he cupped her face in his hands. And then he kissed her with heartbreaking tenderness, slowly, wetly, deeply.

"Please. Oh...oh, Grantham," she whispered against his mouth, wanting him so much. "Please."

He leaned back a fraction and his eyes found hers, the amber gaze penetrating. Watching her face, he pushed inside, his throbbing flesh easing in, parting her, making her cry out. She'd waited so long. He pushed again. And again. Until the slick sheath of her closed around him completely.

When he was buried deep, he released a long sigh of satisfaction. Withdrawing completely, he took her again, this time with a slow, deep thrust calculated to take her where only Grantham could—to completion. To a self she'd never had before she'd met him. To the self in her that was really the person they'd become together. Her breath stuttered, its stops and starts loud in the quiet.

"Come to me, angel," he whispered.

Then he surged into her like the waves. But he was a wave of fire. Riding with him, she felt herself crest and draw back, only to surge again. And each new wave burned through her blood, carrying her farther and farther out to sea.

Everything seemed to break apart. Her senses started to collapse. Fire seemed to be everywhere—in his loins and deep in her belly. The fire was upwind, on the beach, and yet bathing her breasts as Grantham's fiery tongue lapped at them. And yet, in spite of all that fire, she was flooded. Drenched. The very air seemed wet. Somehow Grantham's gasps seemed to come from her throat. Kissing his shoulder, she tasted salt from the sea. Nothing made any sense at all—except him and the love she felt for him. And that last cry that pulled her right over the edge.

She came with her legs wrapped tight around him. He was so deep inside, he could do nothing more than gasp as she pulsed around his flesh. Sensing how hard she was falling, he caught her in his arms and held her as if he'd never let her go. When she reached rock bottom, he went wild. He'd held back. But now he finished taking her—swiftly, urgently—with stark need that had become sheer agony, with desire that had become a sweet torture. With a strangled gasp, he exploded. "Phoebe," he sobbed. "Phoebe. Phoebe. Phoebe."

She'd never forget that—how he'd called her name. It bespoke her power over him. His need. And most of all his love.

He said he loved her later.

Much later, when they were twined together, holding each other, their bodies still damp but long-ago sated. He brushed away the hair from her face and stroked her cheek, his eyes full of tender anticipation.

"Phoebe," he whispered, "I don't *like* you. I love you."

Tears touched her eyes. "Oh," she said in a quick rush. "I don't like you, either." Her lips curled into a soft smile. "I really love you, too."

Grantham pressed his face to hers so the bump of his eyebrow locked perfectly into the hollow above her cheekbone, and her thumb found his chin and dipped into the cleft. He whispered, "Will you marry me, Phoebe?"

"Yep," she whispered shakily. "Oh, Grantham, I want that more than anything."

"GRANTHAM?"

Had she whispered it aloud? The future Mrs. Hale wasn't sure. She dreamily breathed in the clean scent of the silk sheets, her limbs sliding on the slippery, luxurious fabric as she snuggled beneath the covers. Hugging the cool pillow, Phoebe Rutherford, soon to be Hale, felt deliciously, scrumptiously, decadently happy.

Everything had clicked into place since that night in Genesis—the nitty-gritty nuts and bolts, the big picture. Everything. Nowadays, when she and Grantham weren't busy making love, they were chattering like crazy, planning the future. Next week they were getting married, quickly and privately, to avoid the press. Then they would split their time between the city and Genesis, but move to Genesis when the kids were school age. Grantham would start commuting. They'd discussed all the things people were supposed to before they married, which meant countless topics headed by numbers and initials—PTA, IRA, 401K, the IRS. Not to mention school districts, college funds and life insurance.

Everything.

"Hmm." Phoebe snuggled deeper, her humming strangely like a purr. Even their sweet, perfect babies were cooperating. All were sleeping peacefully through the nights, including Stanley, who was tucked into his own crib.

"Grantham?"

Phoebe was sure she said it this time. She heard her own voice—scratchy with sleep, heavy with satisfaction. She stretched, catlike, relishing the pleasurable aches she felt all over. Her fiancé's continual rigorous lovemaking had introduced her to muscles she'd never even guessed she'd had.

"Just go back to sleep," he whispered.

"But I thought I heard the phone ring," she murmured. She'd left Granddaddy Winslow countless phone messages to tell him tomorrow's court session was no longer necessary, since she and Grantham were engaged—which meant they'd sentenced themselves to be parents together forever. But the judge was still out of town. Phoebe's lawyers remained on standby, ensconced in their suite at the Plaza Hotel. If the judge didn't call back tonight, they'd all have to show bright and early tomorrow morning.

"Grantham, did Granddaddy finally call?"

"Just go back to sleep, angel," he whispered again.

She glanced at the digital clock through sleepy slits of eyes. It wasn't yet midnight, but the instant they'd put the babies down, Grantham had pulled her into bed. As usual. She smiled again, her body warming at the thought of his stamina, her blood quickening. Just thinking about it made her want him snuggled next to her, buried lusciously deep inside her. Nope, she'd never known loving could be like this, so easy and satisfying. Her smile broadened. Or so astonishingly never-ending.

Her eyes found him again. He'd pulled on briefs that were a flash of bright white in the dark room, starkly silhouetting his enticing manhood. Another ripple of awareness shimmered through her. Blissfully, she yawned, shut her eyes and drifted. Then she felt the mattress beside her depress. A warm, strong hand that was every bit as silken as the sheets slid beneath the covers and rubbed her naked back.

"Phoebe?" he whispered. He fluffed her hair then smoothed it with his hands.

"Hmm?" She half turned. Realizing Grantham was dressed, her sleepy eyes narrowed.

"I have to go out for a few minutes," he whispered.

"Now?" she croaked.

He nodded. "I'll be right back."

She fought to keep her voice even. "Okay," she whispered, her voice groggy, belying the fact that she was waking up fast.

He patted her side. "Back in a flash."

From where? Phoebe's mind screamed. Who had called? Did this concern another woman? Or the missing money Grantham refused to account for? Was he in trouble? Would the white limousine come for him again? Who was inside that car? As Grantham left the room, emotions overwhelmed her—anger, fear, betrayal. Love and maddening curiosity. The need to protect her own heart and all the babies. Of course, she knew better than to ask him about this. He wouldn't tell her. Nico never had.

Which meant she had only one option left—spying.

As he opened the foyer coat closet, she silently slipped from bed. Tugging on jeans, her sneakers and a sweatshirt, she stared at the video monitor. Could she really risk leaving the babies? She was damned if she did, damned if she didn't. Fear pricked along her skin. Well, the babies were sound asleep, and they'd been sleeping through the night. Hooking the high-tech, phone-style monitor to the waistband of her jeans, she reminded herself that the device was the latest on the market, good for the length of two football fields. All over America, mothers used these while hanging laundry or cleaning a far-off part of the house. And she was just leaving for a minute.

The front door closed.

Go! Hurry up, Phoebe! Court's tomorrow. This is your only chance to find out what Grantham's up to! You have to know—especially if you're really going to marry him! She raced for the door, stopped to grab a windbreaker, doubled back to the library for the binoculars, just in case.

He was already gone! In the hallway she watched an old-fashioned, gold arrow-style metal pointer above the elevator door move downward, from five to four.

She bolted for the fire door, then hit the stairs at a dead run, taking the steps two at a time. The flights zigzagged, making her head spin, as if she was running in circles. By the time she reached the bottom, her heart was thudding dangerously. Breathlessly she peered through the tiny window in the stairwell door. Above the first-floor elevator, the gold arrow moved from three to two.

Fortunately the desk attendant was so engrossed in a novel that he glanced up just long enough to see she was a tenant, then he buried his nose in the book again. The golden arrow moved again. It hovered on one. The elevator was going to open!

Phoebe ran. The doorman wasn't outside the double glass front door. Good. As she hit the street, her eyes darted left, then right. Had the elevator opened behind her yet? Was Grantham staring at her through the glass doors? Diving left, she sped toward a service entrance and ducked inside the recessed stone doorway. She stared at the front awning, suddenly registering the chilly night air. It was cool on her cheeks, making her breath foggy.

Where was Grantham?

Suddenly the glass door opened.

Grantham stepped into the night. It was hard to believe he'd been in bed a minute ago. He looked so in control, his hair tidy, his long raincoat distinguished. In his right hand he was carrying a brown paper bag.

What was in that bag?

He glanced around. Phoebe sucked in a panting breath. Holding it tight, she hoped he wouldn't notice the fog of it on the air. Was she really hiding from her fiancé? The man who'd been buried deep inside her body earlier tonight, climaxing in her arms?

Her heart pounded. She had no choice but to exhale. She sucked in another breath. With it came the smell of the recess where she hid, the musty smell of damp old stone. If the babies cried, Grantham would hear them through the monitor. And if he turned left, coming south, he'd be walking right toward her. *Oh, please, no. He'll catch me for sure.*

He walked west.

Except for cabs on the avenue, it was quiet, and she could hear his steps—long strides on the pavement—

until he started across Park. She waited, her heart thudding, as he headed west on Eightieth. Then she slipped from the dark doorway and jogged halfway across the avenue, to the wide grassy median.

Suddenly, she realized she was fully exposed under the streetlights. If Grantham turned, he'd see her. She lurched forward. Reaching the brownstone on the opposite corner, she pressed her palms against the cold stones, anchoring herself as she peered around the corner. Grantham strode quickly toward Central Park.

She stared helplessly at the windows of the apartment, as if she could see the babies from street level. Sighing, she lunged forward again, using everything in sight for cover—saplings planted in the sidewalk, trash cans, newspaper machines. The few people on the street didn't seem to notice—a couple clutching theater playbills stepping from a cab. The three or four harmless carousing teenagers laughing behind her. An elderly couple taking a late-night stroll.

Phoebe's eyes stayed riveted on Grantham's back—and the brown paper bag.

At Fifth Avenue, she knew she had to quit following him. She couldn't risk being any farther away from the babies. Guiltily, she leaned against a building, hiding in the shadow of the massive stone edifice.

Grantham crossed the street to the museum side, then turned, as if to head for Seventy-ninth, but stopped again. Had someone called his name? She was bracing herself, she realized, expecting another woman. No doubt because of Nico. Anger surged through her. What was she doing here? She should trust Grantham. However suspicious this looked, Grantham wouldn't do anything wrong. With every kiss and every touch, hadn't he put her crazy doubts to rest?

But old voices died hard.

She lifted the field glasses. Street lamps lined the park, and the floodlights of a museum fountain illuminated jets of frothy white spray.

"What's in that bag?" she whispered urgently as a man stepped from behind the fountain. She drew in a sharp breath. The man was shorter than Grantham, stocky and powerfully built, wearing a black windbreaker, black pants and a black cap. Phoebe focused the binoculars on the thug's brutish face. He appeared to be angry, arguing with Grantham. He showed Grantham some things in an envelope.

Grantham's face froze her blood. It was so cold, without expression or emotion. How could those eyes—so unflinching—be the same eyes that had brightly burned for her in the dark privacy of their room?

Her heart skipped a beat as Grantham opened the bag and tilted it toward the man, letting him look inside. The man nodded brusquely, then took the bag. Glancing around quickly, he reached inside.

It's money. Phoebe blinked, fighting the urge to turn around. In the periphery of her vision, she could swear light had flashed, as if from a camera, but it was nothing. She watched the man pull out stacks of bills bound in paper loops. He quickly counted, though she couldn't see the denominations. Was Grantham being blackmailed? If so, what horrible dark secret was he trying to hide? Or did he have a hidden vice. Gambling? She gulped. Well, the man had the money now, and she'd better get out of here.

Pure terror suddenly seized her. She froze. She was

in love with a man who was doing something terribly wrong! For a second, she couldn't move.

Then she edged backward, spun on her heel and ran. She knew it was stupid—Grantham would probably see her—but she was too hurt and scared to think. She ran like the wind, her feet pounding. One hand clutched the binoculars, keeping them from thudding against her chest. The other gripped the baby monitor.

She ran as if the hounds of hell were on her heels. And maybe they were.

Grantham was, at any rate. Darn it. Why hadn't she worn a hat? The green knit cap to her Halloween costume had been within easy reach. From behind, Grantham would see her blond fluffy hair flying. *But I didn't wear a hat because I'm not a thug. I don't think like a thug. And I'm sure as heck not going to marry another one.*

At Park and Eightieth, Phoebe whirled. Her lungs were aching. Gasping for air, she doubled against a sharp pain in her left side. She had to rest, to calm down. But there was no time. Maybe he hadn't seen her. She bolted for the apartment door.

Inside, the desk attendant glanced up briefly.

If she rang for the elevator, Grantham might find her waiting. Gasping, Phoebe grabbed the knob to the stairwell door. The door was locked! But she'd just come out of it! How could it be locked? She wrenched the knob again.

This time it turned. Her panicked hands pushed. Mustering the last of her breath, she dove upstairs. Once she was inside the apartment, she stared at the door. How many of the three dead bolts had Grantham locked when he'd gone out? Her mind raced. One, two—all? Would he remember?

She locked two of them.

Then she fled toward the bedroom. The babies hadn't moved. No one was crying. Thank God. Within seconds, Phoebe was undressed and under the covers. She shoved the binoculars under the bed.

And then she waited. Everything was dead silent. In her ears, blood was rushing, pumped by a hammering heart she thought would explode. Her skin was cold, her mouth bone dry, her throat and lungs burning.

And he was home.

She tried to steady her breath. Feigning sleep, she turned on her side as he came into the room. He shrugged out of his raincoat and tossed it to a chair. She heard his slacks drop to the floor. A moment later, he slipped beside her in the bed.

"Phoebe?" he whispered.

Somehow, she'd stilled her breath. He said nothing more. She was sure he was lying there, staring at the ceiling.

What was he thinking?

She started to roll over and demand the answer. But so far he hadn't indulged her. And Nico Adair had taught her that when men were deceitful, they only told lies.

And so she waited.

After a while Grantham turned toward her. Ever so softly, seemingly not wanting to awaken her, his palm molded the whole length of her side, smoothing the covers over her waist and hip. He gently kissed her cheek, whispering, "Good night, angel."

Tears burned her eyes. Long after his lips were gone, she could feel them, warm against her skin. Beneath the pillow, her splayed fingers pressured the mattress, digging into it. Somehow she had to anchor herself, because this man was rocking her whole world.

The next hours were the longest of her life. She watched the minutes click by on the digital clock. Otherwise she stared at the video monitor the whole time, watching the babies, determined to find out what was going on for their sakes. She couldn't make another mistake, the way she had with Nico, and let all the babies down. She waited, listening for Grantham's deep, steady breaths. Then, quietly, she slipped from beneath the covers.

In the study, she turned on a lamp. Slowly, methodically, Phoebe began checking drawers and going through the file cabinets. Maybe Grantham would catch her, maybe he wouldn't. She no longer cared. It was late, and she was tired. She had only one priority now—the truth.

Phoebe squinted. From the file cabinet, she plucked out a file labeled Big Apple Babies. Surely, this pertained to the kids, since they'd been processed through Jake's agency.

She opened the file and drew in a sudden, sharp breath. Because this had nothing to do with the babies. Inside were bank statements that charted the movement of vast sums of money through various accounts. Ten months ago, for instance, seven hundred and fifty thousand dollars had been routed from CitiCorp to Federated Trust to Chase, and then to a numbered foreign account. Clearly, Grantham hadn't wanted the money traced to him.

But on the numbered account, and in handwriting she recognized as Grantham's, a personal check for seven hundred and fifty thousand dollars had been made out to Jake Lucas.

Why was Grantham paying people off? That man in the street. And the amazing sum of seven hundred and fifty thousand dollars to Jake? The thought of so much money made Phoebe woozy. Her heart hammered wildly, and her shaking fingers silently turned the statements in the file.

Then her blood ran cold. Because she saw a deposit for the missing million dollars Nico had left the babies. As with the other sums, it had followed a similar pattern after it left Nico's West Coast bank.

On the day Grantham had taken custody of the babies, he'd written yet another check to Jake Lucas. And this one was for the missing million dollars.

So was this how a rich, single man who was desperate to be a father finagled the difficult adoption of six babies?

A soft cry was torn from Phoebe's throat. Grantham had paid Jake. Sweet heaven, had he *bought* the babies—like commodities on the black market!

Chapter Thirteen

Grantham woke with a start.

The picture in the video monitor—just a long line of empty cribs—was as motionless as a still shot from a grainy old black-and-white movie. On the bedside table, the sound monitor was silent. Phoebe and the babies were gone.

Grantham blew out a soft, murderous sigh. The man who'd phoned last night was a threat to his family, so when Grantham went out, he was pumped up and tasting adrenaline, his ears straining, his eyes watchful. Of course, he'd seen Phoebe. On his way home, she'd been running a block ahead of him, the fluffy silken hair he'd so often tangled through his fingers flying in the wind. He'd given her an extra minute to assemble herself before he'd come inside.

"Phoebe?" he'd whispered.

But she'd feigned sleep. He'd considered forcing the issue, explaining about the blackmailer. But instead, he'd kissed her cheek, which was still chilled from the night air. Later, he'd heard her rise and go to his study.

Oh, while lying in bed, staring at the ceiling, his first impulse had been to confront her and tell her he'd just paid off a man for her protection. But he was a

Hale. Call it pride or arrogance, but he'd done nothing wrong and didn't have to defend himself. Besides, silence was probably the best revenge. She'd find nothing incriminating, and she'd feel like a fool. And there was something else. Something Celia had taught him long ago—that loving meant accepting people, not trying to change them.

Well, Grantham loved Phoebe Rutherford.

She could be impossible. Meddlesome. Enthusiastic to a fault. And she didn't trust him.

But he still loved her.

He even loved her for those brave faces she showed the world. For how she'd try to keep smiling for others, even when her heart was breaking. His father would have said she'd make a fine Hale woman. She'd understand how to put aside petty personal matters, if need be, and show a smiling public self.

Unfortunately, it was Grantham the man and father—not Grantham the Hale—who wanted Phoebe. And he didn't want Phoebe Queen of the Brave Face. He wanted Phoebe the woman. But how much more of himself could Grantham give? How much longer could he pursue her when she wouldn't give her trust? He'd done everything he could. Emotionally, they'd begun a family. And physically... Even now, he was haunted by the feverish heat of her skin on his lips as she'd writhed beneath him, sobbing his name.

With a groan, Grantham threw back the covers. When he'd finally slept, he'd slept like the dead. He hadn't returned last night's phone message from Cy Lynde, though he hoped it meant Cy had new information. And how had Phoebe moved all six kids out of the apartment without so much as waking him? She must have dressed them elsewhere. At her grandfather's, or at the Plaza Hotel where her lawyers were staying.

"Or maybe you've got it all wrong," Grantham muttered.

Maybe she'd gone to Judge Winslow's to make sure he canceled the hearing. Maybe she and the kids would come home any minute now with a surprise breakfast—warm bagels, cream cheese and fruit.

"Keep dreaming," he whispered.

When he heard a creak in the silence, his heart skipped a beat. "Phoebe?" But it was nothing—just a creak and wishful thinking. *Don't give up on her yet. Maybe she'll come through for you and show she really trusts you.*

Heading for the shower, Grantham knew he'd soon find out. Because in less than an hour, he and Phoebe were squaring off in court.

IT'S SHOWTIME, sweet ladies.

From the painting at the front of the courtroom, the three Fates smiled placidly at Grantham. They were just as he remembered, angelically draped in ethereal white gowns, spinning, gathering and clipping the threads of fate. But Grantham had been in court with Phoebe less than five minutes, and he already suspected the Fates weren't going to do him any favors today.

"All rise!" A middle-aged black woman, whose desk plate said Ms. Cooke, rose and faced the court. "Court is now in session. The honorable Judge T. Winslow presiding."

Grantham's eyes bored into Phoebe.

She bounced Nicolas in her lap, studiously avoiding the gaze. Grantham knew she felt it, though. Her posture was too practiced. The pulse was ticking wildly in her throat. He bit back his temper. That he'd given a man money on the street was definitely suspicious—he'd admit that much—but it wasn't damning. Or it wouldn't be if Phoebe loved and trusted him. Grantham sighed. At least he was fairly sure there was nothing incriminating in the apartment. Still, he wished Phoebe had chosen to confront him, not spy on him in the dark.

Not that it mattered. After the evidence Grantham would put forth in court, she'd know he'd always had her best interest at heart. Hell, it was easy for a man to say he loved a woman. But it was a man's actions that told the truth of it.

Phoebe watched her grandfather approach the bench, leaning heavily on his cane, his long black robe sweeping the floor. She was so heartbreakingly beautiful. These weeks they'd spent together—so full of loving and parenting—had left her looking vibrant. She was wearing a simple navy suit that deepened the color of her eyes. Grantham had chosen an austere single-breasted suit of dark gray.

He was suddenly glad they were inside the gated area at the front of the courtroom, with the curious crowd and reporters behind them. Phoebe was seated at a table to Grantham's left, flanked by her lawyers, Joyce on one side, Orsen and Bert on the other. All the babies except Nicolas were in their two triple strollers. Although Phoebe had paid for the room at the Plaza Hotel until the end of the week, the lawyers' garment bags were propped behind them. That meant they expected the hearing to be brief. Grantham didn't know if that was good or bad.

"I wish Jake was here," James whispered.

Jake had come down with the flu. Grantham leaned closer to the lawyer. "Everything'll be fine."

Judge Winslow slammed down his gavel. "Before we proceed—" His lips trembled in a fleeting movement that might have been a smile. "It has come to my attention via my personal phone answering machine that the principal parties involved in this case, Mr. Hale and Ms. Rutherford, have become engaged to be married. Is this correct?" His piercing blue eyes fixed on Grantham.

"Great," Grantham muttered. *Ask Phoebe.*

Judge Winslow raised a liver-spotted hand to his temple, then leaned forward as if Grantham was particularly daft. "Mr. Hale," he intoned, "marriage is a serious matter. Surely, you must *remember* if you proposed!"

The man was staring at him as if he was an idiot. "I proposed."

Judge Winslow turned to Phoebe. "And so you're engaged?"

Grantham glanced at her with more than mild curiosity. She still wouldn't look at him. He noticed circles under her eyes from the long night. Like dusky butterflies that never landed, her eyes flitted toward him, pleaded for an instant, then were gone.

"I said yes," Phoebe said nervously. "But now I—well, there are a few questions that really need to be cleared up—"

Judge Winslow looked positively appalled. "Do you mean to say," he roared, shaking his gavel in Grantham's direction, "that this man proposed marriage and that you, Phoebe Rutherford, are considering declining?"

She scooted back in her chair, as if to escape her great-grandfather's wrath. "Well, yes. I mean no. I mean we've got some—" Her voice quavered. "Some questions and—" Phoebe glanced helplessly around.

"I just want to do what's right. I—I have an obligation to the babies. We have to find out the truth."

"The truth?" Judge Winslow exploded, his eyes bugging in horror. "You have a criminal record and you need to know the truth?" He rolled his eyes heavenward. "By all means, then, let us proceed. Ms. Moon, I'm sure you're exceedingly anxious to begin assassinating Mr. Hale's character."

Joyce shot to her feet, her straight dark hair swinging. "I take offense at that, Your Honor! I'm here to defend my client's right to have custody of her own children as best as I can. In no way do I mean to disparage—"

Judge Winslow's gaze stopped her cold. His voice was as dry and cold as dry ice. "Just get on with it, Ms. Moon."

Carrying a file, she circled the table. "Very well. We call Cappy Nelson."

James leaned toward Grantham. "Who?"

Grantham shook his head. "I don't know." When the man entered the room, Grantham's heart hammered. It was the blackmailer. Today he wore a dark suit. Apparently, his black cap had hidden frizzy red hair.

"Recognize him?" James urged.

Grantham considered. "Let's just see what he has to say."

James's frustrated sigh made Grantham feel lousy. All along he hadn't made it easy on James or Jake. He counted both men as legal counsel and as friends. But Grantham's love life was on the line. He had to do things his own way. He believed in the truth of deeds, not words. And he had to seize this moment to determine whether Phoebe's actions would prove her love.

Cappy Nelsen was sworn in, and Joyce started questioning him, getting right to the nitty-gritty. "So you knew Mr. Hale slept with a woman in the Wilshire Arms in Los Angeles?"

Phoebe gasped. "No! You can't use that, Joyce! You said you wouldn't—"

The judge's gavel thudded down. "Ms. Rutherford!"

"But—but Granddaddy—" Phoebe sputtered.

"Another word," he thundered, "and you will be removed from this room and held in contempt. You're the one who's so anxious for the truth!"

Phoebe glanced around, her lips parted in unspoken protest, her eyes meeting Grantham's, begging him to believe she hadn't meant this to happen.

Cappy answered the question. "Yes. I, uh, work as a stringer for the newspapers, getting information on public personalities. Anyway, I was looking for a story. And, uh, completely by accident, I became privy to the fact that Grantham Hale was having an affair."

Grantham could merely shake his head. A stringer for the newspapers? What rubbish. Joyce showed Cappy a number of papers. Some looked like photographs. "And these are the documents you collected?"

Cappy nodded.

Joyce waved the papers. "We're marking these into evidence."

Before the items were labeled for later referral and identification, James asked to examine them. Grantham's heart ached when he viewed the pictures of him and Phoebe. The stills from the security videotape at the Wilshire Arms were grainy. Only he was recognizable. Phoebe was conveniently shown from the back or with her hair, which was shorter and dark red then, in her face. There were also signed statements from hotel personnel who'd seen Grantham with a red-haired woman.

"I'm sorry, Grantham," James whispered insistently. "But I have to ask. Was Celia still alive at this time?"

Grantham slowly turned to James. How could his friend ask such a thing? "Of course not."

James's relieved sigh pricked his temper. "Well, then, we can fix this on cross-examination." Raising his voice, James continued, "We have no problem with marking these into evidence."

Cappy stepped down.

"Next we would like to call Mr. Grantham Hale."

Grantham glanced at Phoebe. She looked stunned. Clearly her lawyers had overstepped their bounds. Grantham should have felt relieved, but something beyond anger flared inside him, a strange, detached curiosity about where all this was headed. Phoebe's dream team wanted it to seem as if he'd slept around on Celia. And Cappy Nelson was no newspaper stringer.

Standing in the witness box, Grantham placed his left hand on a Bible and raised his right. Ms. Cooke said, "Mr. Hale, do you swear to tell the truth, the whole truth, and nothing but the truth, so help you God?"

He glanced over the crowd—the sketch artists, the reporters and photographers. If asked directly about the missing million dollars, Grantham decided he still would not answer the question. "I do," he said, then seated himself.

Joyce approached, her dark eyes glittering as she came in for the kill. "Could you state your whole name for the record?"

"Grantham Hale."

"You reside at number eighty, Park Avenue?"

"I do."

Grantham answered the standard questions about his business, his habits, his background. All the courtroom's curious eyes were on him except for the only two that counted—Phoebe's. She was staring into her lap at Nicolas. Grantham felt another rush of temper. Had he really made love to her last night? Had their love-damp bodies really been joined in ecstasy? What the hell did Phoebe think she was doing here today?

Finally Joyce got to the point. "Some new evidence has come into our possession concerning your finances. As you know, you are not on trial, but we hope follow-up will be made to the information we're about to present."

Phoebe gasped again.

Grantham stared at her. Shifting Nicolas, she stood. Warily Grantham took in the angry, nonverbal exchange between the two women. The Big Apple Baby file, he thought. If Phoebe had found that, there would be hell to pay. But surely that file had been locked in his other cabinet.

Judge Winslow bellowed, "Ms. Rutherford, take your seat!"

"I won't!" She stared at her lawyer. "Joyce," she said, her voice laced with betrayal, "when I showed you those, it was for your opinion, your advice, your—"

"One more word!" shrieked the judge, his face turning purple with rage. "You asked to hear all this!"

"But, Granddaddy—"

Orsen grabbed Phoebe's suit jacket and yanked her into her seat. "Sit," hissed the lawyer.

Phoebe gaped at him, looking utterly at sea. If Grantham hadn't been the lawyers' intended target, he might have felt sorry for her. Her dusky blue eyes darted around in panic, as if she wanted help from somebody, but she didn't know who. As if she was a spider suddenly caught in her own web.

Don't look to me for help, angel.

Joyce continued, "I have evidence of money transfers...."

Bracing himself, Grantham listened as Joyce marked his private records into evidence, lying about how she'd obtained them and detailing how he'd routed funds from American to overseas banks.

"Mr. Hale," she said, "did you make these money transfers?"

He considered for a long moment. "Yes, I did."

"Including the transfers of money to Jake Lucas, who you know is the head of the Big Apple Babies adoption agency?"

He supposed he had no choice but to answer. "Yes."

"And you made two payments to Jake Lucas, as I've described. One ten months ago. The second on the day you received custody of your children, which transferred the missing million dollars from the babies' account to that of Mr. Jake Lucas?"

Grantham considered again. He decided he would answer anything—except the reason he made the payments. "Yes."

"And so you see, Mr. Grantham Hale admits making direct payments to Mr. Jake Lucas!" Joyce whirled on the court, as if to emphasize the import of what she was about to say. "Cash for babies," she intoned. "Six innocent babies, bought and sold like chattel by a rich man who wanted to be a father. By a rich man who was willing to buy and sell human flesh, the way he might stocks and bonds and real estate. Isn't that right, Mr. Hale?''

Grantham was utterly stunned.

Even worse, Phoebe was watching him, as if she expected him to answer such a question. Dear God, was that the conclusion *she'd* drawn? The depth of her distrust was astonishing. Inside him, something broke. Suddenly those babies in the strollers weren't his only babies. Phoebe was his baby, too. Something inside him cried out, *Damn you, Adair, how could you destroy her like this?* He hated the man who'd ruined Phoebe's ability to trust. Because without trust, a relationship with her was impossible. Love was unthinkable, marriage out of the question. Grantham was vaguely aware of the flashing cameras. Pencils scribbled. James was objecting.

Joyce's voice was low. "Mr. Hale, did you buy those babies?"

Yes. He considered saying it. Hell, it was what they all wanted to hear.

Judge Winslow whispered, "Take the Fifth."

Joyce exploded. "The Fifth!"

Without waiting for Grantham to respond, Judge Winslow banged his gavel. "Mr. Hale takes the Fifth. He may step down."

Everything around him exploded. Noise, murmurings, protests, questions from reporters, Judge Winslow crazily banging his gavel. As he seated himself, James whispered, "What the hell's happening? What's this about you and Jake? What's this about buying the babies? Start talking to me, Grantham, or you're in serious trouble."

He stared at James.

"Grantham, please. I trust you. But without knowledge of the full facts, I can't make an effective rebuttal.''

"No rebuttal," Grantham said.

The court was quieting down. James gaped at him. His voice was hushed, insistent. "We *have* to cross-examine."

Grantham shook his head. "Just bring out Cy Lynde."

James's eyes bugged. "Grantham, Cy's got new information you haven't even heard yet. You can't go through with this, not after what she just did to you."

As he looked at Phoebe, Grantham's heart broke. His eyes drank in the hair he longed to touch, the mouth he longed to kiss. But he'd given and given to this woman—and look what she'd done! It didn't matter that her eyes were pleading with his across the courtroom, or that she was shaking her head in denial. Hell, the lawyers were in her employ. Hadn't she let them do her dirty work and voice all her secret fears? And the babies. His sweet sons and daughters. Grantham couldn't even look at them right now. Damn it, he was going to lose them. She was going to take them away.

Calmly, he turned from Phoebe. He no longer wanted to clear her name. He was finished. Used up. She could say she loved him a thousand times. But with this show of her complete distrust, she'd thoroughly betrayed him. And no one betrayed a Hale. He wasn't proud of it, but he really wanted to hurt her. And nothing would hurt more than this act of love. No, nothing ever hurt more than the truth. He glanced at James. "Please, just call Cy."

James sighed and rose. "No rebuttal, but we call Cy Lynde."

Judge Winslow groaned as if he knew exactly what was coming. "The court calls Cy Lynde."

EVERYTHING was going wrong.

Phoebe leaned forward, staring at Grantham, pleading with her eyes, trying to get him to look at her. He wouldn't even turn around. *Please, Grantham. Just look at me!*

She could kill her lawyers. She'd gone to them for help this morning, and they'd used things she'd told them not to, publically voicing all her most secret, crazy fears about Grantham. She was sure the man from the park last night wasn't a news stringer. He'd seemed so familiar to her lawyers—almost as if they knew him. They'd made it sound as if Grantham was having an adulterous affair—without even bothering to mention that it was with her. And then Granddaddy wouldn't let her put a stop to it. She *had* to talk to Grantham.

Please, her mind screamed. *Please, Grantham, look at me.* She pushed with all her will, as if she had secret telepathy that might get him to turn around. *Please.* She clutched Nicolas tight, her eyes riveting on the man being sworn in. Cy Lynde? Phoebe's mind raced. She'd never heard the name.

Ms. Cooke said, "Do you swear to tell the whole truth…"

The truth, Phoebe thought bitterly. The truth was she loved Grantham. She knew he was no more guilty than she'd been when Nico raked her over the coals. Grantham's clear countenance in the face of the charges against him proclaimed his innocence. He was the best man in the world. And the best father for the babies. She was sure he hadn't squandered their money.

James paced in front of the witness box. "And what's your occupation, Mr. Lynde?"

"I'm a private investigator, employed by Mr. Hale. He felt Phoebe Rutherford had been maligned by her ex-husband, Nicolas Adair, so he hired me to clear her name. I've found ample evidence that Ms. Rutherford *is* innocent of all previous charges against her."

Phoebe's lips parted in astonishment. Grantham had hired a PI, not only to find her, but to restore her good reputation? She thought the room was shaking, then she realized it was her insides. In shock, she listened while Cy explained that she was never rehabilitated at A New Leaf. He explained how Nico had coerced people into tampering with her credit ratings and driver's record, into saying she was a drunkard.

Finally James said, "And Sven Nordstrom is here?"

Cy nodded. "We flew him in from the West Coast."

After Cy stepped down, the other witnesses testified. "I met Nico at our sports club," Sven Nordstrom said. "He threatened to have me physically hurt if I didn't lie."

"Phoebe was the most wonderful mother," said Selena, the babies' nanny. "You should have seen her with those babies. Her eyes lit up and her face glowed. But Nico...it was like he wanted to own her."

A lady from the woman's shelter said, "That poor girl. I always knew she was telling the truth. Her husband had used his money against her, but she was so honest."

For so long Phoebe had yearned to hear the record set straight. But now she couldn't stand to listen. Because Grantham wouldn't look at her. While she was doubting him—sneaking around and spying on him—

he'd been restoring her good name. Now *he* was the maligned. And *she* was the vindicated. Now she had everything. And he had nothing. Phoebe wanted it to stop. Nothing could have punished her more than the selfless way he was standing up for her.

"In full view of the proof before me," Judge Winslow finally intoned, "I hereby give full legal custody of the quadruplets—Lyssa, Kirby, Nicolas and Langdon Adair—to their rightful mother, Ms. Phoebe Rutherford. Because of pending investigations against Mr. Hale, I rule that the twins, Stanley and Devin Hale, remain with Ms. Rutherford until such time as permanent arrangements are made." Looking livid, he slammed down his gavel. "This court—or is that circus—is now adjourned."

Stunned, Phoebe couldn't move. In a heartbeat, it was all over. Noise broke out. People rose from their seats.

Joyce grabbed her garment bag. "Phew! Well, I've got a plane to catch. But congrats! Chalk one up for the good guys!"

The good guys? Moving past Phoebe, Orsen and Bert quickly shook her hand. Grantham was talking to James, his back intentionally turned. Granddaddy Winslow had vanished into his judge's chambers.

"This way, Ms. Rutherford!" Two security officers materialized at her sides, each taking a stroller. One settled Nicolas into his seat, then gripped her arm. "Come on, we've been instructed to take you out the back way to avoid a scene."

"But I have to talk to Grantham!" Phoebe wrenched around as she was forcibly maneuvered toward a side door. Raising her voice, she shouted, "Grantham!" He didn't turn.

"Sorry, ma'am, you might catch him outside."

Outside. The word played nonsensically in Phoebe's head. As far as the security clerks knew, she and Grantham had been locked in a custody battle, and she'd just emerged victorious. They had to keep her from the press and Grantham, to insure no fights broke out. But they had it all wrong. She fought their grasp.

"C'mon," one said roughly. "We're just doing our job."

They strong-armed her to the street. Gary was at the curb, waiting for her and the babies behind the wheel of the limousine, his nose buried in a book. He didn't see her. But she saw Joyce, and gasped. She was chatting merrily with Cappy Nelson. Pushing one stroller and pulling the other behind her, Phoebe raced toward Joyce, watching in horror as Joyce pressed money into Cappy Nelson's hand.

The man grinned, then darted down the street. Phoebe's hand closed over Joyce's upper arm. "What was that about?" she demanded.

Joyce stared at her. "Look, you wanted to win, didn't you?"

Phoebe gaped at her. "Not like this! What was that money for?"

Joyce shrugged. "We figured we'd show Hale proof of you and him together and blackmail him. We'd use photos of the payoff to show his shame over the affair. But we wound up not even using that stuff." She shook her head. "You want to know the weird thing?"

Phoebe's body shook with rage. The man she'd seen Grantham pay off last night had been hired by her lawyers! The woman Grantham had slept with was her! "What?"

"I don't think it was his reputation he was trying to protect, Phoebe, I think it was yours."

Fury such as she'd never known pulsed through

Phoebe. There was only one word for this person. "You bitch," she whispered.

Tossing her dark hair, Joyce spun on her heel. Over her shoulder she called, "You hired me. And you got exactly what you wanted, didn't you?"

Phoebe sagged over the strollers, feeling as if she'd been punched. Then she saw Grantham. He was walking away. Pushing both unwieldy strollers, she hurried toward him. "Grantham! Grantham, wait!"

Very slowly, Grantham turned toward her, so austere in his dark gray suit, his eyes hard and fierce. His face looked stark, the high cheekbones, noble nose, and the deep cleft in his chin all planes and shadows. His body bristled with anger and integrity. He waited wordlessly.

She spoke in a rush. "I had no idea what they were going to do! I told them they couldn't say those things! I tried to stop them! I—" Her breath caught, her throat feeling tight with unshed tears. She wanted to fling herself into his arms and beg for forgiveness. Somehow she kept her brave face intact. "Oh, Grantham," she continued quickly. "I'm so, so sorry. And thank you! I can't believe what you did for me. All this time you were trying to clear my name."

His voice was deceptively soft. "You mean, while you were spying on me, watching me pay blackmailers to protect you. Or was that while I was paying cash for human flesh—for babies?"

"I didn't know what to think! I—"

"In court it was pretty clear what you thought."

"That's not true!"

"You never thought I paid for the babies?"

Only for an instant. "Please, Grantham! I said I'm sorry! What do you want me to do?" Pure panic seized her. If he'd just show some emotion. Just get mad. But he was so calm.

"Phoebe." Grantham's voice was strained with carefully reined-in temper, and his angry eyes were touched with sadness. "No marriage between us will ever work. I love you, but we don't have enough trust to stand a chance. It's just not going to happen. I know we both wanted it. I'm very sorry."

Phoebe blinked rapidly, fighting tears, her foolhardy attempt at a smile nothing more than a wince. "But, Grantham, I tried to ask you what you were doing."

His eyes pitied her. "Not very forcibly."

He was right. As usual. She'd always backed down so easily. Maybe she hadn't really wanted to know. She'd feared that, like Nico, Grantham would lie. She was blinking tears from her eyes so fast that everything around her seemed to strobe. Somehow she managed to send Grantham another fleeting, pleading smile. "I love you so much. Grantham, I—I was so scared—"

"Scared I'd turn out to be a criminal?"

"Why can't you understand? I married one before!"

Frightening fury filled Grantham's eyes with fire. His palm slammed his chest hard, beating his heart. "I am Grantham Hale. I am not Nicolas Adair!"

She felt her whole world shattering. "I know!"

"Do you?"

She saw the Hale in him then. The uncompromising pride, the king's arrogance. Then his eyes settled on the babies, and he dropped to a crouch in front of the strollers. Abruptly, totally controlling his emotions, the tension left his voice. "Say bye-bye to Daddy," he said softly.

A deep sob caught in Phoebe's throat. Silent tears

started coursing down her cheeks like a hot rain. She couldn't muster one of her trademark smiles. She knew she'd never smile again. "No, Grantham," she whispered.

He ruffled Lyssa's hair, then Kirby's blond ringlets. The kids, sensing something horrible, had turned quiet. Grantham kissed them, first the girls, then the boys. When Devin tugged his sleeve, Grantham hoarsely said, "Be a good boy." And when Langdon's arms stretched toward him, Grantham swiftly hugged him tight. After a moment he pried away the little fingers. "C'mon, Langdon. Daddy's got to go bye-bye now."

When Grantham rose, he showed no sign of emotion except a barely perceptible quiver of his cheek that immediately stilled. Kirby's choked sob sounded first, moving through the strollers with a domino effect until all the babies were crying.

"Grantham," Phoebe croaked, "we need you. You can't leave us."

His voice was raw. "Really, it was you who left me."

As he backed away, she grabbed his arm and held fast. "Please! You hired a PI to find me and clear my name. No matter what, you kept loving me. We can fix this. I know we can! You can't walk away, not now! Not after all this! You can't!"

"I *am*, angel."

Carefully disengaging her hand, Grantham slowly turned and walked away.

"I assume you're satisfied?"

Phoebe whirled on Granddaddy Winslow. Her face was wet with tears, her heart broken. No, she wasn't satisfied! Her babies, who now had no father, were screaming. Grantham's long strides were eating up the pavement. He wasn't coming back, either. Nope, when a man like Grantham Hale made up his mind, he never changed it. Her shoulders hitched with a dry sob. She was such damaged goods. How could anybody love her? "You didn't even believe in me, Granddaddy," she suddenly accused him with a rush of rage.

"Of course, I believed in you!" he thundered. "But what I believe is immaterial! Truth and law are sometimes two different things, Phoebe. As a judge, I must side with the law."

Granddaddy Winslow hadn't believed Nico's lies? Her head pounded with pressure, and fresh tears fell. "Granddaddy, all I wanted today was the truth!"

"The truth?" Granddaddy Winslow's blue eyes pierced right through her. "You want the truth? Well, here's the truth—but you must swear never to speak a word of it."

Phoebe's heart lurched. "I swear."

"On the day she died, Celia Hale asked her husband to make an anonymous private donation to Big Apple Babies. It was the last conversation Grantham ever had with his wife."

Another gasping cry was wrenched from between Phoebe's lips.

"But I found out about Grantham's generosity," Granddaddy Winslow continued. "So I asked him to become a secret backer for Big Apple Babies." His eyes fixed on hers. "I and some others have long funded Big Apple Babies. And we needed one million dollars—the money Jake Lucas just received—for the new teen facility. Because of cash flow problems, Grantham had to temporarily borrow from the babies' bank account to make his personal contribution. Tomorrow he'll replace their money. Grantham kept his donation secret because of his vow to his deceased wife, and also to avoid any hint of impropriety, such as what your lawyers suggested in court today.''

Phoebe lifted a hand from a stroller and blindly wiped at her tear-stained cheek. Granddaddy Winslow was a Big Apple Babies backer? Grantham had made a secret vow to Celia?

"And now I must go," the judge intoned.

A white limousine had pulled to the curb. Phoebe watched in shock as a back door opened and Thurman Newland, Dani Lucas's father, emerged. He motioned Granddaddy Winslow toward the car, and he waved his cane, as if to say he was coming.

"Thurman Newland?" Phoebe whispered. Had Grantham had meetings with Thurman in the white limousine?

"Thurman is helping us fund the teen facility." Still looking furious, Granddaddy Winslow lifted his cane again. Stabbing it on the sidewalk, he roared, "It would be breaking an oath, but somebody ought to tell the newspapers the truth about Grantham." He glared at her. "Damn it, Phoebe," he exploded. "That man's a saint!"

And maybe Granddaddy Winslow was, too. She'd been so wrong about him. And Grantham? She'd stripped him of everything he loved. How many times could he have spoken out, broken his promise to Celia? Or said Phoebe was the woman in the Wilshire Arms? Grantham had seen so much tragedy—and he deserved so much better. Her babies deserved better, too.

Knowing what she had to do, Phoebe quickly starting pushing the strollers, saying, "Granddaddy, I— I've got to go."

"Damn it, Phoebe!" he roared. "Where?"

But she was already past him.

"Phoebe!" he thundered.

She wrenched around. "I'm just no good, Granddaddy," she cried out. And then she whirled again and headed for Gary and the car.

GRANTHAM WENT straight to the bedroom. Everywhere else, toys were strewn on the floors, each a reminder that he'd lost custody. Maybe he'd go out to Genesis for a few days to escape. Hell, he couldn't go to Genesis, either. He'd just wind up in the master bedroom, remembering the love he'd shared with Phoebe there. His eyes settled on the night table. Hadn't the sound monitor been there this morning?

Sitting on the rumpled bed, he shut his eyes to block out the pain. Then he realized he could smell her on the sheets, a scent of roses and musk. Had he demanded too much of Phoebe? Had he wrongly expected her to trust—to share herself and the babies— with the same graceful ease as Celia? Maybe. But Phoebe wasn't Celia. She'd had a much rougher life. She'd been living in a homeless shelter....

Grantham heard a soft sigh. He opened his eyes and glanced around. Then he noticed the video monitor. All six babies were in their cribs! Grantham strode to the nursery. A folded note was taped to a rail of Stanley's crib. Grantham's heart lurched. It was written in a crazy, rushed scrawl.

Grantham—

This time, I'll say goodbye. I didn't at the Wilshire Arms because everything was so perfect. That night, you were my fantasy dream lover, and so I was afraid to meet the real you. But now I know the real you is even better. You're not just a dream lover and a knight in shining armor and a saint—you're the best parent our babies could ever have. I love you.

Phoebe

The sound monitor! She'd been waiting nearby, listening to make sure the babies were fine until he found them. Grantham crossed to the window. Phoebe was staring from the sidewalk. His voice caught. "Phoebe. I know you can hear me through the monitor." But what did he want to say?

It was a moot point. Because she set the monitor on a newspaper machine, where he could retrieve it. Sending him a bright, brave smile through her tears, she lifted a hand and waved goodbye. And then she turned and started walking away.

"Oh, angel," he whispered. She was so bound and determined to set things right. And she did love him. Loved him so much that she was willing to entrust the babies to his sole care.

Beneath his shirt, he felt her ring, pressed against his chest. And he thought of the inscription. *Love isn't love until you give it away.*

Was *he* ready to give away everything—even his Hale pride? Was he ready to give more than he got, until all the damage Nicolas Adair had done was healed?

WITH TREMBLING FINGERS, Phoebe inserted the key into the lock of the room at the Plaza Hotel. The lawyers were gone, so at least she had somewhere to go and think. Swiping away another tear, she was suddenly reminded of another hotel room, another time. Of that beautiful night in the Wilshire Arms. Oh, she'd been degraded and slandered by Nico, and she'd had her babies taken away, but that night, in a sudden twist of fate, she'd met the most marvelous man....

Later, she'd wanted her revenge. Her justice. But now she knew the man on whom she'd wanted that revenge was dead. And it was her inability to let go of the past that had cost her the man and family she truly loved. The door swung inward. The suite was fresh, the housekeepers had come and gone, and Grantham—

Phoebe sucked in a quick breath.

Grantham was here.

It was like a fairy tale. Like magic.

She couldn't move. She was so sure she was dreaming. But the babies—all her well-behaved, precious babies—were neatly lined up, seated in their strollers in front of the TV with the late-morning Barney program playing low.

"Can we start all over again?" Grantham said softly.

He was standing in front of a window in his gray suit. Autumn sunlight kissed his golden hair and danced on his skin, and in his hand he was holding a single, long-stemmed white rose.

Phoebe started across the room on shaky legs. He met her halfway, catching her in his arms. Somehow her fist wound up around the rose stem while his strong arms lifted her off the floor. Her arms wreathed around his neck, and her legs wrapped around his back.

Her voice was hoarse. "Start all over again?"

His eyes settled on hers. "Sometimes I expect too much."

Renewed tears welled in her eyes. "I'm so sorry," she whispered. "I don't do things right all the time."

"I don't, either," Grantham whispered back, right

before his lips tenderly brushed hers. "But I do love you, angel."

Her heart flooded with happiness that rushed through her bloodstream in a current of joy. She glanced toward the babies.

"Do you really think we all have a chance together?"

"More than a chance." That fierce Hale energy touched his eyes. "I'll do anything to keep us together."

"So will I!" Phoebe said with a rush of tearful enthusiasm. "I know we can stay together, Grantham."

"Yes," he said simply.

Her throat closed with emotion. She flashed him a bright smile through all her tears of joy. "How did you find me? And how did you and all the babies get here?"

"Luck and a little common sense," Grantham said with a whimsical smile. "Now kiss me, angel."

And she did. He kissed her back with a tender probing, gently easing apart her lips, then delving with the warm velvet of his tongue, lovingly inviting hers to duel with him.

From somewhere, far off, three angelic women draped in ethereal white dresses looked on in approval. One spun the threads of fate, the second gathered, the third clipped.

And they were all smiling.

They had so many good things planned. A Hale-Rutherford wedding. Phoebe's surprise pregnancy next year. And at this very moment, a cantankerous old judge who couldn't bear injustice was busy breaking his solemn oath and exposing all Grantham Hale's secret charitable contributions. By tonight's six o'clock newscast, Grantham would be the toast of New York again. Someday, there might even be a Winslow-Rutherford family reunion. One thing was absolutely certain, though. All six babies—Lyssa, Kirby, Langdon, Nicolas, Devin and Stanley—would be raised in a two-parent household. And they had long, rich lives of love and happiness in store for them.

But for now, the three Fates were content to smile placidly on Phoebe and Grantham's loving kiss.

"Hmm," Grantham sighed. With Phoebe still in his arms, he started walking toward a bedroom, murmuring, "You know how engrossed the kids get when they watch Barney."

"So?"

"So I love you, angel."

"I know," Phoebe whispered throatily. "But where are you taking me?"

"Where I can show you just how much," Grantham whispered back. He tenderly lay Phoebe across the bed. And the soft, feral light in his eyes said he meant to take her the way he always would. With abandon and passion. And the light in hers said she wouldn't just take. She would give, just as he did. With her whole heart and soul. Because their love became deeper and stronger each time they gave it away.

...And there's more
BIG APPLE BABIES headed your way!

Don't miss the next book in
Jule McBride's exciting
Big Apple Babies miniseries
coming next May.

Verdict: Parenthood

The courtroom drama's not over yet!

Big Apple Babies pediatrician, Winston "Doc" Holiday, is used to other folks' babies. But when the strapping urban cowboy's honeyed drawl lands him neck-deep under the covers with a virtuous virgin, it looks as if Doc might just have to wrangle with matchmaking Judge Winslow—and become a proud papa himself!

* * * * *

*Watch for More Big Apple Babies
in May 1998!*

COMING NEXT MONTH

#701 IN PAPA BEAR'S BED by Judy Christenberry
Once Upon a Kiss

In a cabin in the woods, runaway Jessica Barnes rested in a chair that was too big, ate leftovers that were too small, and slept in a bed that was just right. When Rob Berenson and his kids returned home, one look at the naked blonde between his sheets and as much as he had his own secrets to hide, Rob didn't want this Goldilocks to run away!

#702 A DARK & STORMY NIGHT by Anne Stuart
More Than Men

Katie Flynn sought shelter from a storm but on a windswept cliff she found a moody recluse named O'Neal. Trapped, she fought his sensuality, but she suspected that something haunted the man...something that only O'Neal himself could reveal....

#703 OVERNIGHT WIFE by Mollie Molay

Ditching her Christmas Eve wedding, Arden Crandall fled to the airport in time to take the honeymoon by herself, but she ran smack into a snowstorm and the mysterious Luke McCauley. The man was trouble, but she thought she could resist him—and then came the announcement that the airport would be closed all night....

#704 MISTER CHRISTMAS by Linda Cajio
The Holiday Heart

Holly had to help Raymond Holiday find his heart by December 25th or he'd lose it for good. He'd dodged love for years, from his family, friends, women—though he had a way with the latter, and with female elves like herself. She only hoped he found his heart before she lost hers....

AVAILABLE THIS MONTH:

#697 SPUR-OF-THE-MOMENT MARRIAGE
Cathy Gillen Thacker

#698 PLEASE SAY "I DO"
Karen Toller Whittenburg

#699 VERDICT: PARENTHOOD
Jule McBride

#700 MR. WRONG!
Mary Anne Wilson

Look us up on-line at: http://www.romance.net

HARLEQUIN®

A M E R I C A N ◆ R O M A N C E®

You asked for it...You got it! More MEN!

MORE THAN MEN

We're thrilled to bring you another special edition of the
popular MORE THAN MEN series—and thrilled
to bring you another unique book by the inimitable,
RITA Award-winning author Anne Stuart.

Like those who have come before him, O'Neal is more
than tall, dark and handsome. All of these men have
extraordinary powers that make them "more than men."
But whether they're able to grant you three wishes, or live
forever, make no mistake—their greatest, most extraordinary
power is that of seduction.

So make a date with O'Neal in...

#702 A DARK & STORMY NIGHT
by Anne Stuart
November 1997

The Gentleman & The Hell Raiser

Don't miss these captivating stories
from two acclaimed authors
of historical romance.

THE GENTLEMAN by Kristin James
THE HELL RAISER by Dorothy Glenn

Two brothers on a collision course
with destiny and love.

Find out how the dust settles October 1997
wherever Harlequin and Silhouette
books are sold.